HOT SAND & COLD BLOOD

F. Washington Brown

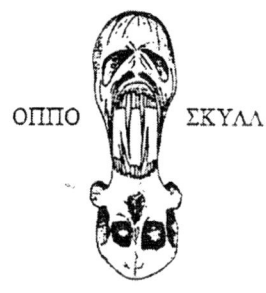

ΟΠΠΟ   ΣΚΥΛΛ

"Hot Sand & Cold Blood" ISBN 1-58939-325-2.

Published 2002, 2008 by Virtualbookworm.com Publishing Inc., P.O. Box 9949, College Station, TX , 77842, US. ©2002 F. Washington Brown. All rights reserved. No part of this publication may be reproduced, stored in a retrieval system, or transmitted in any form or by any means, electronic, mechanical, recording or otherwise, without the prior written permission of F. Washington Brown.

Manufactured in the United States of America

The OMNI agent stepped out with the raised P-89 and started shooting.

The hundred and twenty grain copper-jacketed rounds ripped through Kansi like shooting a paper target. Ryder was close enough to see his bullets hitting the terrorist in a tight group; but having no effect. The rounds were knocking the terrorist around like a rag doll sending blood splattering here and there but he was not going down. Instead, he seemed to be looming larger as his face started to reshape and become inhumanly reddish gray in color.

Ryder kept firing until the Ruger's slide action slammed back and locked sending a wisp of smoke curling from the gun's chamber. The OMNI agent had hit Kansi with every round but the bullets seemed to be about as effective as snowballs.

Then Kansi raised a .380 Smith and Wesson automag and opened fire as his hideous sounding voice boomed out, "Now it is my turn, you annoying insect that has plagued me for over two of your earth years. Now your end has come."

Ryder yelled with pain as a .380 round tore through his leg. He involuntarily fell to the floor, looked at his empty gun -- and knew that time had run out . . .

<u>Time can be your ally</u>
<u>Time can be your enemy</u>
<u>It all depends on how you use it</u>

Chapter-1

The battered old Boeing 707 gradually lost altitude as the pilot attempted a crosswind final approach onto the main runway at Beirut Airport. The captain slipped the nose slightly into the hot, sand-filled winds until the airplane corrected onto the runway's centerline, and then holding that position, descended until the main gear made a less than smooth contact with the asphalt. The tires announced their protest at the hard landing with a loud squeal, punctuated by a short burst of bluish-white smoke.

The giant cargo plane continued speeding down the runway as the pilot applied brakes and reverse engine thrust, slowing the winged juggernaut to a point where it could be steered off the runway and taxied over to the loading ramps next to the main terminal. After finding the numbered parking space the tower controller had assigned Mid-East Oil flight 521, the pilot applied brakes one final time, bringing the weather-beaten flying machine to a halt.

The old bird was the second 707 to roll out of the Boeing plant at Seattle, Washington some eighteen years previously. Shortly after that, United Airlines had purchased the aircraft, painted it with their colors and put it to work hauling passengers. Two years ago Mid-East Oil Inc, bought the plane, gutted it out except for a few seats then pressed it into less glamorous service - ferrying oilrig equipment.

Lance Ryder currently occupied a window seat just aft of the port wing. He sat stoically looking out through the Plexiglas window, peering at a metal patch that covered a hole in the wing. He'd noticed that a couple of the rivets had popped loose during the flight over from Frankfurt and decided that maybe he should mention it to the pilot or maybe the first officer.

He stood, walked forward toward the cockpit door and was just about to reach for the handle when he saw it turn. To avoid being tapped by the door as it opened he stepped back and waited for the person to enter.

The door opened and a tall thin man appeared before him wearing a soiled tan uniform of sorts, complete with short-pants and tan knee length socks. The three stripes on his shoulder-boards identified him as the first-officer or co-pilot. His name was Pierce Wellington and Ryder had met him when he came onboard in Germany.

He smiled and speaking with a clipped English accent mused, "Oh, Mister Ryder, you shouldn't stand so close to the door, might get your nose bumped, ol' boy."

"I was just coming forward to let you know there's a patch coming loose on your wing," Ryder announced casually.

"Yes, I know, the company should give us hazardous duty pay and parachutes to fly these ol' buckets." The tired looking co-pilot was about to facetiously expound further on the ills of the job, when someone gave him a slight shove from behind, forcing him to take a couple of awkward steps forward.

A woman who looked to be somewhere around thirty years old was now standing in the doorway. She was wearing a similar colored uniform, except that it was clean and sported four stripes at the shoulders, indicating that she was the aircraft captain. Even in the old ragtag cotton uniform, it was obvious at first glance that the word Goddess had been coined for one such as her. Short reddish-auburn hair and beautiful heart-shaped face accented the woman's perfectly sculptured body, although the current grimace of impatience she displayed temporarily detracted from her overall beauty.

She glanced at Wellington with a look that conveyed indifference; her voice filled with tired stress she lamented, "Wellington, I don't give-a-damn' if you stay onboard this four-engine trash hauler and complain for the remainder of the day, but at least get the hell out of the way and let me pass. I'm tired, hot, and I need a shower."

In deference to her rank Wellington took a step back and politely said, "Sorry, Lisa. By the way, this is Mister Ryder, the passenger we picked up in Frankfurt. I think you were already up in the cockpit running through pre-flight checks when Ryder came onboard." Wellington glanced at Ryder, and then added, "Mr. Ryder, this is Captain Lisa Anne Nickels, Mid-East's chief pilot."

The woman threw a surly glance Ryder's way along with a caustic verbal acknowledgment by pithily spitting out, "Hi Ryder and bye Ryder." And with that, she exited the aircraft and disappeared into the terminal building.

Wellington, seeming a little embarrassed by the situation hesitantly said, "Well Mister Ryder ... welcome to Lebanon".

Yeah, Ryder thought, *the word welcome could only be described as an oxymoron at this time and this place. It's the latter part of nineteen-seventy-three and the Yom Kippur war is turning the Middle East into a twisted battleground, what with Egypt and Syria trying to reduce Israel to a parking lot.*

The daytime temperatures were very hot and dry with cool nights, which was standard for this part of the world most of the year.

Ryder casually reached up and ran a hand through his sweaty brush cut blond hair and decided to deplane; it had to be cooler inside the terminal. "Thanks for the ride Wellington. I think I'll step into the terminal and see if I can get something for this thirst."

"Good show, Ryder. I think that after I secure the plane, I shall do likewise."

As the tall blond spy entered the building, he looked the place over and saw no trace of Lisa. *Now that was a lady in a hurry* he thought. He approached a lean dark Arab who was standing behind a ticket counter. "Excuse me, can you tell me how I can find the El Kadeem Hotel, and also do you have something cold and wet?" he asked.

The young Arab eyed Ryder curiously while reaching down to pull a soft drink out of an ancient Coke cooler and smiled as he set the beverage on the counter. His pearl-white teeth stood out in stark contrast against his brown skin. With thick accented English He replied, "Yes sir, but it would be a long walk. Perhaps if you took a taxi it would be better, and all the drivers know where it is."

"Thanks." Ryder downed the Coke, set the bottle and a coin on the counter, then turned and started for the main double-doors leading to the street. He was only a couple of steps from going through them, when he heard a voice behind him – more like a whisper actually.

"Excuse me, Major Ryder?"

Ryder's mind and feet froze, and then he turned to see who owned the voice, almost bumping into the short balding man following him. Who was this little guy who knew his rank, and obviously his status? The two men eyed each other for a couple of seconds, then the short man, peering through thick horn-rimed glasses, again addressed Ryder with a low pitched raspy voice. "Major Ryder, my name is Ben Dove, code name, El Dorado. I was sent here to meet you."

Ryder stood six-feet tall, wearing a white linen business suit and white Panama hat. He should not have been recognizable to anyone as an officer and agent of OMNI, except to another known agent. He looked the man over a second longer and then with some apprehension, said, "January five, sapphire."

The man hesitated for an instant, and then replied, "Delta-seven, jade green."

Ryder's facial expression conveyed a look of relief. The man facing him, using a designated OMNI code system had just identified himself as an operative from the agency. "Mr. Dove, my code ID is Proteus, and how did you recognize me?"

"Ryder, I know it's not normal OMNI policy, but I instructed the agency to wire fax me your picture, but it was done with a scrambled signal to reduce the amount of people who will know your whereabouts."

Wire facsimile data transfer via analog satellite signal was new state-of-the-art top-secret technology that could not currently be compromised, but still, Ryder was a very unhappy camper. In a low, almost hissing tone, the words spilled forth rapidly as he replied, "Listen, El Dorado, AKA, Brain Dead, or whoever the hell you are, I get orders for a sensitive assignment and the first thing out of the bag, some nitwit blows my cover by plastering my goddamn' picture all over the wire."

Dove, a little surprised at Ryder's reaction, took a step back and said, "Pardon me Major Ryder, but don't you think you're overreacting a bit? I know how you feel, sometimes I get the shaft too, but it can't be helped. I had to be sure of whom I'm working with. There's just too much at stake here. Look, you're upset and we can't talk here in public. Go to your hotel, relax and have a drink. I know where you're staying – I'll be over in an hour and we'll talk."

"Damn' right we'll talk, and you'd better have something to say that I want to hear," Ryder replied as he turned and hurriedly left the building.

Showered and wearing fresh clothes, Ryder felt a little better as he ambled across his hotel room and stepped out onto the balcony. He looked down into the noisy, dirty street and idly watched a herdsman, who was busy, driving six camels through a crowded open-air market by riding the lead camel and smacking him across the neck with a stick while leading the remainder crude but effective. As he stood there, letting his eyes wander over the activity below, his mind began to relax and slowly drift back to the events of the past month. Suddenly, for a few seconds, chilling mental pain gripped him as he relived the memory ... Mai Ling was dead; his wife of less than three weeks had been gunned down in a busy airport by a maniacal drug runner. That event, for a time, had put his mind into limbo.

ONMI officials, sensing his need for a break from the business, had released him for a month with near carte blanche spending. In other words, he would spend money and OMNI would discretely pick up the check -- within reason. He had caught a C-141 Starlifter shuttle flight out of Binh Hoa Air Base, Vietnam, to Honolulu, and then a commercial flight bound for Monte Carlo, to catch up on a little sun, gambling and whatever. He had been there a little over two weeks when he had gotten the call from Dante. Dante was an agent one-step higher on the food chain than Ryder. To be precise, when OMNI gave Ryder an assignment, it was usually Dante who delivered the news. Ryder had been lounging by the pool when a club steward brought out a phone and plugged it into one of the outlets near the relaxed spy's chair. The club employee handed the phone to the OMNI spy, as he said, "Call for you Mr. Ryder".

Ryder took the phone and put it to his ear. "Ryder."

"Ryder, this Dante. I warned you that I had heard unofficially that your next assignment would be in the Middle East, well OMNI just made it official, and I've been elected to give you the preliminary briefing. You're to leave at first light. To be explicit, tomorrow morning you're to catch a commercial flight for Frankfurt. After you arrive, go to the American Embassy and see a guy named Earl Duke. Officially, he's assigned there as a minor diplomat but that's just a cover. He's actually a deputy commander and number four in the OMNI hierarchy. His current position is coordinator for Middle-Eastern counter-intelligence. He'll get you a passport and papers identifying you as an equipment buyer for Mid-East Oil Inc. This will allow you to travel in that part of the country without generating suspicion or being forced to act like a tourist. After you get your credentials, make arrangements to catch a Mid-East cargo bird out of Frankfurt for Beirut. They have aircraft in and out daily hauling parts and shit like that. Once you arrive, check into the El Kadeem, you'll have a room reserved. One more thing, someone from the agency will contact you. Well, Ryder my man, I guess that's it. Good luck."

"Wait a minute! What the hell do you mean, good luck? You haven't told me why I'm going or what the assignment's about."

"Look, Ryder, I'm using a limited echo pocket scrambler that only allows me to give you class-one details, meaning travel instructions, besides I don't have the deep information. You're aware of how OMNI works, if you're not involved they don't give you access. The agent that contacts you should have some instructions. Gotta go Proteus, goodbye and thanks again for the help you gave me in Thailand."

"Yeah, hell of a way to repay me, by cutting my vacation short two weeks. I – hello, hello." Ryder slammed the phone down, for the last five seconds he had been talking to a dead line.

Ryder's memory of the past five weeks was suddenly spirited from his mind by a loud knock on the door. He took his eyes from the busy, camel-dung-littered street, and peered into the room. "It's open."

The door slowly opened, exposing Mr. Dove, standing in the hallway with one hand on the doorknob, and a somewhat apprehensive look on his face.

Ryder eyed him casually, his anger now dissipated. "Well ... come on in, Dove."

The short man entered the room and quietly closed the door, saying nothing.

Ryder stepped into the room from the balcony and motioned for him to take a chair. "If you're the operative that's been assigned to brief me on the problem that's cropped up here, be advised, I want all the info and details available. I don't like going down a road without a map."

Dove walked over and straddled one of the armless wooden chairs, placing his forearms on the backrest. "Yeah, I'm your contact and I've also been instructed to steer you around the rough spots. I've been in this part of the country for a while so I know where all the bodies are buried so as to speak. Originally, OMNI put me on assignment with MI-6, working with the Brits, which lasted for two years, and then the Mosaud, when the Israelis encountered some espionage problems, but understand, I deal mostly with the paperwork and don't much get involved with the blood and guts."

"Well, speaking of blood and guts, why have I been assigned to this area?" Ryder asked.

"Ryder, maybe I can explain it this way, as I sit here looking at that weapon in its holster, lying on the table across the room there ... that's the reason you're here. You're a deep operative, authorized to kill people, you're good at it, and I'm not. When diplomacy fails, we bring in your kind," Dove replied, his voice showing a hint of aloofness.

Ryder felt his temperature starting to rise but controlled it. Dove was right; Ryder was nothing more than a paid legal assassin, working for a Western international spy organization. His job was to handle military problems that world leaders could not solve with words. "Dove, what you're looking at, is a P-89 Ruger equipped with a BA2 mini laser sight. It's accuracy will allow me to kill a man at a hundred yards and sometimes it's just damn' necessary. I keep it topped off with a fifteen round clip of hollow-point hot loads. I came here to do a job, maybe somebody will get hurt, and maybe not. All I can say is, I'll try not to make a mess and try to keep from getting killed in the process. Now that that's out of the way, why don't you give me a rundown on the situation?"

Dove, momentarily seemed almost at a loss for words, then said, "Well, I'll tell you, the situation is sort of convoluted, that is to say, it's twisted, there's no black or white. Sometimes the bad guys seem like the good guys and *vice versa*, but we're here to assist the Israelis so we're going to assume they're the good guys."

"That's a hell of an attitude to take. Damn' man, it's a well-known fact the Israelis are our allies and have been so for years."

"On the surface that's true, and you can reinforce that argument by quoting a copy of the New York Times, Time Magazine, or any other damn' liberal rag in print these days. Actually, the American State Department doesn't give a rat's colon about Israel, except to use them as our junkyard dog. In addition, that's partly because they would steal a defense secret from us as quickly as they would from the Russians and a few other things that we don't have time to get into but, we do need a buffer between the Arabs, and they and us are it. Wise up Ryder, its every man for himself."

"And I assume that all the major players in the Israeli government are aware of that."

"You're catching' on Ryder, just like a whorehouse full of Johns and hookers, everybody fuckin' everybody. Look man, the operative word here is oil. Let's look at the mentality of the situation, the United States and the rest of the West needs oil and lots of it; most of the world's black-gold is right here, and the Western industrialized nations will have it one way or the other."

"What you're saying makes sense, and I think most people know we need oil, but Israel and the Arabs are fighting over land" Ryder said.

"True, everybody has their priorities, the Jews need a place to live, the Arabs, being religious zealots, are afraid the Jews are taking sacred territory like Jerusalem, the Gaza Strip, and whatever in hell else they deem holy, and us ... we want oil. That's the big three ingredients in the cake: land, religion and oil, and believe me, that baby is cooking as we speak. There's a forth of course, the American and European economy, but for simplicity sake we're going to leave that out of the equation" Dove added.

"Why not factor out the Jews, make their fight over land a separate issue and deal directly with the League of Arab States on oil, it seems like things would be simpler, or is there something I'm missing?" Ryder asked.

"If we put it on strictly a business basis, all the goddamn' rag-heads in North Africa, not to mention the Latinos in Brazil, would band together, get organized and OPEC could drive up prices to where the Western countries would go bankrupt in a year. Hell man, they'd own us."

"If they get organized ... and what's to stop them?" Ryder asked.

"Us. We're goin' to stop them. OMNI and the CIA, but primarily OMNI. If we keep things stirred up with a healthy amount of distrust among everybody, then OPEC can't effectively organize." Dove replied.

"Why not just give OPEC an ultimatum? We just set a fair price per barrel of oil and simply tell OPEC that we own all the big guns and will kick the shit out of any oil producing country that doesn't comply?" Ryder asked.

"Ah, Ryder, now you're thinking like a military dictator. America, and other Western countries which pride themselves on being a democracy, can't afford an image like that. No, the answers are dividing and conquer." Dove condescendingly answered.

"Like how?" Ryder asked with increasing interest.

"You're a military officer, a Marine I believe, at least on the record. I'll set out a scenario to which you can relate. If one analyzes an army, the first thing you realize is that it's not a democracy, because in a battle environment, orders have to be followed immediately without question, but, after a short period of time, with officers giving orders without explanation and enlisted men carrying them out, one can quickly see how resentment would build into revolt. It's a black and white situation which has to be defused and – "

Interrupting, Ryder finished his sentence for him. "And that's where the sergeant or NCO comes into the picture. The officer gives the sergeant the order, and the sergeant passes it along to the enlisted swine"

"Bravo, that's exactly right. The sergeant gets his ego massaged because the officers gives him a certain amount of authority and a little more money, in return for being used as insulation, and the soldier will more readily accept the order coming from the sergeant, a guy that he perceives as being a fellow enlisted man. A psychological ploy on a grand scale that's worked since man started building armies. A simple case of more power-hungry and diabolical humans taking advantage of less perceptive humans." Dove said.

"I'm not sure I totally agree with that assessment, but I do understand the concept. So, by having the Jews as the wild card, they are being used to muddy the waters and take the focus of the real issue."

"Yeah, simply stated that's pretty much it. You see, the Arabs have oil, and we have technology, all kinds of technology, jet fighters, tanks, guns and rockets of every description. If you can keep everybody fighting and thinking they need all that weaponry, then it's business as usual. They sell us oil; we in turn sell them guns and planes to get the money back and everyone's happy. Hell, they destroy all that hardware by fighting with each other and give the Western worker jobs building more of the shit. It's good for the economy. Hell, man, arms sales are the biggest business in the world, bigger than dope smuggling. Even the Arabs understand that it's better to exchange oil for weapons than simply have the oil taken from them. It gives the leaders a method for saving face, and controlling their people, and keeps the West from looking like bullies. They also understand that no matter how many weapons we sell them, we'll always keep the biggest and best for ourselves, that way they'll never be tempted to start a serious war with us."

"It seems to me, based on what you're saying, and with what's going on with the current war raging, that everything is in balance," Ryder said

"If it were just the standard players involved, that would be true, but recently there have been some new developments," Dove countered.

"You mean it's possible to have a situation more screwed up than what you've just laid on me? *Christ*, man, how much worse can it be?" Ryder asked.

"Yes Ryder, and that's why you were called in. I've recently received some communiqués from one of the American CIA operatives here, stating that there's a group of militant Arabs formed from several of the Arab states, which has put together what we believe to be a secret organization, of what size I don't know. There is also speculation that they've managed to obtain a quantity of weapons grade plutonium, enough to build a device ranging in the four-kiloton weight class. Now that's a serious bomb by anybody's standard, capable of taking out New York City, or an area even larger, depending on terrain. The CIA also claims this group has gotten hold of a nuclear trigger, which they brought into North Africa from England."

"Does the CIA know how they got it into the country?" Ryder asked.

"Hell Ryder! You have to quit thinking so microanalytical. At this point, it doesn't matter how they got the damn' trigger into the country. What we need to know is what they plan to do with the damn' bomb, if in fact they do have one, and how they plan to smuggle, it to the intended target," Dove replied as if speaking to a subordinate.

Dove's attitude was once again causing Ryder's temper to raise its ugly head. "Look Dove, I'm here to tell you, the small shit does matter, and it could tell us something about their *modus operandi* … Now do we have any information on the details of this situation?"

Dove, looking a little resigned, replied, "Well for starters, we think the name of the terrorist group is, 'El Sakaka,' but we're not even sure of that. We're also not even sure about them having the trigger, except that one came up missing from Lakenheath Air Base, England, and the group's name, El Sakaka, it has turned up in a couple of memos, and don't ask me who coined the phrase, or which CIA weenie turned up the name. Some of these intelligence operations are so screwed up, the right hand never knows what the left is doing, but for now we're calling it El Sakaka for identification."

"Do you have any clue, no matter how vague, of the organization's size, or how it's structured?" Ryder queried.

"Not a clue, not a guess, I told you, nothing." Dove answered, a little irritated at Ryder's redundancy.

"Well, at least you're making' it easy." Ryder sarcastically replied.

"If it was easy, Ryder, you wouldn't be here."

"I assume you want to get started on this right away?"

"I'm already started. Why don't you take a day or two in order to get your bearings, and then take a plane to Casablanca? After …"

"Casablanca! Damn' man, that's in Morocco. What the hell's in Morocco?"

"It appears this octopus may have far reaching tentacles. As I was saying before you so crudely interrupted … after you get there, check into the Marrakesh Hotel, as Dorian Anton. Some spook from the CIA, will contact you and he'll update you with any information he has on the situation, which probably won't be a whole hell of a lot. He's also there to lend interagency support should you need any. The CIA agent at that location gave us the last info that we have on this thing"

"And if I'm not?" Ryder asked.

"Not what?" Dove responded, a little puzzled at Ryder's question.

"Not contacted." Ryder replied.

"Wait three days and if nothing happens, fly back to Beirut, and we'll start from scratch."

Ryder asked, "So what else do we have?"

"I'm afraid that's all I know Ryder, you're as well informed on the problem as I." With that, Dove stood and headed for the door. Reaching it, he paused for a moment then turned and said, "One last thing Ryder, I'll be your conduit to OMNI. You will keep me informed on events as they unfold, and I in turn will pass along your instructions from OMNI."

"I gotcha." Ryder condescendingly replied. Giving Ryder a puzzled look, Dove turned and left, closing the door gently.

Ryder walked over and sat down on the bed to ponder the situation. To his way of thinking, it just didn't make sense, these people were crude ... sure, they could handle T-72 Russian tanks, pipe bombs, dynamite, RPG rockets and weapons like that. In addition, even fly high performance jet fighters like the Mig-25 Foxbat and they had a handle on most other conventional killing devices, but nukes, it just didn't wash, unless things had changed since the last time he'd been here. And how would they transport a device like that? There sure were a lot of ifs in this situation to Ryder's way of thinking. He was starting to formulate some opinions. He would chew on Dove's story, but he wasn't going to swallow any of it until he got a bigger piece of the picture, a picture that he could translate into something tangible, and something to go on. What had his dad told him years ago ... ah yes, it was, keep you mind open to new ideas son. Maybe this CIA gumshoe in Casablanca had come up with something since Dover had last conferred with him. This business was already starting to get on Ryder's nerves, and then his thoughts turned to the bar downstairs that also doubled as the El Kadeem's lobby. Most Arab countries don't tolerate liquor, but it appeared this hotel was occupied primarily by Westerners, in which case, the unwritten rule was, usually most of the regional Arab governments would turned a blind eye; if the liquor was confined to American and European compounds or bars. Yeah, what Ryder needed was a drink, maybe it would help him think better, then again, maybe not, but he intended to find out.

Chapter 2

As Ryder walked into the lounge, he noticed there were approximately fifteen or twenty wooden tables that accommodated four chairs each, with a long wide ornate horseshoe bar positioned in the center of the room. The lighting was subtle and overall it looked fairly comfortable.

As he approached the bar, a short, well-built, dark haired lady bartender spotted him and ambled over to take his order. She looked up and gave him a casual smile and said, "Hello, my name is Margaret, and what can I get for you today, my blonde headed Nordic one?"

Returning the smile, Ryder replied, "I'm not Nordic, I'm an American, but I can tell by your accent that you're not. Oh, by the way, you can call me Ryder, Lance Ryder"

Her smile broadened a little, as if maybe there was an invitation somewhere in those pouting red lips. "Of course not Mr. Ryder, I'm from Amsterdam," she said.

Ryder was starting to take a mild interest in this woman. "And what's a nice girl from Holland doing in a den of sin like this?"

With a mock look of disgust, she replied, "I thought you guys had quit using that tired line. Anyway, a lady has to make a living."

"And I thought you ladies had quit using that antiquated line." He was about to reply with a little additional repartee, when a bearded roughneck down the bar yelled at the bartender for service.

"Margaret, you big bosomed winch, bring another round, and make haste or we shall surely perish of thirst. Damn! A bloke can't get his whistle properly wet these days."

She turned her head slightly and eyed the loudmouth. "Keep your bloody hat on, I'm comin'."

Ryder watched her cute round oscillating buttocks as she shuffled away, then turned his back to the bar rail to get a look at the kind of a crowd that would hang out in a place like this. He was scanning the large room, right to left, and then he spotted her, Lisa, the cute mega-bitch. She was sitting alone at a table near the back wall. *What the hell*, he thought. *I may as well give it a shot.*

He stepped away from the bar and started back toward her table. She had ditched the uniform and had replaced it with a white silk low cut blouse. She balanced her casual look with designer jeans accented by a pair of low white heels. When he was about ten feet from her, she looked up and spotted him.

Without a hint of expression in her voice, she said, "Well Mr. Ryder, I see you found your way off the airplane."

"Mind if I join you?" Ryder smiled.

"Look Ryder, I've heard all the bullshit pick-up lines and I'm in no mood to listen to some clown trying to maneuver into a position so he can use my body for a fucking trampoline and I do mean that almost literally."

"I don't want to use anyone. I know you fly into Beirut frequently and I thought maybe you could help me with some information."

"That's not original, but I haven't heard it in awhile. It'll get you an A for effort and a half-hour at the table . . . sit down."

Ryder took a chair. "Listen, why don't you call me Lance?"

"Shit, I knew it. It'll be Lance now, and Darling at two in the morning, when your head is laid back against one of my pillows, and you're smoking the proverbial cigarette, feeling smug about your latest conquest."

"Whoa there little fly-girl! What the hell makes you such a hard-ass? Did your mother make you wear tight diapers when you were small?"

With a slight sneer, she spat out, "That's it! Ryder, get the fuck away from my table."

Ryder knew at once that he had made a serious mistake. "Look, I'm sorry. I know that was the, no shit, wrong thing to say. It's just that you seem so pissed off at the world ... Can we start over? I really do just want information."

Lisa paused and looked at Ryder with an icy stare that seemed to go right through him and then with a voice that was calm but filled with resolve, said, "Give it a rest, Ryder, you're just not plumbed right for me."

"What, what do you mean?" Ryder said, totally taken by surprise.

"I mean I don't like men." Lisa said with an expression and tone that conveyed, touché.

Well ... that sure cleared up a few things. In a strange sort of way, Ryder was almost relived; at least this was not an attack on him personally. "Lisa, can we just sit here for a few minutes and discuss some non-personal stuff, like the local people, geography and possibly some useful things you might give me on the area in general. I'm looking for any kind of information that will help me with my job."

"Like what?" Lisa suspiciously replied.

"Well, I don't know exactly. I guess if I knew what I was looking for I wouldn't be asking. For instances, does things seem normal? Are there new people in town? Have you noticed anything going on lately that just strikes you as being out of the ordinary in the way people look or behave?"

She relaxed a little and her manner became a bit more passive. "Okay Lance, maybe you're really not on the make. However, I have to tell you, those are some strange and convoluted questions you're asking. Specifically, what's on your mind?"

"For openers, how often do you fly into the Middle-East from Europe?"

Screwing up her face slightly in thought, she replied, "Oh, on the average I would say ... four or five times a month. Why?"

"Just curious. How long have you been working for Mid-East Oil, and in particular, flying the Europe to North-Africa routes?"

She hesitated for a moment, giving him a mild quizzical look, and then replied, "Oh, maybe five years, give or take a month. I started with Mid-East, flying right seat as a co-pilot. Now let me ask you a question. You came in on one of our planes, so I assume that Mid-East Oil employs you. What do you do?"

"I'm a buyer; I try to get the best prices on oilrig equipment, you know, save the company a little money here and there. Look, in the past five years that you've been ferrying equipment in here, have you noticed anything that's changed in the way of certain people's attitudes, or maybe the mood of the people, particularly in the time frame just prior to the war starting? Have you noticed any new militant groups materializing in the region?"

"Well, first of all, I don't know if you could call this a war, people are predicting this thing will only last a matter of weeks. You know the Israelis caught hell in the beginning, but it looks like they're starting to turn it around. As far as your question about new militant groups springing up; there is always a group of people here or there, pissed off about something" she replied.

"Yeah, that's what I understand. How about people—have you noticed anything unusual or different in the people you've brought in or that have come in on other aircraft?"

"Oh, I don't know, haven't paid that much attention. It's been mostly equipment, but in the way of people, I've brought in a lot of roughnecks, mainly because they don't seem to be able to train these damn' lazy-ass rag-heads to work the rigs. Once in a while I'll fly in a company VIP, who wants to look things over. You know of course, it's just our headquarters that's in Beirut, most of our workers are disbursed to Saudi Arabia, Iraq, Kuwait and other North African countries where we have business interests"

"Yeah, I know. Say, the people who work the rigs, and hang out in the local bars, as well as the Arabs, are they pretty much always the same people, and do you know some, or most of them well enough to know what they do, and what their political feelings or affiliations might be?"

Lisa's face was beginning to take on a perplexed, but interested look. "It's intriguing."

"What's intriguing?" he asked, again wondering if he had triggered some hostility in her.

"These questions that you're asking me; why would an equipment buyer want to know so much about the local roust-a-bouts, rag-heads and militant factions in the area?" Lisa asked, wondering if there were more to the question than Ryder had put forth.

"Simple, as a buyer, I need information about the type of soil they're drilling in and the kinds of people who are using the rigs. It's important to know if the political climate is calm so the oil flow out of the country is not in jeopardy of being disrupted. You know, general data like that," he said, hoping he didn't sound defensive.

"You could get that info from the engineers; they'd know more about that kind of shit than I would." Lisa replied, pressing the issue.

Getting the feeling that he was starting to arouse suspicion he decided to drop the subject. "Yeah ... maybe you're right. Forget I ask."

Inquisitively she said, "Lance, I gotta feeling you're looking for more than good deals on oil rig equipment. Could I be right," She was unknowingly and unintentionally backing him into a corner.

He was starting to feel a little pressured. It was obvious she was more intuitive than he had anticipated. "Look, let's drop it. I'm just an inquisitive person."

He was temporarily caught off guard by the slight tight spot she had unintentionally put him in and let the conversation slide into momentary silence.

He was starting to draw a mental picture of how she might perceive him, generally on the positive side he hoped. Most men by this time would have shown a little more aggressiveness in trying to get her into the sack, or at least tried to establish a connection for the purpose of moving in that direction, after all, she was better looking, and radiated more sex than the average woman. He felt that she was use to having guys falling over her and that was probably part of the turn off when she met men; no challenge. What he didn't know was what had happened to her when she was fourteen.

To her way of thinking, men were just base, crude animals, bent on self-satisfaction and sometimes violence, but Ryder, she had a hunch was different somehow. It was nothing she could put her finger on, it was his demeanor, mannerisms and not what he said, but what he didn't say. There was a lack of brashness that most men on the make always bandied about. She was surprised by the sudden realization that she liked him. It was not that she wanted to bed him down, but his rough exterior couldn't conceal the vulnerable something inside, something she felt he was trying to deal with - the memory of a bad experience maybe. Feeling the need to find out if he was real, and if she was right, she slowly reached across the table, took his hand, and gently squeezed.

Ryder hesitated, and then responded likewise.

His lack of sexual aggressiveness was reassuring and had a tendency to dissipate her long held fear of men. She looked into his eyes, and saw the deep sadness of a man that had at one time or another experienced a great loss. She raised her other hand and touched his face as she softly said, "Lance, don't get me wrong, I meant what I said about men. I've always felt like they are human beasts who feel that instant gratification isn't quick enough, but I get the feeling you need a shoulder right now." Why was she getting these strange feelings about this guy? And why did she feel a need to touch him. It was crazy and inexplicable. She felt like there was a locomotive of emotion pushing her along against her will. Okay ... maybe he could be a friend, but her life was settled, and she knew what she was. She had a lover back in Stuttgart and she wasn't going to complicate her life by entertaining thoughts about this man, but she was starting to let these thoughts bother her. Damn', was it possible that she was bi-sexual? In addition, what about the other side of the coin? The thought of becoming a bull dyke, twenty years down the road, sitting in a dingy bar somewhere, waiting to swoop down on some young female novice. That thought didn't exactly appeal to her either. Now suddenly there were all of these strange new feelings starting to flood into her mind, flipping all her long held concepts into the wind. The scariest feeling of all was the fact that she was attracted to this guy far more than her safety net would allow. Then she realized that somehow in this short time, he had all but destroyed her sexual prejudice against men. With that barrier gone she was starting to see him through different eyes. This was too much, too fast; she attempted to clear her mind. "Lance, I know this'll probably sound crazy, but I'm starting to feel a little restless, would you mind going for a walk with me?"

Ryder had lapsed into silence with his thoughts divided between Lisa, and the impending investigation. He responded to her question. "Uh ... you know, that's a good idea. Lets take a turn around the market and see what the local merchants are peddling."

Lisa retrieved her purse as they stood and then preceded Ryder as they left the hotel bar.

As they stepped out into the throng of people and started down the street, Ryder took her hand and with a smile, softly said, "I advise you to watch your step."

"Yeah, I know what you mean, but you know, I lived on a farm for a little while when I was growing up and I don't mind the smell of a little cow shit, or in this case camel shit." She thought about what she had just said, and it seemed strange that she could be saying something like that to a guy she'd just met.

Ryder laughed. "You know Lisa, I love the way you sugar-coat a delicate subject."

Suddenly embarrassed and at the same time, she wondered why she even cared what he thought about her but it occurred to her that she did. Suddenly she wanted to change the topic. "Lance, do you mind if we talk about something personal?"

"Like what?"

"Sex."

F. Washington Brown

"I like talkin' about sex, almost as much as I like indulging in it. What's on your mind?"

"Do you think I'm abnormal because I like women?"

"Well, homosexuality is not my style and I don't understand it, but I say to each his own. To put it another way and this may sound like a worn phrase or cop-out, but I really don't judge people. You know, speaking of sex, these Arabs have some strange sexual habits by our standards."

"Like what?" she said intrigued by the possibility of hearing something new.

"Are you familiar with the philosophy of Islam?"

"Are you referring to the Muslim religion?"

"Yes." he replied.

"Well, let's see ... I know most of these people here subscribe to it, Allah is their God, the Koran is their bible and something about Mohammed being the major prophet, but what does that have to do with sex?"

"Well I'm getting' to that. Have you ever heard of Ramadan?"

"No." she replied with increased interest.

"Well, a certain sect, or group of the Moslem Arabs, I don't know which, maybe all, incorporate Ramadan into their religious rites, it's kind of like lent for the Catholics in as much as it's celebrated once a year except it lasts for thirty days and nights. During this thirty day period of Ramadan they are not allowed to eat in the daytime, only at night."

"If they don't eat in the day, what do they do?"

"Sleep, they sleep most of the day and celebrate their religion most of the night."

"Interesting, but weren't we talking about sex?"

"Yes, and I'm coming to that. They, like Christians, believe God or Allah, is coming back to earth, but they also believe Allah is coming back to earth, born from a man, so during Ramadan, the holiest time of the year, the men participate in anal sex as part of the religious ritual, but only with other men. This is done in the belief that a holy man who's a true believer in the Koran, will be carefully selected to conceive and bear Allah; thus bringing much honor upon himself. I guess you might say, something like the Virgin Mary. Women are excluded from the ritual presumably because a female is not worthy of such a lofty feat. You understand of course that over here women are held pretty much in low regard, someplace just above a camel and are only good for bearing mere mortals."

Stunned, Lisa lapsed into momentary silence, then after taking few seconds to recover, said, "You've got to be kidding."

"Well, that's what I thought when I first heard about it but that seems to be the case and it gives you an idea of just how strange religion can be."

"That qualifies as the weirdest thing I've ever heard of and all the time I've been flying in and out of here nobody has ever mentioned it to me."

"Yeah, it seems to be one of those things you never hear about." Ryder took her by the elbow to guide her across the street as he said, "Come on, there's a meat market with fresh heads on poles, lets go check it out."

"Oh no Lance, I don't want to go and look, that's such a disgusting practice they have for advertising fresh camel meat," she protested, while all the time enjoying the touch of his hand on her arm.

He laughed softly and said, "You mean because when they butcher a camel or sheep, the merchant sticks the animal's head on a pole to let people know there's fresh meat? There are no newspaper flyers, how else can they advertise?"

"It's not just that, they have no refrigeration, and in this heat, the meat quickly spoils and gets encrusted with flies and maggots," she said as she laughingly placed her hand to her forehead, faked a swoon, and pressed against him for imagined support.

Ryder smiled. "That's a good reason for advertising, sell it before it gets rancid, besides if you cook it real good, a few maggots won't hurt you. Its just more protein." He was having a good time watching her face contort with disgust. "By the way Lisa, have you ever eaten camel meat?"

"No. Have you?"

"Yeah, a little like beef, except it's a little stringier and doesn't have as much fat, hardly any at all actually." He could hardly keep a straight face.

Smiling she said, "That's it Lance, I've had enough, take me back to the hotel."

As he walked her to her door, he found that her room was only a couple of doors down the hall from his. "Lisa, I've really enjoyed this evening. I'm glad it turned out this way."

She turned to face him and mused, "Me too."

Softly he said, "Lisa I don't want to ruin a perfect evening by appearing too pushy, But I was wondering if you would have breakfast with me in the morning? Maybe if you have time afterward we could walk the streets and do a little shopping?

"Sure Lance, I think we can do that."

His face lit up with a smile as he said, "Good. I'll see you around seven a.m. in the dinning room. He once more gently squeezed her hand and softly said, "Good night." He released her hand, turned and started for his room.

Lisa watched him walk down the hall for a moment, then as if making up her mind she called to him, "Lance, wait a minute."

He stopped and turned with a questioning look on his face as he said, "Yes."

She was feeling a bit apprehensive and a little afraid of plowing this new ground because she knew he could perceive this move as taking their relationship beyond the boundaries of friendship. Did she want to take it beyond friendship but was afraid to admit it even to herself? "Lance," she said, "come back I want to talk to you."

Ryder approached her and said, "Is something wrong?"

She looked up at him and said, "No nothing is wrong, maybe just the opposite. You know Lance, I was thinking about something on the way back to the hotel and I want to talk to you. Would you mind stepping into my room for a little while?"

Ryder noted the somber, but thoughtful expression on her face and decided that maybe it was something he should hear. "Sure Lisa." he whispered as he reached up, turned the doorknob, pushed the door open and followed her inside.

She walked over to the far window and stood looking out at the dimly lit city, saying nothing, as if trying to gather her thoughts.

Ryder strode slowly across the room and stood behind her, likewise gazing out at nothing in particular and making no body contact. He had a feeling that something was weighing heavily on her mind and he didn't want to give the impression that he was pressing her to talk about it.

Slowly raising her hands to the sides of her downcast face, which now had taken on a sad expression. She appeared to be trying to hide tears as she finally spoke with a voice that had an almost little girl quality about it. "Lance, this is insane. I have this compulsion to tell you something … something I have never told anybody … not people who are close to me or that I have known for years … not my parents … not even … well that's not entirely true; I told Connie."

"Connie who?"

"Never mind, it's not important but what I'm about to tell you is." She paused.

Lance, sensing the magnitude of the moment and wanting to make it easier for her, reached out, placed his hand on her shoulder, and tried gently to pull her to him.

She resisted as she whispered, "No Lance, I don't want you to hold me and if I look at you I won't be able to say what's on my mind".

He dropped his hand and stood quietly, saying nothing more, waiting for her to continue at a pace that was comfortable for her.

"Lance what I'm about to tell you is nothing new, it's happened to other women before and will no doubt happen to women in the future. To hear about it is one thing but to have it happen to you is trauma that is indescribable

F. Washington Brown

...When I was fourteen, my parents went away to Aspen Colorado for a weekend skiing trip, leaving me and my brother Jon at home. Chester, an older neighbor boy who was sixteen at the time came over to see my brother Jon. They were friends and played high school sports together. I told Chester that Jon had gone to a movie, but he wanted to come in and wait for Jon to get home. To make a long story short and because I don't want to dwell on it, well ... he came into my room and raped me. It was violent, I screamed and fought him, but there was nobody to help. You have to understand; Chester played high-school football, stood five-feet-ten inches tall and weighed around one hundred and seventy pounds. When it was over, he said that if I ever told anybody it would ruin the family name and that I would be sorry. He also said that for my silence, it would never happen again, and it didn't but that didn't keep me from feeling humiliated to the point of contemplating suicide, or worrying about being pregnant for the next three or four months. I can remember that happening as if it were yesterday and as much as I wish it weren't so, it's burned indelibly into my mind. I believe that incident altered the course of my life because thereafter I could never feel comfortable having a man put his hands on me—until maybe now."

Suddenly, Ryder felt like a mental voyeur; he knew he had reached her inner being and it made him feel uneasy, almost lost for words. "Lisa, I really don't know what to say, I—"

She turned and faced him as she placed her hands on his chest. "Don't say anything, the unpleasant things have already been said. I had to tell you that so you would understand what I'm about to ask you to do now."

Trying to ease her pain by lightening the conversation with some trivial humor he smiled and replied, "At this point I think I would do anything you ask, short of robbing a bank or killing myself."

She looked up at him, placed her hand on his arm, smiled, and said, "I'm glad you feel that way, you see I want to know if there is a man in the whole world who is considerate enough to put a woman's feelings and wishes above his own, even in a situation where the temptation is great to do otherwise."

"How do you mean?" Ryder asked somewhat perplexed.

"Well for example, if we stand here with our clothes on and discuss non-sexual related things and I ask you to leave, I'm sure you would. Is that not right?"

"Yeah, I'd go." Ryder replied, a little curious as to where she was going with the question.

"What if we were standing here naked and I ask you to get dressed and leave, would you do it?"

"It would be tough, but if that's what you wanted."

"I haven't been near a naked male since I was fourteen and now I'm getting ready to take the biggest gamble of my life because you have stirred feelings in me that I didn't know existed until now. If I'm right it will probably change the rest of my life, if I'm wrong I will never look at a man again as I'm looking at you tonight."

No doubt about it, Ryder was feeling pressure. "Lisa, are you sure you want to do this, I mean if it were different circumstances, I—"

"Lance, don't talk, just take your clothes off."

"What?" he asked, more than mildly puzzled.

"I said, take your clothes off." With that, she reached up and started unbuttoning his shirt.

Ryder knew he wasn't the smartest guy in the world, but he could take a hint. He slowly unbuttoned her blouse and in moments, they were standing next to the bed completely naked. He leaned down, kissed her softly, and then started to lift her gently, to lay her on the bed.

She reached out and grasped his wrist. "NO! . . . I don't want you to put me on the bed and jump on me; I want you to make love to me . . . like a woman would."

This little turn of events sure put a twist in his thought processes. "What, what do you mean?"

"Slow down . . . don't be controlling . . . gently, I want you to think about me and not yourself, now get on your knees."

"Okay sweetheart, you're in charge." He settled to his knees in front of her and waited for her next move, deciding to take a passive roll and let her run the show.

She spread her feet about eighteen to twenty inches apart, leaned her hips toward him and placed her hands on the back of his head, pulling him in as she leaned her shoulders back for balance.

Ryder caught a glimpse of her soft little auburn velvet triangle as it closed with his face, while at the same time he reached around, placing both his hands on her well-shaped buttocks, and with great abandon did what he was born to do. From the moment he had first saw her on the airplane through all of the fateful events that had transpired since then to bring them together, Ryder had never entertained a serious thought that this moment would really ever happen. It was as if the heavens had opened up and the gods had smiled on him, especially Diana the goddess of love. Before long he could feel her body tense up as she emitted gentle moans of pleasure and softly whispered words like, "yes ... that's it ... more ... Oh god! I love it".

Ryder could feel the pressure on the back of his head as her hands pulled him in tighter, his nostrils catching her musky female fragrance, his lips and tongue tasting her salty womanly essence as she became increasingly moist.

Slowly, she tilted her head back and cried out, not a loud scream, but more like an audible gasp. For a long moment, he wasn't sure he would not suffocate, and then she relaxed her grip as a slight trembling sensation rippled through her body. She stood for a few minutes with her eyes closed, saying nothing and then she stepped back and looked down at him with an expression of pure satisfaction in her eyes. Finally, she said, "Good night Lance. I'll talk to you tomorrow ... like you said, we'll have breakfast."

Ryder slowly stood, feeling somewhat perplexed and with a slight rasp in his voice said, "Lisa isn't this sort of premature ... I mean I thought we were ... what about me ... is this it? Are we done?"

Her expression changed and became passionless, almost cold. "Believe me, Lance, we're done. I know that I'm in a compromised position and if you want to take me I won't protest or try to stop you because you've earned it, but it would be against my will and in my mind it'll be rape, so I'm asking you to put your fucking clothes on and leave."

He paused for a moment tying to make sense out of what she was saying, finally he replied in a subdued tone, "Yeah, sure, why not." Now he knew what Led Zeppelin meant by Dazed and Confused, but what could he do? He picked up his clothes, got dressed, and left the room. Walking down the hall, he was still trying to make sense out of what had just happened. Not in his whole life had he ever encountered a woman like Lisa. Was this lady warped or what? The word, bitch, kept cropping in his mind. As he entered his room he began to rationalize the whole situation and decided it was for the best, after all, he was here on assignment and this woman would just serve to take his focus off the business of tracking these terrorist or whatever the hell they were. Realizing the need for a cold shower he decided to take a bath, brush his teeth, go to bed and forget the whole damn' day ever happened.

Ryder stepped out of the bathroom with his robe on, padded across the room and got into bed. He was about to turn out the light on the nightstand when he heard a soft knock at the door. He glanced at the door for a second and then yelled, "Look Dove, whatever you want to tell me can wait 'til morning. I'm tired, good-night."

There was another soft rap at the door then a woman's voice. It was Lisa.

"Lance I have to talk to you." she said softly.

Ryder took a deep breath to control his irritation and then replied, "Lisa, listen, I'm tired. Couldn't we discuss whatever it is tomorrow? Anyway, you're bad news, mean spirited, shit like that, go away and get into the wind. I don't know anymore descriptive adjectives so go torture some other poor bastard."

"No Lance, you don't understand. I have to talk to you now."

"Look, lady! What part of, go away, don't you understand?

Her voice changed slightly, trembling with anger. "No, you look! Lance, open this fuckin' door now or I'll scream."

Well this sure put a new spin on, who was in charge. "Okay, okay, just shut-up wait a minute. I gotta unlock it." *Damn'*, he thought, *this woman is two and zero... Lisa wins two and Ryder wins zero.* He got up, walked over, flipped the latch on the door and opened it.

She was standing in the doorway wearing a red housecoat that flew open as she rushed in and threw her arms around his waist. She wore nothing beneath it.

"Lance I had to be sure! I hope you understand," she said, sounding like an excited high school cheerleader who's just found out about boys.

Ryder, by now was completely confused. He pulled her to one side and closed the door. "Lady, it's late, you're going to wake-up the whole damn' neighborhood and how did you know which room I'm staying in?"

Grinning, she replied, "To answer your question, I saw you come to this room after you checked in and I don't care if I do wake-up everybody. Lance darling, don't you understand that I had to be sure?" Smiling, she spun around like a ballerina and added, "I'm throwing caution to the wind, and yes I'm sure this is right."

Looking a little puzzled Ryder replied, "Sure? Yeah I'm sure that you screwed up my mind tonight."

"I apologize for what happened. When you left the room, it was all I could do to keep from stopping you but I had to know that you really would leave after us going that far and you did. I think I've been living a lie, I'm not a lesbian ... and Lance, honey, I want it all ... Let's don't talk anymore just take me to bed."

Ryder certainly had no problem with that. As he scooped her up and headed for the bed he whispered, "Lisa, I've only got one thing to tell you before we hit the sack ..."

"And what's that, big boy?"

"They don't call me Ryder for nothing."
She smiled and mockingly whispered, "Prove it."

Chapter 3

The sun's rays, like long golden knives slashed their way in between the wooden shutter slats that covered the window and fought their way into the room, attacking Ryder's eyes. He awoke and looked at Lisa. She lay there beside him asleep, naked except for the sheet partially covering her legs. The woman had a body that didn't need clothes to hold everything in place; she looked incredibly beautiful, dressed or not. Ryder thought about last night. It was amazing how all those pent-up years had affected her and how she had reacted when the dam finally broke. He felt fortunate that he had been on the receiving end of that release as this wild river of a woman had flooded over him in an untamed torrent of emotion, although at times, wasn't sure he was going to be able to, like a Holland Dike, contain her. Suddenly he wondered if that were how lesbians came to be known as dykes. He chuckled to himself for a second as the bazaar thought, like a sail-boat, floated through his mind, then admonished himself because he knew that, dyke, was a label that didn't apply in her case. Reluctantly he dropped the train of thought and decided to get up, call the airport, and see what he could do about getting a flight out to Casablanca.

He rolled over gently, trying not to wake her, and was just about to drop his feet on the floor when he felt a warm hand grasping his arm.

Lisa's voice was a husky sleep filled whisper, spiked with a hint of passion as she adamantly growled, "No Lance, you're not getting out of this bed. I'm not finished with you. Until last night, I hadn't experienced a man's lovemaking in my entire life. I have a lot catching up to do and … you're the guy that's going to help me by giving me what I want when I want it". Her bright expression dimmed a little as she said, "I only have one regret. What do I tell Connie, and how can I break it gently ... the news that I can't see her anymore?"

Ryder looked into her glistening emerald green eyes. "Who's this Connie, you're talking about?"

"Connie Lindsey, my lover who is currently working in Germany. She's a stewardess for British European Airways."

"You'll just have to break it to her as easy as possible. You know it's the right thing to do."

A little sadly, she replied, "Yeah, I know." Suddenly her eyes brighten. "Let's drop it for now and just think about you and me."

As he took her in his arms he had a feeling he wasn't going to be able to get that airplane out of Beirut today and somewhere in the back of his mind a little warning alarm was going off, saying, Ryder what have you gotten yourself into.

They made love off and on all day and into the night, getting out of bed only to shower or go downstairs to eat.

The following morning Ryder awoke early, eased out of bed, dressed, picked up his bags, and tiptoed out of the room. He looked back at her just before he went through the door. She was sleeping peacefully and he would have liked to remain indefinitely but he knew there were planes to catch and things that had to be done.

As he entered the airport terminal, Ben Dove approached and fell into step with him. "Ryder, I noticed you picked up a companion; the lady pilot who flew you into the country, I believe."

"What are you, Dove, some kind of a fuckin' peeper?"

"Not exactly, but we have people keeping an eye on you; it's for your own protection. Incidentally, do you think it's wise to be getting mixed up with a skirt while you're on assignment?"

"Pull off your dogs. I can take care of myself and don't worry about the lady, she's my concern."

"Can't do that entirely, if something happens to you, ONMI will want to know."

"Okay, but if I get into a shoot-out or a tight situation and I'm not sure of who is who, I'll take out your man just as quick as I'll take out a bad guy, so if you've got somebody in the field, you or he had better let me know ... or let him know. "

"Fair enough. I've arranged for a Lear jet; the airplane will be at your disposal while you're in country. After you get to Casablanca and settled into the Marrakesh, wait until six in the evening then go to Rick's Cafe Americain. It's a nightclub patronized exclusively by Americans and Europeans, and it's located one block east of the Marrakesh."

"You've got to be kidding. You're referring to Rick's Cafe Americain? You mean like the classic gambling casino in that nineteen-forty-two movie, Casablanca ... lets see, I think it starred Humphrey Bogart and Ingrid Bergman?"

"Well, Proteus, I'm surprised. I would have never guessed that you were a classic movie buff. Anyway, it seems that six or seven years after the movie was made, there was this enterprising French businessman who, already having some holdings in what was French Morocco at the time, decided to put in the bar, thinking it might attract tourist. I guess it was a good idea because I understand it does a brisk business and succeeds in attracting some of the strangest people on the continent. You should feel right at home. Oh ... I almost forgot; do you have a brown suit?"

"Yeah, why do you ask?"

Dove reached into his pocket, pulled out a lapel pin, and tossed it to Ryder.

"This Mid-East Company pin and your brown suit is how the CIA is going to know you."

"Is there anything of importance I should know about my contact in Morocco?"

"His name is Chico Baronga, code-name is Don Juan, and I believe he has a partner by the name of Holt Malloy. I don't know much more than that, but remember one thing, these guys are Company operatives, so be careful about how much information you share with them particularly concerning OMNI or you may wind up getting screwed."

"Company?"

"Yeah, THE COMPANY. Insiders refer to the CIA as, The Company. Incidentally, your airplane is the blue and white bird with Mid-East Oil markings on it and it's sitting on the ramp just to the left as you exit the boarding gates. Well, good-by Proteus, and good luck. By the way, officially the reason you're going to Casablanca is to inspect new equipment that's bound for Mendoub".

The two men stopped to shake hands as Ryder replied, "Same here, Dove. I'll try to keep you informed so try and monitor your D50 mini UHF radio as often as possible or at least keep the low wattage beeper activated." Ryder turned and disappeared through the gate.

Dove paused long enough to watch Ryder walk through the door then he turned and went to a telephone booth. Picking up the receiver, he attached a small device to it and dialed a number. "El Dorado here, Operation, Rolling Thunder is in play. Proteus the lion is out of the cage." He removed the device, dropped the receiver into the cradle, and turned to leave. Precisely at the same time, two crimson stains appeared on his shirt. He slumped to the floor, without so much as uttering a sound.

The Lear sliced quickly and quietly through North African skies, giving Ryder a chance to reflect on the key elements of his last mission, a mission in which he had been assigned to take down a ring of drug-runners at Long-Binh Vietnam. He had accomplished the task and came close to getting killed in the process, which wasn't unusual. He had out of necessity put himself in harms way on other assignments. That's what he was paid to do but the last mission had been distinctly different. He couldn't help but wonder about the way Eddie Slade had died. Ryder had no doubt seen a suit of black armor rise out of the drug runner's burning body. He had tried to rationalize the event away by forcing himself to believe it was a stress-induced hallucination, but it was no good, he knew it wasn't his imagination. Ryder had also looked into Eddie's indigo eyes before he had died. Eddie had not been human and what was worse, Ryder had a feeling that the evil phenomena would come back to haunt, or even try to kill him.

The feeling and memory was shook loose when he felt the aircraft's nose pitch down slightly as the pilot brought the small twin-engine passenger jet around for a final approach. The airport at which they were getting ready to land was once an American installation called, Nourasur Air Base. The U.S. Air Force had constructed and used it to stage B-47 bombers as a deterrent to Russia's strategic threat. Nourasur was one of two bases abandoned in the mid-sixties when strategy changed and money got tight. Now the Moroccan government used it as sort of an international airport due to its close proximity to Casablanca. The second former American air base known as Sidi Slimane A B had been built two hundred miles inland and to the south in the Moroccan desert. Because it was isolated from any major city it had no value to the Moroccan government and had been left abandoned and in disrepair since the Americans had evacuated. However two months ago, the word, abandoned, was a term that had ceased to exist for Sidi Slimane, as Ryder was about to learn.

The Lear touched down smoothly and the pilot taxied over to one of the VIP parking spaces near the main terminal, parked the bird, and shut down the engines.

Ryder was about to get his bags and deplane when the cockpit door opened and the pilot, upon entering the passenger cabin, said, "Sir I was told by one of the company reps that you were coming here on an inspection tour to look over the new drilling equipment that is soon to be sent along to the Mendoub oil fields in Saudi Arabia. I was further instructed to be at your disposal in the event you had business in various other parts of the country."

"Uh ... yes ... that's correct. I don't know how long I will be here. Incidentally, what's your name and where will you be staying in case I need you?"

"The name is Brad Hymen and I'll be stayin' at the Morong De Frontera. If you need anything, just call the front desk and leave a message. And you are ...?"

"Anton ... Dorian Anton."

"Well, Mister Anton if you have nothing more, I've got to see one of the local mechanics about our instruments. Twenty minutes before we landed I started having trouble with the attitude indicator and I want somebody to check it out."

"Yeah, go ahead, and thanks. I'll be leaving the airplane as soon as I gather up my bags, and Brad, if anything comes up, I'll be at the Marrakesh."

"Fine, Mister Anton, take your time." Hymen departed the plane.

Ryder relaxed for a moment to let his mind go over the events to date and see if he could start drawing a picture, but finally decided that until he talked to the CIA people it was just to early.

He picked up his bags, and departed the Lear. He walked on through the passenger lobby, exited the main front door facing the street, and hailed a taxi.

The Marrakesh was an old hotel, built just prior to World War II. Ryder could see by looking up at the fancy ornate guardrails along the balconies, that French architecture had greatly influenced the look of the building.

He entered the hotel, checked in, went to his room, took a shower, and put on his brown Brooks Brothers suit. After attaching the lapel pin, he checked his watch. It was still an hour until the CIA spook was to meet him at Rick's Cafe, but decided to get there a little early in order to check the place out.

As he stepped out onto the worn old sidewalk, he figured that maybe all cities of the Arab countries looked and smelled pretty much the same. The street was busy with French made Citron and other foreign built automobiles. The street smells were strong from gas and diesel fumes, food aromas of sidewalk cafes, mingling with open sewage. The combined odors were indescribable, not good, not bad, but just different from what one would find in the cities of America. It seemed like the drivers here all used horns rather than brakes, which, combined with the sounds engines devoid of mufflers, made for a fairly noisy environment.

It took him hardly any time to walk the one block to Rick's Americain. Upon arriving, he stopped and gave the place a once over. He remembered seeing the movie Casablanca when he was a boy. He tried to visualize how the front of the building looked in the movie in order to compare it to this place. Deciding that it was probably close enough, he stepped through the front door and looked around. It was pretty impressive, and appeared to parallel the movie set, in the way it was laid out. A large grand piano stood in the center of a huge room, which served as the gambling casino. Panning his eyes left, he spotted the long, well stocked, antique mirrored bar that hugged the left wall, while not missing the tall arches that supported the high ceiling. An immense white spiral staircase led upward to the inside open balcony and owner's offices. The Italian marble topped tables were fitted with silver ornate lions paw legs, while the four overstuffed chairs that surrounded each of the tables were covered with French wove, natural red dye velvet, with black Persian leather backs. Low-level defused lighting glowed just bright enough to allow one to appreciate the luxury, and marvel at the money invested in this hi-dollar watering hole. Large crystal and brass chandeliers hung from the ceiling like condemned murderers, framed by the pearl white paint that covered the entire interior, except for the black marbled floors that was inundated with gaming tables and roulette wheels. It was also flooded with hi-rollers and booze. All they needed now was a black guy to sit down at the piano and play, 'As time goes by.'

He treaded over to the bar and ordered a scotch-straight-up and decided to nurse it because he had a feeling he would need all his brain cells functioning for the upcoming pow-wow with the CIA guys. He looked around and picked a table, which was strategically located where it would give him a good view, especially of the front door. He sat down, took a small taste from his drink, and waited. He didn't have to wait long. He'd no sooner gotten the red velvet seat cushion warmed up, when the broad, teakwood front door opened, and in she walked. He couldn't believe his eyes. Oh Jesus, he thought, how did she find me? It couldn't be, but there she stood, Lisa. It was as if he were having a flashback, suddenly, the famous line of dialogue from the movie drifted through his mind. He felt like Humphrey Bogart ... and the line, how did it go? ... Oh yeah ... of all the gin joints in all the towns in all the world, she had to walk into mine. It wasn't Ryder's bar of course, but considering the situation, the phrase seemed appropriate, meaning; she could be instrumental in screwing up the meeting of the decade. He stood, in order to get her attention.

She was looking around, seemingly searching for somebody, and then her eyes found him in the crowd. She smiled, raised her arms slightly, and started toward him, but as she came closer, her smile slowly disappeared, for Ryder didn't seem happy to see her, in fact he seemed real unhappy.

He looked down at her as she approached the table. "Lisa, what are you doing here?"

Feeling and looking a little uneasy, she replied, "When I woke up, you were gone so I checked with the airport flight planning section, and they said only one pilot had filed a flight plan for Mid East Oil that morning. I figured that had to have been your pilot. They said you had filed for Casablanca. The company owes me a few days off for crew rest, so I took one the three Lears assigned to our offices in Beirut and followed you here. When I arrived, I checked the tail numbers on the Lear that you came in on and I knew that Brad Hymen had been assigned to fly that jet, so I called around to all the hotel registers and found that Brad had checked into the Morong De Frontera. I used to fly with Brad; he's a real pig. Likes his females' young, too young.

Anyway, I had them ring Brad's room and he said his one and only passenger, was a Mister Anton, who was staying at the Marrakesh. I didn't ask him about the name, Anton, I figured you had a reason for using the alias and I didn't want to blow it. Anyway, I arrived at the Marrakesh just in time to see you leaving, and I followed you here. Lance, I'm pissed at you because of the way you ran off without telling me you were leaving. Why aren't you happy to see me, and what are you doing here, and why are you using a fake name, and—"

"Be quiet for a minute and listen", he said lowering and softening his voice. "I don't have time to explain, just trust me, go back to the hotel and wait for me. I'm staying in room 211. I'll be along as soon as I can."

Her pretty face registered both anger and hurt, but she understood and trusted him. With glistening emerald eyes, she looked at him for a moment, and then said, "Be careful Lance, and please come soon." She turned and left.

He watched her disappear through the front door, and then sat down to wait. It occurred to him, that not only was she good looking and good in bed, she would also probably make one damn' good detective.

Ten minutes later he took his eyes off the half-full glass in time to spot a guy enter, wearing a tan trench coat. Christ, he thought, don't these CIA types have any imagination? Hell, trench coats are for the movies.

The guy paused for a brief time, discreetly looking around the room, then approached Ryder's table. He had a bad haircut, and his washed-out pale brown eyes bore into Ryder like two overpowered missiles, as he said, "Ah, excuse me, I'm looking for a Mr. Dorian Anton. Might you be him?"

Ryder stared back, unblinking. "Might be ... and who's asking?"

As Mister Trench Coat took a chair, the corners of his mouth turned up slightly to form a cruel little almost noticeable smile. "Mister Anton, my name is Baronga, Chico Baronga. The Company has directed that my partner and I contact you for the purpose of conducting an operation."

"Where's your partner?"

"Mr. Malloy is currently on an errand. Now Mister Anton, down to immediate business. I won't discuss details here—this place is not secure. My only purpose for coming is to establish contact and schedule a future meeting. There's a road called, The King's Highway, that leads southeast from Casablanca along the Mediterranean coast. In four days my partner will complete his errand and will be able to join us. On Friday morning you will rent a car from the service near the tourist information office and drive approximately sixteen miles out on the King's Highway. Keep looking to your right; you'll come to a dirt road marked with a small sign that says, SIDI SLIMANE. That'll take you due south; follow it for sixty miles until you come to some metal buildings twenty yards off the road to your left. We'll meet you there. Get there between eleven and noon. One more thing, are you packing heat?"

"Yeah." Ryder answered.

"Good. I carry a .44 Desert Eagle. It'll knock a man dead at two hundred yards. A little advice Mister Anton, until this assignment is complete, or until you are dead, always carry your weapon. My partner or I may have to count on you to back us in a firefight. It probably won't happen, but then again, you never know." CIA agent Baronga pushed his chair back and stood. "Until Friday Mister Anton."

As Ryder watched him walk away, he softly whispered to no one in particular, "Yeah, I'll see you Friday Mister Baronga."

Ryder contemplated the short meeting with the CIA agent and the comment he had made about carrying a gun, as he walked along the dirty cobblestone street. He was also thinking about the man, that had been setting four tables behind him, wearing a blue blazer, who stood as he as was leaving. That wasn't so strange, but the fact that they seemed to be going in the same direction was. Just to be sure, Ryder had walked a couple of blocks out of his way, and now he had no doubt; the guy definitely was following him.

Ryder quickly sidestepped into the next alley, took two steps, and then flattened out against the wall. The brown suit in the dark alley was almost invisible. He waited until he heard footsteps approach the alleyway, and then he stepped back into the street. Grabbing the man by his lapels, he threw him into the ally. Ryder heard the unmistakable metallic sound of a gun, after it flew out of the man's hand and clattered across the cobblestones.

Ryder's moves had totally taken him by surprise. He slumped to one knee, but was immediately back on his feet and pivoting on his left foot, as he spun counterclockwise with a round-kick, aiming for Ryder's ribs, but Ryder had been down this road before.

He stepped back as the guy's foot missed by an inch, then did a half left, leaning sideways for balance while bringing his own leg up, immediately kicking straight out from his side with full force, catching the attacker between the shoulder blades.

Ryder heard the man grunt with pain as he pitched forward, then a sickening crunching sound as the man's teeth, nose and forehead impacted against the brick wall. He slid to the cobblestone and except for the street noise—all was quiet.

Ryder reached down, rolled him over on his back and checked his pulse. He was dead. He was also an Arab. The bone, which formed the bridge of his nose, must have broken on impact and was driven into his brain. Suddenly, Ryder wondered if his cover was blown, and if so, who had ratted him out. Was it Dove? ... Naw, he was an OMNI spook. There is no way that was possible. Then how about Lisa ... she seemed to be sticking pretty close ... but he had come onto her, or was those sexy blue-jeans she was wearing no accident ... no it wasn't Lisa, his instincts told him different. Maybe the pilot who flew him into Morocco, Brad Hyman, but how would he know that Ryder was from OMNI. No, he could be ruled out. That left the CIA operatives, who were rival agents, but still, everything considered, both OMNI and the CIA worked for the same side, the only difference being the CIA was strictly a USA owned company, and OMNI was a US, French, and British, cloak-and-dagger operation. He had no options; all he could do was watch his back and hope he found the rat, before the rat found him. Meanwhile, he would try and devise a plan to make that happen.

As he entered the hotel room, he spotted Lisa sitting on the bed looking a little morose. He walked toward her, and as she stood to greet him, he grabbed her, lifted her from the floor and dropped her on the bed, face-down, placing his knee against the small of her back, then roughly taking her wrists and pulling her hands and arms around behind her back. Holding both her wrists with his left hand, he jerked the P-89 from its shoulder holster and placed the muzzle against the back of her head.

She screamed in disbelief and terror, "Oh god! Lance, please don't kill me." Her words became unintelligible as they disintegrated into a kind of terrified wailing sound, something akin to a hurt animal.

His words were harsh as he spat out, "Shut up bitch and just answer my questions, and if you lie to me I'm gonna cancel your fuckin' ticket, right here and now." His instincts told him her fear was real and she would answer truthfully, and if his instincts weren't enough, he watched as wetness spread across and darken the crotch of her tight jeans, followed by the faint smell of urine. This alone told him she was in a state of mind to answer his questions. "Did you set me up tonight?" He waited for an answer, but all he could get out of her was wailing and blubbering. He looked at her eyes, which were open wide and filled with pure fear but seeing nothing. It was obvious that the lights were on but nobody was home, then she started hyperventilating. He knew that if she were a trained agent she would have maintained enough cool to convincingly answer his questions in order to try and save her own life. Suddenly it dawned on him that if he didn't back off, she may lose her mind.

Quickly, he dropped the Ruger back into its holster and released her hands, rolled her over and pulled her up into sitting position. He went into the bathroom, wet a towel with cold water, brought it back and began gently washing her face. Slowly her breathing began returning too normal as Ryder, feeling uneasy, spoke to her in a low, soothing, reassuring manner. "Listen Lisa, I'm sorry, I didn't mean it. I mean maybe I've sort of gotten use to this kind of thing and didn't realize how it might affect a civilian. Jesus, how can I say this, or what can I say to make it right or to make you understand ..." He continued talking to her in low tones with no apparent effect, and was starting to seriously worry about her mental state. "Sweetheart, talk to me, it's been almost an hour and you've said nothing. Honey I love you."

Slowly, she looked up at him with tear-filled eyes, then softly and gradually with a voice that sounded like she had regressed back into some sort of psychological self protecting state, said, "Really, Lance ... are you really sorry for what you did to me."

He looked into her eyes—they seemed so far away. Now he was gravely concerned that maybe he had caused her to have some kind of mental-breakdown. "Please Lisa, tell me you're okay?"

Suddenly, she bolted to her feet and began pounding him about the head, shoulders, and chest and anywhere else, she could land a blow with her small fists, while screaming at the top of her lungs, "HELL NO, I'm not okay, you brain-dead shitbag. You scared me out of twenty-years of my life you goddamn' maggot infested puss-bucket. You shit for brains, I'm gonna make you sorry your mother ever downloaded your mangy ass onto this fuckin' two-bit planet."

Relieved beyond words, he grinned, and let her get it all out. He also knew he shouldn't laugh because it just made her angrier but he was so happy he couldn't help it. *Damn*, he thought, *she hits pretty good for a woman*. Deciding maybe he should exit for a while and let her cool off, he stood, faked a step to her left, sidestepped back to her right in order to get around her, then beat feet for the exit. As he slid through the door, he closed it behind him and headed down the hall. Walking toward the hotel lobby, he could still hear her yelling behind him.

She flung the door open, stepped out into the hall and hollered, "Come back here you cowardly son-of-a-bitch, I'm not done with you."

He could tell she was getting tired and starting to wind down, there was a certain conviction lacking in her voice, but he decided to go for a walk anyway and let her get it completely out of her system.

As he stepped onto the street, he figured this would be an opportunity to extend his rat search and decided to have a heart-to-heart with Mister Hymen just to make sure he was who he said he was. He hailed an old beat-up Mercedes cab and slid into the back seat. "The Morong De Frontera."

The cabby swiveled his head around and gave Ryder a toothy smile. "Yes sir. I am Mohammed Kaleed, and sir I know all the places of interest. Would you like Mohammed to take you on the tour? I can show you the King's summer palace, the waterfront where all the big ships come in from every part of the world, and—"

Returning the smile, Ryder interrupted. "Listen my friend, just take me to the hotel."

At the prospect of having his fare fee reduced the cabby's smile faded slightly. "Yes sir." He put the cab into low gear and pulled away from the curb as the worn-out old engine grumbled, accompanied by the clouds of blue smoke that curled from the car's rusty exhaust pipe. Ryder wasn't sure, but he thought he also heard the cabby grumbling

As the ancient German built auto bounced along the pothole-plagued streets, he thought about Lisa and knew he had to make it up to her for what he had put her through; maybe he could take her on the cabby's tour. No it would have to be something more elaborate than that. He decided it would require more thought and imagination and put it out of his mind for the present.

F. Washington Brown

After what seemed like hours of bone jarring torture, the cab finally ground to a halt in front of a large dingy two-story building. Putting the car into neutral, the cabby reached back for his fare. "Sir, two dollars, American, or six Moroccan francs, please."

Ryder paid the man, exited the cab and stood looking the place over. It was the granddaddy of fleabag hotels. Without a doubt it had once been elegant, but over time, slowly fell into disarray. A couple of broken windows were boarded up and the paint on the large sign in front had peeled off leaving it to read, 'MORON_ DE FRO_TERA'

He went inside and approached the check-in desk that was currently being attended by an old Arab woman, wearing a black berracan or sometimes known as a berka. It was a large garment resembling a sheet that covered her entire head and body, save one eye, and her feet. The garb was derived from Arab custom, which dictates that women are not to be seen by any man, except her husband.

Casually, he asked, "Excuse me, and can you tell me if you have a Mister Hymen registered here?"

Slowly, she cast her one visible eye down at the ledger on the desk, and after a moment, replied, "Yes, he is in room fourteen, first floor."

"Thank you." He turned and headed down the wide hallway, checking the numbers on each door as he passed, and found it to be the last room on the left. As he stopped, raised his hand and started to knock on the thin wooden door, he could faintly hear a male and female voice inside the room. Judging from the moaning and the bedspring squeaks, it sounded like two people engaged in sex.

He hesitated for a second longer, wondering if he should interrupt, but decided his mission was too important to put on hold. He rapped on the door, and after a moment heard some shuffling around inside the room, and then the male voice called out. "Who is it?" This time it was loud enough to be recognized as belonging to Hymen.

"Anton. I need to speak with you."

"Hold on a second." After a moment, the door opened just a crack, as Hymen's face nervously appeared. "Listen

Mister Anton, couldn't this wait? I'm kinda busy right now, I could meet you someplace."

"Now, Hyman." Ryder's tone was more command than request.

"Okay ... come on in and tell me what's on your mind." He opened the door wider and stepped back to allow Ryder to enter.

As Ryder walked in, the first thing he noticed was that the place was a littered mess of liquor bottles and clothes, the second thing that caught his eye was the girl setting up in the bed. She looked scared as she pulled a sheet up to cover her naked body. She was blond, brown eyed and couldn't have been over eleven or twelve years old.

He was immediately enraged. "Hymen! You goddamn' low life chicken-hawk, you get this girl's things together and get her back to her parents or wherever she belongs, and I mean now."

Hyman fidgeted with the tie-strings on his bathrobe. "Now just wait a minute. This is none of your fuckin' business, besides she doesn't have parents no more. I bought this little piece from a white slaver that ripped her off the streets of Miami. She's a runaway."

Ryder glanced at the child. "What's your name girl?"

The girl's eyes remain downcast as she answered, "Karen".

"All right, Karen, wrap that sheet around yourself, get in the bathroom and get dressed. You're leaving on the next plane back to the States."

Doing as she was told, the girl disappeared into the bathroom.

Hyman took a step toward Ryder. "She's not going anywhere 'til I'm done with her."

Ryder wheeled to face Hymen, bringing his right foot up, connecting squarely in child molester's crotch.

Hymen screamed and doubled over in pain. It was apparent that he was no fighter, but at this point, it didn't matter to Ryder if he could fight or not.

Ryder brought a right hook across, catching Hymen in the jaw, straightening him up while propelling him back against the far wall.

Hyman slid to the floor, where he sat moaning in pain.

Ryder looked at him and snarled with disgust. "One last thing, Hymen, you don't have a job anymore. I'll see to that, and if we were in the States, I'd have you brought up on statutory rape charges. Now get your shit, and get the hell out of here."

Getting up on shaky legs, Hymen moved over to the bed and sat down, mumbling something about twelve-year old girls being legal in Morocco.

At that moment, Karen came out of the bathroom, fully clothed. She gathered up her things and put them into a bag.

Ryder looked at her with concern visibly showing on his face as he said, "Okay, let's go kid." He followed as she walked down the hallway and out onto the street. As they stood waiting for a taxi, he wondered, now that he had her out of there, what would he do with her? The only thing he could do, take her back to the Marrakesh and give her to Lisa, and let her contact the authorities, make travel arrangements, or whatever was appropriate. After all this was a little outside his line of expertise.

Chapter 4

Ogar the Zombeast swung his huge scaly head irritably about as he cast his one large bulbous indigo eye over the Isle of Fire; his netherworld of the animated dead. His eye allowed him to look upward into the world of living man, which lately he frequently did. However, being a specter and having no mass, he could do nothing more than observe … unless the Old One allowed him to go forth. He had betrayed the Old One's trust and made a mess of things a couple of earth years ago when the Old One, had sent him to man's planet for the purpose of gathering souls. Lucifer had released him to inhabit the dead body of Eddie Slade, an evil descendent of the even more evil Edward of Lockland. The event had been terminated when Ryder destroyed Eddie Slade's body by fire. Ogar now felt his chances of ever going back to the world of the living were slim. He now just spent his time resentfully watching the activity of Lance Ryder, the one who walks in the light, and who had been responsible for bringing about his downfall.

What was even more humiliating was the fact that Ryder, except for a fleeting moment at the time of Eddie Slade's fiery death, was not even aware that he had defeated the mighty Ogar.

True, Ryder had for a moment, seen Slade's black armored soul leave his body when he died, but had just simply written the incident off as being a stress induced hallucination.

Ogar fumed with a desire for revenge, wanting nothing more than to go back to the world of the living and take Ryder's head with a broad sword. He was frustrated further knowing he would probably never get the chance to carry out his vengeful act. He wanted one more chance to retrace his footsteps back over the ancient spoor, Beelzebub's path to the living, but he knew the revered trail could be used only on very special occasions, maybe once or twice every two or three earth centuries, and in agreement with the Lord of light, for the purpose of keeping creation in balance.

Ogar now watched, as Ryder walked out onto a grimy street in a city on earth known as Casablanca, in a part of the world referred to as Morocco. As he watched, he heard a faint rumble of thunder in the distance. He looked across the desolate fiery void in the direction of the sound and observed a vast dark swirling storm of sand and black clouds being propelled by heated winds accompanied by white hot flashes of lightning. The thunder became deafening as it approached, then as suddenly as it had begun, it ceased, and all was quiet.

The devil had announced his arrival.

Ogar was immediately gripped with fear, for he knew how punishing the Old One could be, and even more so when provoked. He thought Satan had come to inflict more pain on him for his failure to extend his stay on earth and gather more souls.

Ogar, now as always when in the presence of the Old One, found it hard to focus on his master's form. He seemed to be everywhere and nowhere, like a camera badly out of focus. He would become life-like, with his body taking on the appearance of various evil creatures that had came to exist on earth after man had evolved, then explode into a swirling whirlpool of blood, fading into a dark mist, only to reappear an instant later as still another hideous incubus. For this was the devil, the embodiment of all that is evil through out the universe and for all time and would remain so, unless the angel of light could bring him down, but this had not happen since the beginning of time.

While his continuing metamorphous took place, the Old One spoke with a deep thundering preternatural voice. "Ogar, your service to me as of late has not been to my liking. Would you have me take thy head and send you to the greater fire below, what say you?

Trembling, Ogar hesitated, afraid anything he said would be found offensive. "Please my lord, pray tell, what may I do to redeem myself?"

"Ogar, your work remains unfinished. You were allowed to go forth into the world of the living to take souls and defeat the one called Ryder, for he is dangerous to us. Though Ryder is not aware of it, his soul possesses great power."

"But my lord, is it not true that all the male and female of the human family possess power?" Ogar fearfully ventured.

"True, Ogar. Before man evolved into reasoning creatures with the ability to know and do the bidding of good and evil, the Lord of Light and his kingdom, as well as I, Lucifer, with my legions, with all our power, were but benign entities in the universe."

"Yes my lord ... because we have no form."

"Alas, it is true but to combine with living man, we can manifest our power into tangible evil deeds of great proportion before finally taking his soul. You see Ogar most men are not one way or the other. They go to a house of worship to proclaim their allegiance to the lord of light to greedily gain favor for their mediocre souls, but then do they not like to rape, to pillage and steal, yes, and even to kill one another. I say to you Ogar, in the end we shall have them all because in their heart they know it is more pleasurable to participate in an orgy than to sing a hymn."

"I agree Lord Satan, but why the special interest in the one called Ryder. He does not attend worship rituals for the Angel of Light."

"No, but he has what modern man calls principals deep within his heart and because of this, his power is that of a hundred."

"Then we must be wise and win him over."

"His will is too strong. We have but one path, that is to destroy him, and to that end, I have devised a plan".

"But my lord, we are spirits, we cannot physically destroy Ryder ... free will remember".

"Yes, Ogar, but I have two strong weapons. We can entice man's greedy mind with promises of material things, and I can see the future. There is a leader of a terrorist group known to his fellows as Amal Kansi –"

Bursting with enthusiasm Ogar exclaimed, "Yes! I know my lord; as of late I have been watching Ryder in his latest quest to track and capture Kansi, although he has yet to learn Kansi's identity. I –"

"Quiet, you son of an under-demon and listen. Soon things will happen to make it possible for you to inhabit Kansi's body. I have come here to release you to follow the ancient path back into the world of the living. In spirit form you will share Kansi's footsteps until his death by Ryder's hand and then using my seal; make the habitation of his physical presence with such speed as to convince Ryder that his attempt on Kansi's life has failed. Your spirit coupled with Kansi's living flesh will make you stronger than ten mortal men. But remember you will only supply life force and will".

"I know master. Because of the fact that I perished in the fourteenth century I have no knowledge of what living man calls technology in the modern world, so we must retain Kansi's mind to operate man's new inventions".

"All that you say is true Ogar. However, because of the evil life Kansi has lived, once he is dead he is mine and I will draw his soul here to the Isle of fire to await the arrival of his conscious mind once we are though with his physical presence. Without his soul he will loose the little good that is left in him and thus can be controlled totally by you Ogar so use him well in soul gathering. Also remember that once you have gained physical presence you will be able to kill Ryder, so bid your time and do not fail me again. For if once again you fail you will reside in darkness for all eternity with the etops grilling you insides.

Ogar shuttered at the thought and replied, "I will not fail master because I have an advantage. Once I have possessed Kansi's body, bullets cannot destroy it, only fire. Ryder was lucky in our last encounter for it was sheer chance that our battle ended with the chamber that I occupied catching fire and destroying Slade's body which forced me out and back here".

The devil became more animated as a tornado-like wind swept through, and above the din he boomed out, "Don't fail me, Ogar", that was followed by an earth shaking clap of thunder and then he was gone.

Ogar stood silent for a moment, marveling at his master's mode of travel. He was ecstatic that he was once again going back to the world of the living where he could unleash his evil on mankind. In preparation for his journey back across the ancient path he turned, looked up into the living world and started his chant of gothic parables, a chant that served as a prelude to his trek.

Chapter 5

A taxi pulled up in front of the hotel and ground to a halt. Ryder paid the driver, opened the door, and got out, followed by the despondent girl. As they started toward the entrance, she looked up at him with sad eyes that belonged to a woman much older, and asked, "You're not going to hurt me are you mister?"

Ryder studied her tired face for a moment, thinking, *here is a girl twelve years old going on thirty. How in hell does a thing like this happen?* He put his hand on her head to reassure her and said, "No Karen. I'm going to introduce you to a nice lady who will make arrangements to send you back to your parents".

"I appreciate what you're doing mister, but living with my parents wasn't all that much better. I know this sounds weird but I really have nowhere safe that I can go. Mister ... can I just stay with you and the lady? I won't be any trouble, honest".

Ryder usually had all the answers, but at this moment and for this situation, he had none. Searching for the right words he haltingly said, "Karen, first of all just call me Lance. I'm Lance Ryder, and the lady's name is Lisa, uh, Lisa Nickels. Karen, believe me when I say that I would like nothing better than to have you and Lisa live with me. But " He was trying to say exactly the right words because he knew that she was fragile and had been damaged by the people around her. However her changing expression told him he was not succeeding in his feeble attempt.

Her eyes weld up with tears as she burst out, "I knew it! You're not going to help! You're like all of those other bastards. You're going to send me back." Then suddenly she became very quiet, and with a whisper said, "I'm sorry, I didn't mean to get angry ... just help me ... Lance, please help me."

"Come on kid. Let's go see what Lisa has to say about your situation." He took her by the hand and they started up the steps.

Lisa looked up with a bit of surprise when she saw Karen enter the room with Ryder.

In an attempt to explain the situation, Ryder said, "Lisa I want you to meet –"

Lisa shot an icy glance at him and spat out, "Shut up dipshit. I'm not speaking to you!" Then her eyes softened as she looked down at Karen and with a more soothing tone said, "Who are you dear, and how did you get mixed up with this clown."

Karen tried to suppress a snicker but lost control and just let go. The laughter was contagious and Lisa joined in. What Lisa had said was not that amusing but it did serve as a catalyst to relieve the nervous tension and as a result the laughter just followed.

Ryder knew he had all of this coming, so for the moment he just tried to look as dignified as possible and said nothing, but after a brief period he too could not suppress a smile.

Still grinning, Lisa raised her right hand and motioned for Karen to come over and join her on the sofa.

Karen complied and Lisa put her arm around Karen's shoulder. After a rather lengthy period of getting-to-know-you girl talk, Lisa looked at Ryder and said, "Well I guess that you're out of the dog house, buddy, but in the future ya better watch it. Do you have a plan for Karen?"

This is not covered in any of my contingencies, but it seems clear that we're going to have to take her to the American-Embassy and have them arrange to have her flown back to Miami." Ryder replied.

Karen cried out, "No Lisa, I want to stay with you and Lance".

Lisa drew her close and said, "Karen that's just not possible. Lance is here on business and I have a job; we're simply not in a position to take care of you. I truly wish that were not the case."

Karen pulled away and became distant.

The embassy like most buildings here was of French Design. It was constructed during the Victorian period and as a result was inundated with an abundance of Greek style sculpture, wide gates, and large ornate wooden doors.

As they approached the fancy gates, a U.S. Marine guard stepped forward and asked Ryder for his papers. Ryder produced a passport and his ID. After a short discussion the guard saluted and directed them to the ambassador's office. They ascended the marble steps, entered the embassy and proceeded down a long hallway to the envoy's administrative center. Their shoes made a hollow echo that reverberated off the tall ceilings. Over the noise Lisa asked, "Lance why did that marine salute you. You're not in the service—are you?"

"Not now Lisa. We're here for the girl, so let's keep our focus on that."

A little miffed at being sidestepped Lisa curtly replied, "Fine, what ever you say."

They stopped at a door marked, Ambassador John Roberts, and Ryder reached up and tapped lightly on the dark polished redwood. A short time later the door opened and a short jovial looking man said, "May I help you?"

In a polite Ryder tone Ryder said, "Yes, we're here to see the emissary, might you be him?"

"No sir, I'm his administrative assistant. He will be with you shortly, meanwhile why don't you folks have a seat across the hall."

"Thank you."

One hour later the door once again opened and they were called in to meet Ambassador Roberts. He was a tall medium built man with a bit of grey at the temples. His dark pen-stripped suit gave him somewhat of a Chicago gangster look, but Ryder wasn't here to critique his wardrobe. Roberts was sitting behind a large antique desk but came to his feet when he saw Lisa come into the room. He smiled and with a commanding gesture motioned for everyone to have a chair as he said, "Welcome to the embassy and what can we do for you folks today?"

After taking a seat Ryder said, "Mister Ambassador, My name is Lance Ryder, I work for a Mid East Oil affiliate. This is Ms. Lisa Anne Nickels; she is a pilot for Mid East Oil. And the young girl here is Karen Whitmore. She is an American Citizen and We'd like for your office to make arrangements to return her to her parents in the States."

"What is the circumstances that brought her here?"

"Sir that's a rather long story and the important thing is that she be returned safely to her relatives."

Roberts reached over and pressed a buzzer on his desk and a moment later a matronly looking woman came into the room and said, "Yes sir, you rang."

Roberts glanced at the woman and replied, "Yes, Barbara. This young lady's name is Karen Whitmore. She'll be staying in one of the guest rooms for a couple of days until we can arrange for her return the States."

"Very good, sir." Barbara looked at Karen with an expression that appeared to be an attempt at a smile and murmured, "Come with me child."

Karen stood and looked at Lisa with tears glistening in her eyes and a little uncertainty in her voice as she said, "I haven't known you and Lance very long, but I feel like I have. I sure wanna stay with you but I know you can't do it. I just wish you knew what you were sending me back into—at least Brad didn't hit me."

Lisa's heart was breaking as she too stood and put her arms around Karen and with trembling voice said, "Karen, Lance and I care about you, and I'm going to contact the Miami Social Services and see if we can get you a good home."

Karen moved over close to Ryder, kissed him on the cheek and mumbled, "Good-by Lance. I hope you and Lisa can come and see me. I'll be looking for you." With that, she turned and followed Barbara out of the room.

Ryder felt Karen's warm tears on his cheek; but in reality he didn't know if they were her tears or his as he got up and said, "Mr. Ambassador, I want to thank you for your help. I know that this goes without saying, but please be kind to her, she's been through a lot."

"We will Mr. Ryder, and thank you for bringing her to us. Ms. Nickels, Mr. Ryder, it's been a pleasure and Henry will see you out. Good day."

As Lisa and Ryder turned to leave, Ryder said, "Good day to you too, sir."

The two of them were very quiet as they bounced along in the old cab. Finally Ryder said, "Lisa I want you to call Mid East Oil and tell them what happened. I want you to get their assurances that they will fire Hymen, and that I want you as a replacement pilot for the duration of my stay here."

"I hate to say this Lance, but they may not terminate him. They're short on pilots, and here, twelve, and thirteen-year-old girls become wives. I'm pretty sure that's why Brad likes to fly this route."

Little veins suddenly stood out on Ryder's forehead and his voice took on the qualities of a disgruntled Kodiak bear as he said, "Lisa I don't think you understand so I'll rephrase the statement. Tell Mid East to fire Hymen or I'll put him in a fucking wheel chair for life. My job gives me the authority to do just that with no reprisals."

She looked at him with an expression of amazement and stammered, "Lance, I love you, but sometimes the things you do and say just flat scares the piss out of me and I mean that literally."

Immediately cognizant that he was directing his anger toward the wrong person, Ryder abruptly mellowed out while sheepishly mumbling, "I'm sorry," then leaned over and kissed her, snaking his tongue into her mouth.

She bit him lightly on the tongue and a bit factiously said, "I'm warning you pal, you'd better settle down or I'm going to quit letting your tongue visit the beaver."

Ryder smiled and replied, "I'm not worried because the beaver loves the visits way too much to ever let that happen."

She mused, "Pretty damn' sure of yourself aren't you."

I can't take this anymore, he thought, *she's going to kill me and I seem to be powerless to do anything about it.* He could feel the hot sweat as it poured off him and onto her, mixing with her womanly scented perspiration, then rolling down her neck, well shaped breasts, and small stomach; on it's way to the amply soaked sheets below. Even the mattress was becoming a bit drenched. They had been involved in heated sex for three hours and he had to admit that he was totally at her mercy. Rolling off her and onto his back, he just lay there grinning like a satisfied limp wet noodle, trying to catch his breath. Between gulps of air he said, "I'm on to you Lisa, you're not fooling me. You're trying to kill me by inducing a cardiac arrest because of what I did to you a couple of days ago. Come on, admit it."

Smiling, she slid her hand across and wrapped it around his limp wet penis as she said, "I'll admit it, if you admit that you're a wimp and can't handle a little rough sex."

With mock anger he retaliated with, "Oh, that's hitting below the belt. Hell, I did all the work."

"The hell you did. I was on top at least half the time," She retorted.

Feeling his manhood coming to life at her caress, he abruptly sat up, grabbing her as he did. With one fluid motion he flipped her over, placing her on hands and knees as he announced, "Prepare for doggie style." Without further ado, he none to gently buried his large shaft as deep as physically possible.

F. Washington Brown

Feeling a little like she had been rear ended by a freight train, she moaned upon the rather abrupt coupling and breathed, "Oh, Lance you are a dog ... my fucking dog ... my lap dog. Oh god ... Oh! ... yes, just do it you bastard. Just take all of my ... hungry wet pussy. I can't ... believe .. what ... you're doing to me. "

Morning broke with no surprise in the weather; hot and dry was the name of the game. It was approaching time for Ryder to rent a car and go out to see what the CIA spooks had on their minds.

He reached over and lightly slapped Lisa on the butt and announced, "Rise and shine Lisa Anne."

She slowly sputtered to life while he took a shower. After becoming fully awake, she ambled into the bathroom and joined him. They proceeded to soap one another up and down ending with him predictably placing her against the shower wall and once again introducing her to the helmeted warrior.

After getting dressed they went out for breakfast. The outdoor cafe that she picked was sparsely occupied, giving them ample quiet and privacy to discuss their immediate future plans.

They ate in silence for a time then Ryder said, "Lisa, I've changed my mind. I want you to take your aircraft and go back Mid East Oil's headquarters in Beirut. Get back on you schedule or what ever it is they need you to do."

Not sure she understood fully what he had said, she dropped her fork into the table and blurted out, "What? What did you say?"

"You heard me Lisa. I have some job related things I need to get done and you can't go with me."

"Lance, I don't understand. I called Mid East, like you asked and they fired Hymen. You need me to fly you around to talk to the oil engineers, purchase rig equipment. Who will fly you?"

"Lisa, I'm not here to buy equipment for Mid East Oil. They are just cooperating with our government."

"Government? Do you mean the U.S. Government? Oh, I get it; you're really some kind of agent for the government. That's why the marine saluted you, and why –"

"Lisa, stop it. We can't talk about this, and besides for your safety you don't want to know."

Lisa sighed and her shoulders sagged slightly as she picked up her fork and began slowly eating in silence. At one point she looked at him and said, "You're a real asshole Lance." After that the mood changed. They exchanged little more than small talk as they returned to the hotel to pack her things. He escorted her to the airport and as they approached her plane, she turned to him and said, "Lance, tell me again that you love me and that you weren't just stringing me along to get laid."

"Damn, Lisa. Don't you think leaving you is hard enough without you thinking something like that? Hell yes I love you, but I don't have any choice here. Our separation is only temporary and as soon as I complete this assignment I'll come for you. Believe me honey, this is the way it has to be but it will work its self out. Just trust me on this."

With misty eyes she replied, "I believe and trust you, Sweetheart. Just don't forget me."

"Lisa, Honey, you know that will never happen."

They kissed deeply and then she turned, climbed the short four steps and disappeared inside the Lear. Ryder reached down and swung the door up and turned the recessed latch.

She fired the Pratt & Whitney turbo twins, released the brakes, and taxied out. Ryder stood by and watched as she took the runway and got airborne.

Chapter 6

Ryder awoke to an uneventful morning and checked his watch; it was six-thirty. *Yeah,* he thought, *I'm back on the clock and it's time to go to work.* The four days had flown by. He got dressed, checked the P-89 Ruger's clip and tucked it into his belt under his shirt. He also had a hundred round box of spare ammo in a plain brown paper bag. He picked up the bag and went downstairs for a bite of breakfast. After paying his bill he headed to the car rental service that Baronga had mentioned. The rental structure, like a lot of other old buildings was in need of repair but they had a decent variety of cars. From the look of it a guy could rent anything from a low budget VW Beatle and French Citron, to a new Mercedes 500SL.

He thought it over and came to two conclusions. The first was that he wasn't paying for it, and the second was that he didn't want to break down in one hundred and ten degree heat. He opted for the new Mercedes. As he approached the office, a young obviously motivated Arab man striving to beat out his competitors, came out to greet him. Bowing and scraping appeared to be his method of operation as he shuffled up to Ryder with a big smile and announced, "Merci Meseur, how can I ... uh... help you this morning Se' beu' pley?"

His French stunk, but Ryder wasn't here for French lessons. He smiled and replied, "Good morning. I'm looking for a dependable rental for a day or two."

"Yes, but of course I can help you. I have everything. A German VW perhaps."

"No, I was thinking more of something like the new Mercedes 500SL there on the corner of the lot." Ryder said, pointing to the sleek road machine.

Hot Sand & Cold Blood

"Yes, yes, that is a wise choice my friend, and it is only five-hundred francs per day or seventy-five American. Uh ... you will have to buy gas of course."

"Of course," Ryder replied.

After a little more discussion about the details of the agreement they went inside, signed the papers and the Arab handed Ryder the keys. Ryder thanked him, turned and went back out to the car. After tossing the 9-mil rounds through the open window onto the front seat, he got in and drove off. It was one thing to stand on a balcony watching the street traffic; it was quite another driving through it. *Like threading a needle,* he thought. Everywhere there were cars, camels, goats, bicycles, Arabs pulling small two wheel flat bed trailers stacked high with merchandise they hoped to sell in the market. Nobody respected or even noticed his big expensive car. He was forced to pick his way through the seemingly mindless bedlam like everyone else, and with a look of slight determination on his sweaty face he pressed forward at a steady pace. At around eight-thirty he had cleared most of the city traffic and was making good time headed east along the El Camino Real.

Ryder was enjoying the Arabian Desert on the right side of the road and the seaside to the left. There were tall date trees along the highway framed by a background of azure sky and the deep blue of the Mediterranean Sea. In the distance he could see brightly painted Arabian fishing trawlers with their nets over the sides. The ocean breeze drifting in from the north dropped the ambient temperature maybe ten degrees on the beach, but after about a quarter of a mile inland, car hoods were hot enough to fry eggs on.

Ryder kept an eye on his odometer and after traveling a little more than fifteen miles he started keeping his eye peeled for the road to the right that Baronga had mentioned. Yep just as the man advertised, Ryder saw a small faded road sign coming up written in Arabic and underneath in English, it said: SIDI SL_ _ _ _ The wind had apparently torn off the rest.

Ryder turned off onto the southbound side road and immediately decided that the Morocco Government hadn't ran a grader over the camel path in years. It was hot, rough sledding and he was grateful the AC worked. The holes slowed him some but about eleven-forty he was scanning the terrain to his right and spotted a couple of what appeared to be metal buildings. One resembled an office and the other looked more like a garage of sorts. They were about two hundred yards off the road with a lone white four-door Chevrolet Impala sitting in front. As Ryder recalled, the CIA had bought a trainload of them and spread them around the US Embassies of the world. Driving that Chevy was like putting a sign on your bumper that said, 'CIA.' Ryder couldn't understand why they didn't drive something less conspicuous.

He pulled in next to the Impala, killed the engine and surveyed the landscape. Experience had taught him to be cautious. He pulled out the P-89, chambered a round and slid it back into his waistband. While constantly scanning the area he got out and approached the closest building. He was about twenty feet from it when the door opened. Reflexes sent Ryder's hand to the butt of the P-89, not to draw it but just to feel the reassurance of gunmetal.

Baronga appeared in the doorway, took a couple of steps out, and motioned for him to come inside. Ryder dropped his hand to his side and followed the CIA man into the building. In the center of the run down room was a table with some maps and diagrams lying on it. A thin man of average height with black hair stood leaning against the opposite side of the table. He looked up as Ryder walked in but said nothing. Ryder sized him up briefly and decided that there was something he didn't like about the man, but wrote it off as his being bias against CIA people.

Baronga broke the silence with, "Mr. Anton, this is Holt Malloy. Holt and myself are going to be your Central Intelligence Agency counterparts on this op. The reason you were brought in is because you're employed by three countries and have the backup support that we lack, or so that's what they tell us. As a result you're authorized to do things we're not and that's pretty much the whole enchilada. Holt this is Agent Dorian Anton; second tier operative, OMNI.

Malloy eyed Ryder briefly then walked around the table and extended his hand, and said, "Welcome aboard Anton. We can always use a little assistance."

Ryder shook with the man, still not thinking any the better of him but replied, "I just hope that we have talent and information that will serve to our mutual benefit in this endeavor. Oh, by way, my name's not Dorian Anton. It's Ryder, Lance Ryder. The Anton thing was something Dove came up with. After thinking it over I believe the cover name does not serve in the best interest for our working together."

Without another word Malloy returned to the other side of table.

Chico Baronga stepped to the table and with a wave of his hand, addressed the messy stack of documents on the table and said, "OK gents, even with short sleeves it's warm so let's get down to business. Ryder you're coming in on this late so we'll bring you up to speed on what we think we have so far. By the way before we get started I just want to say it's tough about Dove... him getting hit and all."

Shocked, Ryder glanced at Baronga and said, "What, what did you say? Dove got taken out?"

Baronga hesitated for a second then said, "Yeah, just what I thought; you were in route to here when it happened so you didn't get the word until now. Tough break Ryder. Hell Malloy didn't know either until he got back about two hours ago. I got the word from our field office late last night"

Damn, Ryder thought, *I tried to raise him on the vhf radio after Lisa left but when he didn't respond I just thought his radio transmitter was off or malfunctioning.* Trying to appear casual about the news Ryder replied, "I guess that means that I'm working without a control; I'll have to make some adjustments but it shouldn't be a problem."

Baronga, looking relieved replied, "Fine. I'd offer to let you channel your Intel through our office but it's against our regs and I'm sure yours also."

"With out a doubt. I'll just catalog the investigative progress until OMNI sends a replacement to Beirut."

"Good. Now that we have that sorted out, we can begin. We've taken all available CIA reports and put that together with what Malloy and I have found out and came up with pretty much what you see on the table. First let's start with the terrain; Ryder the road you came in on is no secret but it gets very little use."

Factiously berating the rough road, Ryder echoed, "Why is that not a surprise."

Baronga continued on, "The main road is blacktop and cuts off from Kenitra then straight to Sidi Slimane and since we get no traffic through here, it's a no brainer that we're sure they all use the main road. We don't enjoy total anonymity here but we are out of the way and so far have attracted no attention. This place is perfectly located to run surveillance on Sidi.Sidi Slimane was once an American base that was used for bomber planes in the fifties and into the sixties. Now it's rundown and deserted, or was until recently. About a month ago some Berber tribesmen were overheard talking about a small group of Arabs spending a lot of time around the old base. French Intelligence recognized one of the names in this group as Amal Kansi. At the time we were notified, the name meant nothing to us, but since then through the French and other sources we've found out that this guy Kansi is Mr. Clandestine Terrorist Extraordinaire. We believe they have all the makings of a nuclear devise and that they're assembling it at Sidi."

Ryder questioned, "If you have reasonable suspicion, why don't you just get some people together and go in and smoke them?"

"For a few reasons. First, in Morocco, to get their equivalent of a search warrant you have to have overwhelming tangible proof. And second, the Moroccan Government doesn't like foreigners snooping around so we have to be double sure that we're on solid ground before they'll give us any kind of cooperation. And another big reason is that the government and law enforcement here isn't tight like in the

States. They have a kind of 'leis-a-fare' attitude meaning, live and let live."

"So what do you have in mind to get a closer look without incurring legal problems, or do we have to come up with something?"

Malloy spoke up, "Glad you asked that Ryder. Over in the next building we have three high centered vehicles with big knobby tires that were designed for loose sand desert driving. Like a snow cat in the arctic, these things will go though any kind of desert terrain and do it without hesitation. Two of them are for us with a spare in case one breaks. Ryder you'll use the spare."

"And we're going to drive these things all the way to Sidi?" Ryder mused.

Baronga spoke up. "No Ryder we're going to drive them to the launch complex."

Glancing first at Baronga then at Malloy, Ryder muttered, "The launch what?"

Baronga smiled, satisfied with the mini bombshell he'd just dropped on his OMNI counterpart, " Ryder, the complex will be easier to explain when you see it. The pad is five miles due east of here and totally hidden, even by air. It has a sand colored camo net that covers every thing. The British Air Force flew it in at night and air dropped it in pieces. They also parachuted in a small team to assemble it. After they put it together they gave us a crash course on how to fly the two drones."

"Drones." Ryder's jaw muscles flexed slightly as if trying to add something to the single word he'd just uttered and finally managed, "You mean drones like airplanes that the military flies by remote-control?"

With his smile broadening Baronga slapped his hand on the table and exclaimed, "Bingo, Ryder. You got it. They fly similar to the remote controlled model airplanes you've seen kids playing with; only these birds are big toys for big boys".

Ryder's eyes narrowed slightly, and as if almost a question he said, "So you are going to, what, bomb them with these things".

"No Ryder, the drones are not equipped to bomb anything. Tell you what, lets all saddle-up and go have a look. Malloy and I will brief you when we get there. The buggies aren't very comfortable but they'll get you over the dunes. Baronga paused for a moment as if pondering some great truth and then said, "Buggies ... dune, that's it, yeah we should call them dune buggies. With that, Baronga turned and started for the door with Malloy and Ryder following him out, neither impressed with CIA Agent Chico Baronga's revelation.

As they approached the second building, Baronga produced a key and unlocked the wide metal sliding door. He slid it open and they went inside.

Ryder approached and slowly walked around the buggy nearest the door and after a brief inspection, announced, "I don't think they have much of a future. I mean look at it, a cage with four oversized wheels and a VW engine. Who in their right mind would drive this thing for transportation, or pleasure? And what is this cargo box looking thing strapped to the top here?"

Baronga slid into the seat of the second vehicle and said, "I don't know if they have a future but they go where that Chevy won't. As far as that cargo box, it's a portable remote control panel."

Blank puzzlement replaced Ryder's amused expression as he said, "It's a remote what?"

Baronga smiled and said, "Never mind, I'll show you when we get there." He cranked the engine and drove it out of the building. Malloy mounted the third vehicle and likewise drove his out. By this time Ryder had also got his buggy started and followed Malloy. With all vehicles out in the open, Baronga dismounted, walked over, got into the Impala and drove it into the recently vacated building. Following Baronga's lead Ryder too dismounted and drove the Mercedes in and parked next to the Chevy. Ryder returned to his buggy while the CIA man locked the door. Baronga then walked over to Ryder and raising his voice a little to be heard over the sound of the engine, said, "I'll take the lead and you follow Malloy. The gas pedal is a little touchy so be kinda careful until you get use to it. Remember this is a light vehicle for the engine, and acceleration is lightning quick."

Ryder gunned the engine as if to verify what Baronga was saying then replied, "Gotcha."

Baronga went over, mounted his vehicle and thundered off into the desert with Malloy and Ryder hot on his trail.

The longer Ryder drove the better he liked it. As Baronga had said, acceleration was quick and steering was very responsive. *Damn*, Ryder thought, *maybe these things do have a future.* The five miles flew by and suddenly they had arrived. Baronga had been right, it seemed like they were almost on top of the complex before Ryder saw it. They pulled up, shut off their engines, and dismounted.

Baronga walked over to the desert camouflaged netting and pulled back a door-sized flap and stepped in under the netting. Ryder and Malloy followed and Ryder was relieved to be out of the heat. There was no thermometer that he could see but figured it must have been twenty-degrees cooler under the net.

The next thing Ryder noticed was two launch rails about twenty-five feet long. At the lower end sat two cigar-looking vehicles with stubby wings and openings at both ends of the fuselage. Ryder figured they must be powered by some sort of small jet engine; probably a General Electric J-75. The netting directly in front of the launcher had been raised slightly to allow the drone to clear on launch. The drones were painted a flat bluish white color and no markings to avoid visual detection. There was a small pod mounted under the nose and appeared to have the ability to rotate about 180 degrees side-to-side. Ryder walked over and upon closer inspection saw a round hardened glass port on the front of the pod. *So that's it,* he thought. *High resolution, high-speed cameras.*

Baronga stepped around in front of the drone and said, "Do you need any explanation on what we have here?"

Ryder took a close look at the rest of the drone, as he said, "No it's pretty much self explanatory. I guess the hump on top here is a parachute for recovery."

"Yep. To be exact, this seven-foot long model with a ten-foot wingspan is an even smaller version of a subscale jet drone known as the BQM-34. The cameras were developed by NASA and shoot four thousand high-resolution pictures every sortie. To recover it after a mission, we bring the drone in to about one hundred and twenty meters of the complex after we've slowed it to just above stall speed which is around eighty-knots, depending if there's a head wind. Once we have it in this position at six hundred feet altitude we send an R.F. analog discreet command to pop the chute. If we do it right the bird lands on our doorstep."

"I've heard of these things but this is the first one I've seen. So tell me where are your eyes? When this thing is fifty or sixty miles away you're not going to have line of sight."

"Step over to this little control center Ryder and let me show you something."

Ryder followed Baronga to an area that consisted of two chairs sitting in front of a small console. The flat horizontal part of the console directly in front of the chair had two airplane control sticks mounted on it. A CRT type video screen and a plot board were mounted on the vertical part of the console, along with fuel gages, altimeter and an assortment of other instruments. "This is all pretty straight forward. Upon launch we have the drone's surface controls preset in climb position like a carrier launch. Once the bird is off the rail we assume control with one or the other of those sticks you see on the console. It's built to fly two drones simultaneously. However, we always fly just one at a time so the sticks are set up to trade the single drone back and forth between two controllers. The monitor of course allows us to see the drone at all times and the plot board gives us, X, Y, and Z data. The commands are shipped to an antenna mounted on the drone, via Radio Frequency signal through a low wattage tracking radar fifty yards from here. It's under that other piece of netting you saw when we drove up. There is also a small TV telephoto camera mounted on the radar dish support, so everywhere the radar points that's what we see on the monitor, and the radar is always on the drone. The system has a range of over two-hundred miles much more than what we need."

"Who processes the film?"

"Malloy does that. His regular job with the company is, photo recon processor. We have a dark room in the building where the buggies are stored. However, Malloy thinks we have a bad batch of film because we just aren't able to get pictures clear enough to analyze. Today we're going to launch the alpha drone. The bravo drone has a bent rudder tab; it was damaged last week by a rough landing. Another rudder tab is being flown in tomorrow at around 1400 hours. That means we have to be here to install it. The 'Company' has directed that from now on, we're going to fly daily until we get some useable aerial photos."

As they were talking Ryder could hear a faint noise in the distance that sounded like a piston engine powered airplane.

Baronga stopped speaking for a moment and then said, sounds like our drone fuel has arrived. Let's go out and retrieve it."

All three men went out and watched as an old C-123 cargo plane approached at around four hundred feet altitude. The rear cargo door was open and when the aircraft was almost over them, a large parachute unfurled, dragging a large pallet from the aircraft as it did. At that altitude the pallet was down in a little over two-minutes, landing about thirty feet from Malloy's buggy.

Malloy let out a curse and exclaimed, "If that drop had been two seconds later I would have had to walk back to the car barn".

Baronga, wearing an amused smile chimed in with, "Quit your bitching Malloy, those guys planned it that way; you should glad you don't have to hump those gas cans in from a half mile out".

Working quickly, the three agents retrieved the jet fuel and supplies and about two hours later the alpha drone was prepped and ready for flight. Ryder was getting a first hand education in drone operations.

F. Washington Brown

Baronga was looking the alpha bird over in last minute preparations as he said, "Malloy is going to serve as drone controller on launch, I'm going to stand by and remove umbilical cords four seconds before launch. Ryder you stand behind Malloy and watch everything be does".

Malloy walked over and sat down in front of the console and began a calibration check. As he flipped switches he called out to Baronga, "Altimeter check, battery check, fuel level check, radar transponder check. All right Baronga, the panel looks normal". He looked over at Baronga and asked, "Are you ready for ignition"?

Baronga looked at the meter on the DC power pack then called back, "Battery level green, roger on ignition".

Malloy reached over and flipped a toggle switch and the drone's engine started a low whining sound, which increased in pitch as he pushed the throttle up. Malloy watched the RPM gauge and when the engine reached 100% he raised his hand, at which time Baronga pulled the power cord from the drone's fuselage and stepped back. He dropped the cord onto the power pack and walked over to the console.

Malloy yelled over the sound of the engine. "Does everything look OK to you"?

Baronga gave a thumbs up.

Malloy flipped the rail lock switch to, 'off' and the drone sped up the rail like a roman candle. Before Ryder could say drone, the drone was ascending through two thousand feet.

As they watched, Malloy pushed the stick forward to level the drone at two thousand then he pulled the stick right until the heading indicator came to, 180 degrees. The drone was now flying due south and toward Sidi.

Baronga slid into the seat next to Malloy and said, "I'll take the drone, you operate the nose recon camera when we get into range".

Malloy took his hand off the stick and moved it to the switch marked, 'Camera surveillance' as he announced, "Roger that".

Ryder was paying close attention to everything that both men were saying and doing.

The drone flew along straight and level for approx twenty minutes then Baronga said, "Malloy, I'm going to approach Sidi from the north. Turn on the nose TV on and we'll fly a 360-degree circle around the base at two thousand feet. That's high enough for this small bird not to alert anybody that might be there. If it looks like there's activity, zoom in on it and start filming. Go ahead and run your zoom in and out to make sure it's focusing."

Malloy ran a zoom check and everything looked good and gave Baronga a thumbs up".

Baronga brought the drone over Sidi, did a 360-degree circle and on the first pass it appeared that there was no activity.

Malloy said, "I don't know what you see but to me it looks like there's nobody home".

Closely scrutinizing the monitor, Ryder said, "They could have driven their vehicles into one of those hangers or buildings just like we did".

During the next twenty minutes, Baronga made four more passes over the base at different angles and altitudes but the place seemed deserted. Finally Baronga said, "We're going to have to Return To Base and recover the drone; gas is soon going to be a problem.

Ryder was keeping a close eye on the screen as Baronga rolled the drone out northbound to bring it back when Ryder saw the change and exclaimed, "There, did you see that".

"See what", Baronga said.

"The door on the hanger we just flew over was open and when we flew over the first pass it was closed".

Malloy said, "I didn't see anything. Ryder you must be imagining things".

A little annoyed Baronga said, "Well I'm busy flying the bird and depending on you guys to spot activity".

Ryder said, "Make another pass and come in a little lower and slower".

F. Washington Brown

Baronga brought the drone around and as the drone went over the hanger they all saw it. Not only was the hanger door open but there was a couple of late model cars inside. Baronga made one last past then announced that the jet was down to bingo fuel, only enough to recover with a not a drop more.

The drone's chute deployed as advertised and the bird landed twenty-yards from the netting. Baronga pulled out a four-wheeled dolly and they went out and loaded the bird onto it. Once it was back on the rail, Malloy pulled the film out of the camera and they hopped on the buggies and headed back to the office to develop it.

Chapter 7

Malloy's been in that dark room for two hours. How long does it take for him to develop film"? Ryder's annoyance becoming apparent.

Baronga took a drink of the coke he'd brought along and replied, "Easy OMNI man, it won't be long now."

He'd no sooner spoke than the dark room opened and Malloy stepped out and announced, "It looks like we might have something."

Relieved, Ryder said, Well that's good news. Toss the stuff on the table and lets have a look."

Malloy was holding what looked to be around two hundred stills in his hands as he walked over and began laying them out on the table. I extracted these frames from the roll that appeared the have the best resolution."

As Ryder and Baronga stepped to the table to have a look Ryder said why don't we just thread up the film on a magnified projector, it will give us movement and perspective? And it may give us something that you missed."

"Can't do it." Malloy answered. "The track holes in the film is elongated and won't run on the projector."

Damn' Ryder thought, *if I didn't know better I'd say Malloy is either stupid or has an agenda.* "OK then lets see what we have." The Ruger in his waistband was chafing a bit so Ryder took it out and laid it on the stool next to him.

They looked the stills over for an hour or so and came up with additional items and people that the TV camera had missed.

Holding a mag glass over a particularly interesting still, Ryder said, "Baronga, look at this and tell me that in addition to three vehicles, there is also four guys standing near them and it looks like a fifth man is getting into one of the cars."

Baronga studied the picture for a minute and said, "Well we were shooting through the open hanger door so there is some shadows inside but you got sharp eyes Ryder, there sure as hell are five guys there. And judging from the way they're dressed, I'd say they are Arab."

"I agree," Ryder said. "Now the question is do we go in, or do we fly a couple of more recons to make sure? I vote that we go in."

Malloy said, "Now wait a minute Ryder, we can't just go in there with guns blazing like three cowboys."

Irritated, Ryder looked at Malloy and said, "I didn't say guns blazing. I mean lets get some desert camouflage fatigues and sand face paint and go in commando style. We can put silent running mufflers on the buggies and go in to within a quarter of a mile, drop a net over the vehicles and walk the rest of the way."

"I don't agree," Malloy said. "It's too risky, and at the very least we should fly more recons."

Finally Baronga said, "For my vote I agree with both of you. Like Ryder says, I think we should go in silently and scout it out to make sure that we're not biting off more than we can chew. But, I also think we should fly one more recon to get all the Intel possible to give us an edge. I'll throw in one more thing; this morning I received word from the CIA field office in Madrid stating, that because of Ryder's extensive expertise in this type of work he'll be acting as coordinator, in effect Malloy, for this op, we will act on Ryder's suggestions. If Ryder wants to go in, we go in."

From the look on Malloy's face Ryder could tell he wasn't happy. "I've thought about it," Ryder said, "and what Baronga says makes since. If we rush this thing it may fall apart. We'll fly another recon – maybe two. Anyway we've done a good days work. We meet back here in the morning and launch another flight."

Malloy spoke up. "What if the bad guys don't show tomorrow?"

"Then we'll fly a day or two more until they do. If they haven't showed in two days we'll go in regardless. From the reports that I've got, these guys are terrorists in the middle of building a nuclear bomb, hell they don't have time to take off for vacation."

Baronga nodded his head in agreement and said, "Then I guess we have a plan. Lets head back."

Malloy spoke up, "You guys go on out. I've got to put these stills back and secure the developing chemicals."

Ryder and Baronga left the building to get into their vehicles. The OMNI agent started to open his car door when the thought hit him. *Damn, I've left my gun inside. It's the first time I have ever done that. I must be slipping.* He turned and went back into the building. He picked up the weapon, tucked in into his waistband and was starting to leave, when he heard Malloy's voice coming from the dark room.

As Ryder turned and walked toward the darkroom he could hear Malloy in low tones, speaking English with some Arabic thrown in. It sounded like he said; "They bought it." and something like, "Kansi," but he couldn't be sure. He stepped into the red-lighted development room and said, "Malloy who are you talking to." Ryder looked to his left and saw Malloy sitting with his back to the door, holding a transmitter mike in his left hand.

Surprised at the radio, Ryder said, "Malloy what are you—"

"You heard didn't you Ryder?"

"Heard what?"

At that instant Malloy wheeled lightning quick bringing up his Desert Eagle and fired.

The round hit Ryder in the upper arm, spinning him backwards through the door and onto the floor. Before Ryder could recover Malloy was up and standing over the OMNI agent.

Malloy's face was the epitome of anger as he said, "Good-bye you trouble making son-of-a- bitch!"

Suddenly three shots rang out in quick succession and Malloy was instantly propelled backward like a rag-doll and slammed into the far darkroom wall.

F. Washington Brown

Baronga looked down and said, "Ryder, are you all right?"

With a grimace and a grunt, Ryder stood and said, "Yeah, I'm not seriously shot, it's just that those .44 slugs knock you around like a prize-fighter. You know, you expect and look for that kind of treatment from your enemy but not your friends. It was just lucky for me that you showed up when you did."

"It was a little more than luck. I had an advantage because I had started to suspect that he was into something. The errand that he went on was to take a courier pouch full of documents to Madrid, which he did. However, the curious thing is that he routed his flight back through Beirut for four hours of ground time and didn't tell anyone. I found out inadvertently when the 'Company' pilot called my room and wanted to know if anyone would be going back to Beirut because he had unfinished business there and would like to be the return pilot. I didn't think anything about it until Madrid called and told me that Dove had been killed. Apparently he figured that he could keep an eye on, and monitor a CIA operation. However, when OMNI got involved that meant there would be elements that he couldn't have access to so he decided to take out your briefing officer to slow down OMNI getting involved. The question is what was he doing and who was he involved with."

Ryder said, "I think I can answer that or part of it. Just as I walked in on him, he was on that radio and he said something like, 'I think they bought it', and he mentioned Kansi. Do you think that it's possible that he was working with Kansi? And if so it could only have been for money because if he couldn't be loyal to the CIA chances are he had no loyalty to anyone. Was he a big spender?"

Baronga reached down and pulled Malloy's wallet from his back pocket and started going through it. "I didn't see any evidence of heavy spending but he liked to bet the horses. His bookie may have been putting pressure on him. Wow, Ryder look at this, a recent bank draft in Malloy's name, transferring two hundred thousand dollars American, from the Portuguese Bank de Nationa'le in Lisbon to the

Cayman Islands. Not much doubt about it, our boy was in bed with the bad guys."

Ryder looked the bank draft over and said, "I agree, but the thing he said about, 'I think they bought it'. Do you have any ideas on that?"

"He could have meant anything by, they bought it. Maybe some one of his people bought a component for the bomb that they're building. Hell who knows? That's just not enough information to draw any conclusions about. Come on man, you need to get back to town and have a doctor look at your arm. I'll call Madrid and have an H-53 fly in and pick up Malloy's body"

"Yeah, maybe you're right. See you tomorrow around twelve."

Ryder awoke with some stiffness in his arm but otherwise felt all right. The nurse had done a good job the night before of cleaning and dressing the wound. After a healthy breakfast, he climbed into the Mercedes. He arrived at the buggy building around a quarter until noon and saw that Baronga was already there. Ryder entered the building and found Baronga going over the stills. Without looking up he said, "I wasn't sure that you'd be here, because of the wound and all."

"It wasn't bad. It'll take a couple of days to work out the soreness then it should be fine. Hardly lost any blood and the round didn't hit any bone or muscle. Baronga, I was thinking that with Malloy gone who's going to process the film. If we bring in another guy that's going to eat up time that we don't have."

"So what do you have in mind, OMNI man?"

"Malloy may have said something on the radio that could have alerted them. If that's the case we may need to push up our time line. Because of what we've found out about your partner, I've reversed my earlier thinking. I brought some camo fatigues and I think that we should just go check it out. If we go now we should get there about late evening"

"Yeah, Ryder, I'm inclined to agree with you," Baronga replied.

Ryder's shoulder was getting a little sore by the time they reached the estimated quarter mile distance from Sidi's main hanger buildings. The terrain was fairly flat except for a small dune here and there. They pulled up behind one of the dunes so the buggies couldn't be spotted from the old base and shut off the engines. Ryder pulled a pair of field glasses out of his backpack and give the place a once over. He saw no sign of activity and handed the glasses to Baronga. "I can't see anything going on out there, Chico. Have a look, maybe you can spot something that I missed."

The CIA agent took the glasses and scanned the area and came up with nothing. "I didn't catch anything either. Do you think Malloy may have gotten a warning out and they have decided to abandon the place?"

"Naw, but even if he did it makes no difference because they would still have to come back and pick up their equipment and documents and they haven't have time to do that. In the final analysis it makes no difference if there's somebody in there or not, we are still going in because it's the only game it town. Another thing is if nobody's home it may be an advantage; it'll give us an opportunity to look around without having to engage in a firefight."

"Look, Ryder, if Malloy was working with Kansi, then the terrorists would have had to know we were on to them and that they were under surveillance."

"It's one thing to know that you're being watched, and another to know that the law is riding down on you ... but you do have a point, Chico. There's something a little strange with this whole damned op, and putting that together with what Malloy said about, 'I think they bought it', keeps going over in my mind. I can't help thinking that we may be into something more than what we were briefed on."

Baronga put the field glasses to his eyes and once more scanned the hanger buildings in the distance. "Well if you think that we're into something more than what we were briefed on, do you have any ideas as to what it might be?"

"No I don't, but it will be dark in another half hour. Get on your radio and tell your people that we'll be going in and we will give them a call if we run across anything."

"Alright Ryder, you're the boss." Baronga stepped over to his buggy, picked up the radio receiver and said, "Zebra Tango, this is, Red Dog One. How do you read – over?" The radio crackled but nothing came across that was coherent.

Again Baronga repeated, "Zebra Tango, this is, Red Dog One – over."

The radio again crackled slightly and then, "Red Dog One, this is, Zebra Tango, we read you five by five. What is your location – over?"

Chico replied, "Quarter mile north of target, will call if we run across anything important – over and out." He turned the radio off and walked back over to where Ryder was once again scanning the base with the glasses.

The half hour passed quietly and then Ryder said, "Well I guess it's time. Baronga do you have any spare ammo for that Desert Eagle?"

"Yeah, the fifteen round clip is full and I have two spare clips."

"Good. I've got about the same. The approach seems simple and I don't think that we need a plan. When you looked the area over do you recall seeing the big hanger that appears to be the closest to our position?"

"Yeah. It has a two and something painted in Arabic painted on the roof."

"That's the one. Even though it's dark it's still open ground so move as quietly as possible and let's see if we can get to it without being spotted. Lets move out and spread out some so that you wind up at the east end of the building and I'll go toward the west side. When you reach it wait four minutes to give enough time to be sure that we're both near the building. At that point play it by ear. We'll enter the hanger and see if anyone is home. Work your way to the center and we'll meet there. Keep your safety off but let's try not to shoot each other when we meet. It's a good possibility that if it's populated there will be more of them than us, so my suggestion is shoot anybody you see unless he insists on surrendering and giving us information. One more thing, take the radio along to call in to let somebody know in case we run into something that we can't handle. Keep it turned off so it don't crackle at the wrong time and give away our position Got any questions?"

Baronga clicked the Eagle's safety off and said, "It's pretty clear to me, Ryder."

Ryder slapped Baronga on the back and said. "Good. Move out."

Baronga picked up the radio and disappeared into the darkness.

Chapter 8

Ryder stood next to the metal building thinking, *so far so good.* After mentally ticking off the four minutes he moved along the wall looking for a small personnel entry. He turned the corner and was proceeding along the north wall. He'd taken maybe six steps then, Bingo, he saw it; a metal door with the window broken out and standing a quarter of the way open. *How convenient,* he thought, *I don't even have to pick a lock.* Cautiously he approached the door and looked in. Seeing nothing, he quickly stepped inside and flattened out against the wall, holding his gun in both hands using it as a pointer to the potentially dangerous areas of the interior. The area he was in appeared to be a series of hallways and offices. He picked a hallway that looked like it might lead to the center of the hanger and started cautiously walking. After going thirty feet or so he came to an intersecting hallway and carefully looked around the corner. To the right it was dark, but back to the left he saw a light at what seemed like a distance of about three offices. He turned the corner and slowly drew near the lighted room and as he did he could hear two voices speaking in Arabic. The door to the lighted office was missing and this gave Ryder an advantage. He quickly stepped through the door opening and trained his gun on two men that he discovered in the room.

The two Arabs looked up to see a tall blond man wearing camouflaged fatigues instructing them to raise their hands, which they did.

Ryder surveyed the room for moment. One of the Arabs was about five foot eight inches, wearing typical Berber headgear, robe and white pantaloon type pants. The other Arab was around six feet tall and wearing a tan business suit with black tie. Between them was a short wooden table with a few papers scattered on it.

Watching the two men with the alertness of a cat on amphetamines, Ryder said, "Do either of you shit-birds speak English?"

The suit said, "We both do. If you'll permit me sir, to put my hands down. They are becoming tired."

Ryder shook the gun at him and said, "If you twitch, Dipshit, I'll shoot your dick off. You in the suit, what is you name, and if you lie, you know that I'll kill you as soon as I find out the truth."

The suit replied, "No need to be uncivil my friend. I will tell you because you will not leave here alive. I am Kansi, Amal Kansi, and this is, Momar Wahajadeen. If you have come here to rob us I can assure you that there is no money here."

"I didn't come here for money. I came to take your retarded ass to Madrid for interrogation. Now I want you two to get—"

At that instant gunfire erupted at the other end of the hanger. The event momentarily distracted Ryder, giving the robed Arab an opportunity to reach under his garment for a firearm but it was too much of a reach and the OMNI man put three rounds into his chest killing him dead. The time that Ryder expended shooting the robe gave the suit enough courage to try his luck. He reached in between the two lapels of his double-breasted tan coat and came out with a S&W 38 revolver and everything was going great until Ryder put a nine millimeter hollow point round into his gizzard and one into his chest.

Ryder didn't have to check Kansi's pulse to know that he was dead and cursed himself because he had wanted to take Kansi back for interrogation.

More shots rang out and Ryder ran out of the room and down the hallway in the direction of the firing hoping he could get there in time to help Baronga survive the firefight. The noise of the gunshots became increasingly louder and after what seemed like an eternity the hallway and offices abruptly ended and Ryder found himself in the large hanger bay. A round sang by his head and hit the wall behind him. Ryder looked around, spotted what appeared to be the tail section of an old airplane and dove in behind it.

Looking around and taking stock of the situation he immediately realized he was in an excellent position. There were at least three Arabs behind cover and were protected from fire coming from the far side of the hanger which is where he suspected that Baronga was pinned down. However, from Ryder's position they were sitting ducks. The stuff about not shooting a man in the back was good for the movies but in the real world it didn't wash, besides it appeared the good guys were out numbered. Ryder proceeded to shoot all three guys as fast as the P-89 Ruger could spit out the copper jacketed rounds.

Another Arab screamed something in Arabic then jumped up and rushed Baronga's position. Baronga's reply was to promptly shoot the Berber between the eyes.

The Arabs didn't seem to be able to shoot real straight but they were determined to win or die, and die they did. When the smoke cleared there were eleven dead Arabs including the two in the office. Baronga had taken an Uzi round through the rib cage. It wasn't life threatening, but this was where he got off of the marry-go-round. Baronga would go to Spain to spend some time in the hospital and OMNI would either send Ryder another partner or he would proceed on like a one-man posse.

After examining Baronga's wound, Ryder looked the place over and finally found some cloth to bind up the wound and got the bleeding stopped.

As Ryder helped the CIA man to his feet, he asked, "How do you feel buddy?"

Baronga managed a week smile and replied, "How the fuck do you think I feel. I hurt like hell. I always thought you OMNI guys were smart but I swear you're dumber-n-dirt. See if you would have gotten shot then you could take some time off."

Ryder grinned and said, "Quit your damn' bitching and let's go take a look at Kansi. I shot the bastard dead in one of these rooms."

As they started slowly down the hallway with Baronga's arm around Ryder's shoulder for support, Baronga said, "Kansi, you actually shot Kansi?"

Ryder said, "Did that guy shoot you in the ear? I just said I shot him didn't I?"

"How do you know that it's Kansi?"

"Because he told me he was before I shot him."

Looking a little skeptical Baronga said, "Why would he tell you his name?"

"He thought we were never going to get out of here alive, or he could have done it because he has a big ego. How the hell should I know? He just did that's all."

They continued down the hall until they reached the room and went inside and Ryder immediately noticed that Kansi was gone. There was a cushioned chair in one corner and Ryder eased Baronga into it.

Baronga looked at the dead Arab that Ryder had shot first and grunted, "So that's Kansi. He don't look very impressive."

Registering a little disbelief in his facial expression and voice, Ryder replied, "That's not Kansi."

"What? But I thought you said you shot him dead?" Baronga quizzically replied.

"I did man. I put one through his neck and one through his chest and there is no way in hell that he could have got up and walked off."

"Well you may have shot him but you sure as hell didn't shoot him dead because there is a blood trail leaving out of here and down the hall. It appears like that guy is tougher than nails."

"Baronga, keep your gun handy. I'm going after him and I'll be back to get you as soon as I can."

"Adios Ryder, and don't forget where you left me. I don't want to be here this time next year"

Ryder left the room and followed the blood trail back down the hall with it leading him back to the outside door where he had entered the hanger. *Something is really odd here* Ryder thought. *There is a lot of blood in the office where it starts out but the farther it goes the blood tail gets thinner with less and less blood. If he is bled out where is the body.* Ryder stepped through the door and pulled a pin light out of his pocket that he had brought along. Checking the sandy ground he saw only a few drops of blood and footprints leading off in a different direction than he had earlier approached the hanger from. As he followed the prints he noticed two things. The first was that after the first hundred and fifty feet or so the blood trail stopped and only Kansi's footprints continued into the desert. And secondly, not only did they continue into the desert, they became further apart. *Damn,* Ryder thought, *this guy is running through the desert with two bullet holes in him of which either one would be fatal.* Ryder was starting to get that familiar feeling that he'd had in Vietnam. How he had seen Eddie Slade walking across the tarmac on fire and burning from head to toe. And out of that pyre he had seen the hideous black armored rising up out of Eddie's burning body and then disappear, and from that day he had never mentioned the incident to anyone for fear that they would think he was nuts. But there was another reason, Ryder was a practical guy and the thought of someone or something being supernatural was not a concept that his intelligent analytical mind could assimilate. To his way of thinking you were either alive or you were dead and if you're dead you don't walk around, or in this case run around the desert.

At that moment Ryder heard the sound of a small airplane cough and then come to life. It sounded like a Lycoming aircraft engine, probably a Cessna 172 or another of the Cessna series. Ryder broke into a run toward the sound then realized that it was coming from close to a half mile away. The chilling fact was that it had to be Kansi; everyone else was dead except Baronga and himself and if you wanted to believe the unthinkable ... Kansi.

From the sound of the engine it was obvious the aircraft was on a take off roll. Ryder stopped and listened as the small plane gathered speed and got airborne. The next thought to enter Ryder's mind was that he had to get on the radio and get a trace on the airplane's flight path. It could be done because there weren't that many small planes flying around this part of the country at night but he would have to hurry before the bird entered regular air traffic patterns making it close to being impossible to identify. He headed back to have a quick conference with Baronga on the latest events. Walking back down the hall toward the office he kept going over the most recent activity and something bothered him. The bomb making equipment, plans and other material had to be around the hanger or at least the old base somewhere. Would Kansi just fly off and leave all that evidence? It sure didn't seem likely. But a lot of things didn't add up. This had started off as a nice little conventional investigation of a scumbag terrorist organization. Now suddenly it had evolved into a surreal supernatural nightmare. First Kansi is alive, then he is without a doubt dead, and then he is once more alive. Could it be that somebody helped Kansi out of the building and into the plane? It didn't seem possible to drag a dead or dying man that far in that amount of time. Hell, the guy helping him would have to be super strong. But even if he had help, where was the second set of footprints in the sand. No it had to have been Kansi alone and under his own power, and with two bullets in him in locations where either of them would have killed the average guy. Ryder was starting to feel like he had been in this situation before.

As he stepped into office he saw Baronga struggling to get to his feet and said, "Just cool it for a minute Chico. Sit back down and let's discuss our game plan and let me bring you up to speed on what's happened so far."

Sweating, red faced, and grimacing from pain, Baronga sit back in the chair and said, "How far did he get? Why don't you go get a buggy and load him onto it, then you can come get me?"

"Baronga, Kansi is not out there." Ryder said.

"What? Don't shit me Ryder. Kansi has to be out there somewhere and judging from the amount of blood in this room he can' t be that far."

"Damn it man, you're not listening. I said Kansi is gone. He hopped into a small plane and split."

"Baronga looked at Ryder with disbelief for a moment and then said, "You mean somebody put him into a plane."

"No man. I followed his tracks out of here and partway across the desert and there is only one set of footprints. While I was following his tracks the blood trail ceased and just the footprints continued into the darkness. It was about that time that I heard a small plane crank up and take off."

Baronga just looked at Ryder, speechless and then finally said, "Well I'll be damned. What do you think Ryder?"

"Right now I don't want to think about it, but I have no choice. Tell me something about that radio you were using to contact your field office."

"Like what?" Baronga asked.

"Is it, UHF, VHF, or both?" Ryder queried

"It can be tuned on either bandwidth. Why?"

"I think that this part of the desert has to be sparsely populated as far as aircraft go – would you agree with that?"

"Yeah. Except for the re-supply birds we have been getting in there has probably been nothing through in months."

"That's what I wanted to hear. We need to call your field office and get the radio frequency numbers for the Nourasur International Airport in Casablanca. We need them for the tower and radar approach control."

"What do you have in mind Ryder?"

"We are going to call the airport and give them this location and ask them if their radar has picked up a small aircraft coming from this area."

What you're theorizing is possible but not likely. There would be a better chance of picking him up if the radar was close to him on take-off and dedicated to just his airplane unless the transponder in his plane is on. If his transponder is off which is likely because he'll try to avoid being detected, then their sweep radar won't pick him up at all unless they can piggyback from a tracking radar that's able to get a return from the aircraft's skin. They call it 'skin painting'."

"Damn, damn, damn," Ryder was beside himself with anger and frustration. Then he abruptly stopped cursing and his facial expression suddenly changed as he exclaimed,

"Wait! I've got it! Baronga, what about that drone radar; can it skin paint Kansi's plane?"

Baronga's eyes lighted up as he figured out what Ryder was thinking. "Hell yes. Why didn't I think of that? Yeah man it's a track radar and totally capable of painting Kansi's plane? Ryder, help me to the dune buggy. Do you remember asking me about the cargo box that's mounted on top of the buggy?"

"Yeah, and you said that it was some kind of portable remote control panel. I didn't understand it at the time but I think that I do now."

"I didn't think that we would ever use it but man I'm sure glad we have it now. It's a smaller version of the control panel that Malloy and I used to control the drone. The guys explained that if we were ever out scouting and run across something that we needed a better look at but didn't want to risk getting to close we could use the portable panel. I didn't think much of the idea and still don't but the one feature that is workable in our current situation is the radar. Ryder we can use it to remotely power up the track and sweep radar from here. Then once we acquire Kansi's bird on radar, we can confer telephonically with Casablanca 'rapcon', which is an acronym for 'radar approach control'. They can piggyback on our return and pick him up and track him from there to where ever he lands. With his problems he'll have to file a flight plan while he's airborne. He may not file but if he doesn't he runs the risk of being hit by a heavy."

Ryder broke in with, " Wait a minute. Heavy, a heavy what?"

"A heavy is what control towers call commercial aircraft over a certain weight, like a Boeing 707. I would think that he would have a contingency plan for a back-up airport or runway. Now we have a way to track him to there. What do you think, Ryder?"

"Baronga, I think you had better stay here. I'm going to hump it back and get the buggy. It should take no more than fifteen or twenty minutes. Are you going to be alright?" Ryder asked.

"I'm fine, man, you hustle and get back as soon as you can." Baronga replied.

"Keep you gun handy in case one of his buddies decides to pay a visit and get that radio fired up; I want those freq numbers by the time I get back," and with that Ryder was through the door and gone.

Baronga leaned back against the cushioned chair and turned the radio on. It took a little time to raise his office but he finally made contact. He briefed them on the firefight and that he had been wounded. They gave him the radio frequency numbers for the airport tower and rapcon and then wanted to know what other assistance they could lend.

Baronga's reply to that was, "The situation is fluid so stand by and let's see how this radar plan works. I'll get back to you as soon as I know what else we're going to do."

"Roger that, Agent Baronga, we'll stand-by, over and out."

Baronga had just flipped the radio switch off, and in walked Ryder looking much more tired than when he left.

Baronga looked Ryder over and said, "Damn that was quick," then with a smile he added, "but I gotta tell ya Ryder that you look like a bag of dehydrated assholes."

"Fuck you too CIA man. Did you get those numbers?"

"Yeah, I got'em. By the way in case you haven't noticed I'm feeling quite a bit better. I was checking my bullet wound and no vitals were hit. I lost a little blood but I'm over the shock. Hell, as soon as I hit a first aid station I'll be good as new, and then we can get that bastard Kansi. I can't wait to –"

"Forget it, dipshit," Ryder said, "the only place you're going is to a hospital in Barcelona"

"Fine, I'll spend a month hitting on some good looking Spanish nurses and meanwhile you can go get your ass shot off." Baronga retorted.

A slight grin crept across Ryder's face as he emphatically announced, "Baronga, you CIA weasels are always scheming on a way to get laid. Now get off your butt and show me how to fire up the control panel." Ryder reached down and put an arm around Baronga's waist, helped him up and down the hall. As they approached the door leading outside, Ryder stopped and looked around the area near the door jam for an exterior light switch. Finding one, he flipped on and an outside light mounted over the door came on. Ryder figured that Kansi must have installed a generator somewhere to provide electricity. They were too far from civilization to steal it from a line pole. With the area around the buggy lighted up so they could see what they were doing, Ryder, under Baronga's tutelage, set about the task of setting up the small portable control console. For power they used a rectifier that was wired in to the dune buggy's generator. The buggy would have to be kept running while they used the console in order to keep from trashing the battery. While Ryder finished the setup, Baronga got on the radio and raised Casablanca on the frequency the field office guys had given him and apprised them of what assistance they needed and then coordinated the radar interface. After exchanging all the information with the Casablanca rapcon Baronga said, "Ryder it looks like this retarded plan of yours just might work."

Ryder started the vehicle and turned the power switch on the small console. They weren't going to need any of the drone control and telemetry functions, just the downsized low power sweep radar and the track radar function.

Baronga started calibrations on the system for non-transponder skin return mode only. "Ryder this is going to be close because this portable has a hundred mile range and that's stretching it."

Ryder stepped up next to Baronga and checked the radarscope and said, "The scope looks powered up and normal."

"Yeah. Using this little joystick I've remotely lifted the antenna out of its cradle. Lucky for us Malloy left the netting off of the radar dish or we would be operating blind. It seems to be moving on the gimbals properly."

"When he took off it seemed like from the sound of the engine that he was flying almost due north, and that would take him toward something in the vicinity of Rabat." Ryder volunteered

"Yeah, Ryder, or he could have gotten out a mile and did a 180 back toward Casablanca or Tunisia."

"Maybe but I don't think so. He's going to want to go to a big city with an international airport. I've got a feeling that he knows that it's going to be too hot for him around here."

"Alright Ryder, back to the joystick. If I move it up and down that controls the elevation, and if I move it left or right that controls azimuth. Now, assuming that you're right, I'm swinging the dish to the north and we will do a criss-crossing pattern with elevation and azimuth with the acquisition or sweep, as it's sometimes known. If we're lucky we'll pick up a blip around sixty or seventy miles out then we'll start a directional plot on him and talk the Casablanca long-range radars onto our signal giving the latitude and longitude. Baronga played with the stick for no more than maybe three minutes when he said, "Bingo, I have him. Ryder, call the tower and give them the following co-ordinances."

Ryder keyed the radio mike button and said, "Casablanca tower this portable radar, I'm calling to give you our position and tell that we are powered up and we have bogie on radar, over."

"We read you portable radar." the tower replied.

"Casablanca tower we are ready to give you bogie's lat and long position, over." Ryder said.

"Never mind portable radar. We have been piggybacking on you since you came up and we are now tracking your airplane, over."

"Roger that Casablanca. Maintain you track until he lands and we will call in periodically for updates, over."

"Roger, portable radar, over and out."

Baronga turned off the portable unit and said, "Ryder, we got the bastard and the best part is that he doesn't even know it."

"I'm not so sure about that Baronga. We don't have any evidence so we can't get an arrest warrant. All we can really do is keep him under surveillance. You stay in the vehicle and get some rest and I'll go back in and look around. I won't be gone long."

F. Washington Brown

"What ever you say OMNI man. I won't argue with because I'm getting a little tired." Baronga replied.

Ryder went back to the hanger bay and looked it over. He didn't find anything that even looked like a bomb, or bomb making equipment. He found a box of papers near the hanger bay door on a table and went through them thinking there may be some blueprints or plans and instructions for an explosive devise. He came dry. He was starting to think the whole thing was a bust then he remembered that there was a stack of papers on a table in the office where he had shot Kansi. He hurried back to the office but when he got there he discovered that most of the papers he'd seen were gone. A few remained, scattered here and there. A couple of them had blood smears of them like maybe Kansi had grabbed for them but in his haste they got left behind. He gathered up all that he could find and started looking through them. It was difficult because some were torn with blood obscuring the words. Also the information was written partly in both Arabic and English. He found just scraps of sentences and words here and there. On one was written, 'Western States'. Well that made since, the United States was obviously the intended target. On another torn piece was a reference to, 'gas', and he thought it might be possible that they planned to use some sort of gas triggering release for the bomb. He found still another with the word, 'Company'. Ryder wondered if that could have been a reference to the CIA. Could it be that they were planning to blow up CIA headquarters in Langley, Virginia? The only thing he found that came close to sounding like a reference to bomb making material was a small slip of a manila envelop with writing that said, 'R.F. remote signal turn on transmitter 164.5 freq'. Figuring that Kansi's boys were setting up some local communication network, Ryder tossed it back on the table then on second thought picked it up and stuffed it into his pocket. After giving the room a final going over and finding nothing that even remotely resembled plans for a bomb, Ryder gave up and went back out to where Baronga was waiting.

Hot Sand & Cold Blood

Baronga gave Ryder a quizzical look and said, "Well what's the verdict man. Did you come up with something we can hold Kansi on?"

"Dry. I came up dry. There is not the slightest bit of evidence in that hanger. We are back to square one, Baronga. Because of the reports that your agency put out, I can and will continue to keep Kansi under surveillance but as of right now we have nothing concrete to hold him on, that is if we can find him. Do you have any ideas on this?" Ryder asked.

"Naw, Ryder. I'm as much in the dark on this as you are. But I'll say this, where there's smoke there's fire and I believe that Kansi is dirty. We just have to keep digging."

"I agree. Right now we have to clear our tracks and get rid of any sign of us ever having been here. Do you have any explosives back at the office?"

"Yeah. Why do you ask?" Baronga queried.

"We are going to blow up the drone launch pad and then get the hell out of here." Ryder answered.

"Ryder, are you crazy? Those drones cost thirty thousand apiece."

The OMNI agent climbed into the vehicle and asked, "Can you drive the other vehicle?"

"I think so, but I'll have to take it easy around the rough spots. I don't want start bleeding again." Baronga said.

Ryder drove back to where the other vehicle was sitting and helped Baronga into it. "Are you sure that you're going to be alright?"

"I think so, Ryder. If I get into to trouble I'll flash my lights."

Taking it slow they got back to the office building around six a.m. Both men were exhausted and Baronga had started to bleed a little. Ryder got out of his vehicle and went over to help Baronga out of his. "Chico, you are bleeding again and you look like that you're getting ready to pass out. I'm going to help you to your Chevy so you can get some sleep." Ryder said.

"What ever you say ... Ryder. I'm in no condition ... to argue with you." Baronga said, barely conscious.

With Ryder supporting most of his weight Baronga moved along slowly and managed to get into the back seat of the big Impala. He stretched out and immediately fell asleep.

Ryder walked over to the Mercedes, climbed into the back seat to also get some rest.

At two thirty that afternoon Ryder awoke to the sound of a helicopter hovering in the area. He stepped out of the car, looked around and spotted a lone H-53b helo that was in the process of landing. The chopper pilot put the craft down about twenty-five yards from the building. Ryder watched the unmarked chopper with some curiosity as the helo's doors opened and four guys stepped out.

The noise had obviously awakened Baronga who was sitting in the Chevy's back seat with the door open. Baronga was also eyeing the big helo.

As the men approached, Ryder quickly noticed all of the tell tail signs, the hundred dollar sun glasses, buttoned down collars, dark Brooks Brothers slacks and patent leather shoes. They were CIA. The tallest of the four was a black guy with a serious look, followed by a short chunky man with curly red hair. The other two were average and would be hard to pick out in a crowd. The black man ambled up to Ryder and said, "I'm Harold Kolinsky, these are my associates, and you are ..."

"Waiting for you to tell me where you're from and what the hell you're doing here, or more precisely, what do you want?" Ryder asked.

Ignoring the acid reply the CIA agent smiled briefly, "Like I said before I'm Harold Kolinsky. I'm from the 'Company' and we are looking for a Mister Chico Baronga."

Pointing a thumb toward the Impala, Ryder said, "He's sitting in the back of that Chevy."

Hot Sand & Cold Blood

Baronga raised his voice enough to be heard and said, "It's OK Ryder, I know these guys."

The four men turned almost as if in lockstep and headed toward Chico's car followed by Ryder. As they reached the Chevy the black dude said, "Chico you look like hell man. We heard that you took a round. That's why we're here buddy, to give you some assistance."

Ryder spoke up, "It's hot out here gents. Why don't we all step into the building and discuss who's who and what we're going to do."

The curly red haired guy said, "Good idea. We'll exchange some information and maybe come up with a plan. Once in the warm room the smell was quickly noticeable and one of the CIA guys that hadn't spoken until now said. "What the hell is that smell?"

"That smell," said Ryder, "is the garbage you guys were supposed to pick up yesterday."

With his noise crinkling a little, Red said, "Excuse me."

Baronga spoke up, "What he means is, you guys were supposed to pick up Malloy yesterday. He's in the dark room growing maggots and becoming more ripe as we speak."

Looking a little sheepish Harold said, "Uh, uh, first I heard about."

"Well let's haul him outside," Ryder said, adding, "it's bad enough in here with just the heat. Also gents, I'd like to help carry him out, but I'm shot in the shoulder."

Baronga quickly followed with, "Yeah, I'd like to help haul him out too, but I'm shot in the rib cage."

Harold grimaced and growled, "I can see where this shit is going. Butler, grab Malloy's shoulders, I'll get his feet. The shorter of the two nondescript agents followed Harold into the dark room and immediately tossed his breakfast.

Harold yelled. "Damn' it Butler! Watch that shit, you're splattering chunks of puke all over my shoes."

"Sorry Harold, but this mother-fucker smells bad."

"I know that, now grab his shoulders and lets get him outta here before I start upchucking right along with your uncouth ass."

Once Malloy was outside and all the doors were opened the room became almost bearable. Ryder stepped to the table and said, "Alright people, listen up. I'm going to bring you up to speed concerning the activity here in the last couple of days. After that if anyone has information they can ad that will help clear up the situation, volunteer it at that time."

Ryder proceeded to brief the CIA people on the drone flight, the trip to the hanger and finally how Kansi made his exit in the small plane. After he completed his briefing the four stood looking at him with what appeared to be expressions of total disbelief.

Ryder added, "Yeah, I can see it on your faces, if I hadn't been there I wouldn't believe it either. Now if there is no one who has any information to add, Baronga is going to show us where the squibs and comp-4 explosives are and we're going to destroy the drones and get the hell out of here. One of you guys will have to take Chico's company car back to the embassy."

Harold spoke up, "Ryder, your control, an OMNI agent named Dove was killed."

"Yeah, I know. Malloy killed him."

"A scrambled message was passed along to us from OMNI HQ that says you are to go back to Beirut a wait for further instructions."

"Hell I can't go back to Beirut, at least I don't want to but I imagine HQ will raise hell if I don't. I need to follow Kansi while the trail is still warm."

"Agent Ryder, I'm not in your chain of command so I can't advise you. When you get back to Beirut why don't you call your agency, apprise them of the situation with Kansi. Maybe They'll let you continue your investigation without delay."

Fuming, Ryder said, "I know all that, It's just that all the red tape slows things down and wastes a lot of time.

Let's get up to the drone launcher and set those explosive charges."

Chapter 9

Amal Kansi and Momar Wahajadeen sit drinking glasses of sugar thickened homegrown Arab tea at an outdoor café next to a busy street in Rabat. Upon finishing their drinks the two stood and walked toward a waiting French Citron. They entered the automobile and the Arab at the wheel put the car into gear and pulled away from the curb. On the trip out to Sidi Slimane they sat quietly discussing the upcoming events. As the car approached the main hanger, a large door slid open and the driver pulled inside and parked. Getting out of the car, the men headed down a wide hallway toward an office that Kansi had selected to conduct his planning affairs. They walked into the office and Kansi flipped on a light. He was a bit irritated because they had arrived later than usual. Kansi instructed Momar to have a seat at about which time another Arab entered the room and ask, "I'm here to see if there was anything that Sadeki Kansi or Sadeki Wahajadeen might need."

Kansi said, "Yes. Would you find some refreshment for Momar and myself."

The Arab replied, "Right away, Sadeki Kansi, and Sadeki Wahajadeen. He left to get the refreshment that usually consisted of small cups of coffee with scoops of sugar. He returned close to an hour later with the coffee and profusely apologizing for the delay due to a cooking burner not working properly. He set the coffee on the table and backed out of the room.

Kansi took a sip from his cup and said, "Momar I think the beverage is good and worth the wait."

Momar smiled and replied, "I agree Kansi. I'm grateful to be your second in command so that I too enjoy some privileges."

As the two men finished their drinks, Kansi set his cup on the floor and Momar did likewise.

Kansi produced a stack of papers and laid them on the table as he said, "Now Momar, I stayed up late last night and guided by Allah's hand I have thought of a change in plan that will make this process easier and faster. See here on this diagram I –"

At that moment a tall blond American or English looking man appeared in the doorway wearing army pants, holding a gun in his right hand and instructed. " Raise you hands."

With upcoming important events about to unfold, Kansi did want to die as yet so he complied and he and Momar raised their hands.

The American asked, "Does either one of you shit birds speak English?

Kansi thought, *I must humor him,* and said, "We both do. Sir, if you will permit me sir, to put may hands down. They are becoming tired." Kansi was a little worried because now the American was shaking the weapon at him and said that if he twitched the American would shoot off his penis. Attempting to sooth the American, he said, 'No need to be uncivil my friend. I am Amal Kansi and this is Momar." Kansi glanced at Momar and could see that he was tense and that meant, that as sure as there was Allah, Momar was going to go for his gun. A couple of more words were exchanged and then it happened. Momar seeing his chance, grabbed for his revolver. With the distraction Kansi thought he had better help and reached for his own weapon as he watched the American shoot his friend three times in the chest. *By Allah, I must not fail,* he thought as he pulled his gun out to take aim. Then he heard another gunshot and instantly felt something heavy and with tremendous force hit his neck and then again in his chest. At first the pain was overwhelming and then it started to fade, as did the light in the room. Kansi started to drift down and away as if off onto a deep sleep and then beyond that. As he spiraled down he felt as if a part of him continued downward, but another part of him, the reasoning part stopped and hung suspended for how long he didn't know. Then he started to ascend on a return trip of this strange path he had involuntarily taken. Up he went faster and faster as if being propelled by a force outside himself. Then with a shuttering, he felt himself join with his body.

As he slowly became conscious he also started to once again feel the pain in his neck and chest. He opened his eyes and the light slowly returned. He was totally confused by what had just transpired. He lifted his arm and looked at it. He opened his mouth to see if he could speak and said, "By Allah, I live." He noticed that the pain was subsiding and the blood flow had ceased. By now not only was the pain gone but also he was actually starting to feel normal. Then he heard heavy shooting in the hanger bay. Thinking that there was a full-scale assault he quickly made a grab for the papers, smearing blood everywhere but getting most of them, he left the office. He had lost a lot of blood and it had soaked his clothes and now dripped on the floor as he walked. He got through the outer door and started across the desert toward a small plane that he kept under a tent some distance away from the main buildings. It was for an emergency such as this when one day it was possible the authorities would discover him before he could put his plan in play. But now it was too late for the authorities to ruin his plan. Everyone else had already gone to America and now it was his time to go, a week early perhaps but that was all right. It changed nothing. His strength was returning at a tremendous pace. He almost felt that he couldn't contain it and broke into a run. Allah had truly given him the power of ten men.

In no time he reached the aircraft, climbed into it and cranked the engine. Not bothering with a preflight check, he released the brakes and started his takeoff roll. Once airborne he climbed to five thousand feet and brought the bird to a 320-degree northwest heading that would take him back to Rabat. Once there he would fly for the coast and then over the Atlantic side of the Straight of Gibraltar. He was going to Lisbon.

As the plane cut through the night skies on its four hour flight Kansi's mind wandered back to a week earlier when he had volunteered to go with a raiding party into the west bank near Tel Aviv. He remembered the screams and pleas of Jewish children as he cut their throats. He also pictured the Israeli women crying hysterically as he, and the others first raped and then slid knives into their soft bellies and shot them as they lay dying. *Yes,* he thought, *the Jews must die until there is none left in Palestine. The Americans are helping the Jews so the Americans must also be slaughtered like desert camels. May Allah be praised.*

The aircraft's engine coughed a couple of times bringing Kansi back from past memories to concentrate on a possible current problem. He leaned the throttle mixture and the engine seem to smooth out some. He was just in the process of mentally congratulating himself when he heard a voice inside the plane say, "Yes Kansi, congratulate thyself for thee have indeed outwitted your tormenters.

Upon hearing a voice with such clarity caused fear to shoot through Kansi like an arrow. He screeched and inadvertently put the plane into a dive. Sweat popped out on his forehead and his jaw muscles flexed. His mouth opened and closed but no words came out. Addressing the second of his problems first, he pulled back on the wheel and the airplane's nose came up. As the plane became straight and level his first problem returned to his mind. He turned his head to see if someone had hid in the luggage compartment, and saw no one there.

"Thee will not find me there Kansi for we have melded and become one." said the voice.

"Allah, help me for I am possessed," Kansi screamed. He could deal with the problems and pleasures of the tangible world but the thought of a supernatural being absolutely terrified him.

"Fear not Kansi, for I am here to help thee in thy quest for plunder and death. Together you and I will take the lives of many of the infidels."

Kansi was starting to settle down and come to terms with the voice although he could not tell if the voice was inside the plane or somewhere in his brain. Daring to question the entity he spoke haltingly, "Who are you ... and what do you want? Are you ... Allah?"

"Let us say that I have come to you from the ancient path and the old one is proud. In the past you have served him well and now you and I will gather souls for him and we will receive much reward and pleasure in return."

Kansi interpreted this to mean the old one was Allah and Allah had smiled on him for his past deeds. He remembered in the infidel's holy book somewhere that there was a parable that said, the devil deceives, but that was their book not the Koran.

The voice proceeded to instruct Kansi in the ways his life would change and that man's laws no longer applied. He would have any woman of his choice to sexually ravish and then to dispatch and take her soul. He told Kansi that with each soul he gathered he would become stronger until at some point he would be invincible.

Trying to get a better picture of what he was dealing with, Kansi said, "But if you are not Allah then who might you be?"

"I am called Ogar, but to some who have opposed me and felt my wrath, I am known to them as Zombeast from a time centuries past. And for now that is all you need to know." The voice had taken on a certain irritated edge, which conveyed to Kansi a subtle message that he should use caution in his conversations with Ogar.

Kansi asked a couple of more questions but heard no more from his intangible invisible companion. Apparently he only spoke when there was something of substance to say. Could it be that this Ogar was a servant of Allah?

Kansi flew on and was becoming a little worried when his fuel level started to dip into the red. He looked over the horizon and saw the city lights of Lisbon. As he approached to within twenty miles of the airport, he tuned his radio to the guard frequency, picked up the mike, keyed it and said, "Lisbon International, this is Cessna 5001Popa 73Zulu. Do you read, over?"

The radio static made the reply almost unreadable. "Cessna 5001P73Z I read you 5 by 5. State your position, over.

Tower. I am twenty miles due east of Lisbon International and low on fuel. I'm requesting landing instructions, over.

Roger, Cessna. You are cleared to land on runway 22, turn out on taxiway 10 right and expedite we have heavy inbound from Heathrow with ETA of thirty minutes. Do you copy, over?"

"Roger, Lisbon." Kansi pushed up the throttle and within five minutes had a visual on the airport runway's outer marker lights. He pulled the throttle back to almost idle, extended full flaps, and turned onto final approach. Executing a short final, the little plane made a smooth touchdown and Kansi proceeded down the runway with a high speed taxi, then slowing when he saw taxiway 10R. He turned off onto the taxiway and proceeded to the hanger section. He pulled into the rental tie down area and applied brakes. He killed the engine, got out and tied down the airplane. Looking around he saw that the airport passenger lounge and ticket counter buildings were about fifty yards away. He walked the short distances and entered the building by a side door. He continued on until he reached the big front doors leading to the street in front of the terminal building. Walking quickly to a line of waiting taxies he slid into the backseat of one and instructed, "Take me to the El Cabaletta Hotel and make hast, I am very tired.

The Portuguese driver glanced into the rear view mirror and his eyes became wide when he saw the blood on Kansi's suit but he manages to suppress his panic and said, "Very good sir, the El Cabaletta it is, and a fine choice sir. I must say –"

"Be quiet you babbling fool and let me think." He pulled his wallet out of his coat pocket and opened it. Inside were six hundred Moroccan Francs and two thousand dollars in American, all large bills. He checked his pant pockets and came up with thirty dollars worth of Moroccan Francs all in small bills. When they reached the hotel, he paid the driver with the small bills and quickly entered the hotel by a side door. Walking rapidly to a ground floor lavatory he stepped inside and grabbed a hand full of towels and wet them. He entered a stall for privacy and proceeded to clean himself as well as the circumstances would allow. Afterward he left the latrine and went to the desk and checked in. The desk clerk looked at Kansi with a curious expression but did not mention his appearance. She handed him a key and said, "Four-thirteen sir, it's on the forth floor. The elevators are to your right. Do you have any questions?"

"No but I have some requests. As you might have noticed, I've had a small accident and I have brought no clothes with me. I am six feet tall; wear a size 42 large suit, and shoes in a size eleven medium. In suit colors I like a tan or dark with a blue-stripped tie of some sort and a white silk shirt. Please contact an all night haberdashery and have those items delivered to my room. Tell the salesman that I will pay extra for speedy service."

Hesitantly, the clerk discreetly asked, "Sir would you like for me to call you a physician?"

"No I'm fine, actually it was a friend of mine who was hurt in an automobile accident and I made a mess of myself assisting in the placing of him into an ambulance.

Her facial expression changed to a look of concern as she said, "Oh, Mother of Mary, I hope your friend is going to be all right."

"He's fine. A few days in hospital and he'll be good as new. Now, Miss, about those clothes." Kansi was suddenly a bit unnerved by the fact that he was starting to feel an attraction for the woman behind the desk.

She replied, "Oh, yes sir, I'll make the call right away," and all the while she couldn't help noticing that the man before her had very compelling blue eyes. It occurred to her that blue eyes were very unusual for an Arab. She admonished herself for becoming sexually aroused by them.

Kansi said, "Thank you," then turned and started for the elevator.

Hot Sand & Cold Blood

She watched as he stepped into the elevator, and as the door closed behind him she thought, *what a nice man. I hope his friend will be fine.*

Kansi stepped out of the elevator and headed for his room. Once inside he removed his coat, shoes and tie. He turned on the television and relaxed on the bed watching some mindless programming. Right now he just wanted to clear his head and get some sleep. The events of the last twenty-four hour had been very unnerving in some ways and beneficial in others. A humorous and facetious thought occurred to Kansi, maybe the Ogar didn't need sleep but Kansi sure did. Tomorrow he would address the matters at hand.

There was something else rolling around in Kansi's mind. It was the young woman down in the lobby behind the check in counter that he had been talking to in regards to ordering new cloths. It occurred to him that he had a strong and unusual sexual attraction to her. Kansi liked sex just like any other man especially with young women, although normally his sexual drive wasn't as strong as the average man's. It had always been this way and he reasoned that it was because his mind held more lofty thoughts like the political dogma directed toward ridding the world of Jews. In his mind a preoccupation with sex had always been a waste of time but sometimes had to be done for procreation. Why then did the girl suddenly hold this attraction? His thoughts started to center on visions of seeing her naked. He even felt his penis becoming erect and was genuinely mystified by the simple fact that he wanted this woman and a week ago he would not have taken a second look at her. He began drifting off into a deep sleep knowing that tomorrow would be a busy day. Suddenly he was jarred from his slumber by a jangling sound and after a moment realized that it was the doorbell. Half asleep, he ambled over and opened the door and came face to face with a well-dressed man about his height, wearing a navy blue Armani suit. He was holding a shoebox in one hand and clothes hanger covered by clear protective plastic in the other. There was a medium dark pen-striped suit beneath the plastic. He was also wearing a large smile at the prospect of collecting some big bucks for delivering a high dollar suit at this time of night. "Good evening sir. I have an order for an ensemble of men's cloths for this room, I assume this is your order."

Kansi opened the door wider and said, "Come in and put the clothes on the bed," then turned to go retrieve his wallet.

The man followed Kansi into the room and laid the cloths neatly on the bed. Afterward, he said, "If you please sir that will be eleven hundred American and you don't want to know the amount in francs or lira."

Kansi paid the man to which the haberdasher thanked him profusely and left.

Finally, Kansi lay back on the bed and settled in for a nights sleep. It had been a rough and very unusual day.

Chapter 10

Ryder looked at Baronga and said, "You stay here and I'll take Butler with me to help set up the comp-4 Symtex charges. Harold, why don't you guys assist Baronga getting on the chopper and then load Malloy's body and go on back to Casablanca. When Butler and I get back from the drone site, he can take Baronga's Chevy back to the embassy and you guys can meet him there."

Harold Kolinsky's facial expression became something akin to pitiful as he lamented, "Ryder, as bad as that boy smells I'd just as soon leave him here, hell he ain't going to know the difference."

"Yeah, but your boss will when you guys come home one agent short." Ryder glanced at Baronga and said, "Where do you keep the explosives?"

"In the vehicle garage. They're in a box marked, for emergency exit." Baronga said.

"I'm not even going to ask what that means," Ryder said as he headed toward the garage.

Harold and the other agent who's name Ryder never did catch and really didn't want to, set about the business of loading the dead traitor onto the H-53. After getting Baronga settled onboard, Harold approached Ryder and said, "Ryder we're ready to go. Is there anybody you want us to call or contact when we get back to Casablanca?"

As they started walking toward the helo Ryder said, "Yeah, you might call Dante at the OMNI field office in Frankfurt and tell him what's developed so far. You might also tell him that I'll give him a call when I get back and give him the details."

"I'll do that Ryder." Harold extended his hand and said, "I hope they let you pursue this thing with Kansi."

Ryder shook his hand, and then Harold walked around to the other side, climbed into the helo and started running through preflight checks.

Ryder looked up through the open door at Baronga who was in the rear seat with a couple of safety belts securing him in the event they hit some rough air on the way back. "Well," Ryder said with a little devilish smile, "Chico, you got balls I'll give you that. You turned in one hell of a performance in that hanger firefight."

"Thanks Ryder. I was just glad to be there so I could help out."

"Take care of yourself, Chico."

"You too, Ryder."

By now, Harold had the H-53's blades spinning and the dust was starting to kick up so Ryder turned and walked away from the chopper to keep from being sand blasted. The helo lifted off and was soon out of sight and then the desert was deathly quiet.

Butler was standing by one of the dune buggies and now broke the silence with, "We have about half of the stuff loaded, Agent Ryder. But I need to tell you there is only three squibs to detonate this stuff so we had better make sure they're placed in strategic positions."

"That should be enough. Let's go in and get the rest of the explosives and get ready to move out?"

Ryder had just got the last word out when a gunshot punctuated his sentence and the round kicked up sand next to his feet. Ryder dove for the cover of the closest building and Butler did likewise.

"Butler, do you see anybody?"

"No but it sounded like it came from that row of dunes about a hundred yards to the east over there."

"Yeah, that was my assessment also. Can you work your way around and flank them for a better look?"

"I give it a try, Ryder, but I'll tell you that there's a lot of open ground to my left and that's the only way I can go without moving directly into their line of fire."

"All right, make a tentative move to your left as a diversion, but be careful and I'll try to flank to my right. At least we will be spread out and that will force them to divide their attention and maybe smoke them out. I know that it's not much of a plan but we're on low ground and we don't have many options."

"Ryder, I'm moving out, if I draw any fire maybe you can pinpoint and put a few rounds their way." Butler flattened out on the ground and started crawling and had gone ten feet when a couple of rounds from the far dune kicked up sand around him causing him to freeze. From the other side of the building, Ryder was watching and saw the little wisps of smoke as they curled up from the gun muzzles. He quickly took aim at the dune and proceeded to empty a clip into it and the sand came alive flying everywhere as the P-89 rounds peppered the crest of the dune. Ryder heard a muffled cry and once again the desert became quiet. He hollered, "Butler, are you alright?"

"Yeah, I'm O.K. I think that you nailed him Ryder. I heard somebody yell"

"There may be more than one, so keep you head down and don't get in a hurry to find out what happened and remember that we are on low ground so they have the advantage." They stayed low to the ground and didn't move around much for another ten minutes and seeing no movement from the far dune, Ryder decided to take a chance on exposing himself for the thirty feet or so that he would have to crawl to get the cover of the next dune. If he could make it to that point then there was fairly good cover all the way and even including the area that would allow him to get behind the far dune that he had seen the gun-smoke rise from. He slipped another clip into the Ruger and then started belly crawling toward his next position of safety. He just hoped that if he drew fire, Butler would have enough sense and experience to take advantage of it, and shoot who ever it was on that hill. He reached the safety of the next dune and could not believe he hadn't had a single round come his way. He paused for a couple of minutes to have a look around from his new vantage point and then was just about to move further in the direction to flank the far dune when he heard the, ring-ding-ding of a two-cycle dirt bike in the distance. He waited for a minute longer and then rose to his feet in a crouching position with his gun trained on the far dune and broke into a run.

Butler, seeing Ryder charging the far dune, leaped up and approached from the opposite direction. Neither man drew any fire. They reached the dune's apex where the gunfire had erupted from and found no one there. Ryder checked the ground and found the area disturbed with two sets of footprints leading in and out. There were also three empty shell casings from a Kalishnakof machine pistol lying on the ground. "Well, Butler, who ever took those shots at us apparently hauled ass out of here on a couple of dirt bikes. They could be, and probably are part of Kansi's dirtbag gang."

"Do you want to go after them Ryder?"

"It's a long shot, Butler but if those guys are part of Kansi's outfit then we should do everything possible to chase them down and extract any and all information they may have. Can you handle a dune buggy in a high speed chase?"

"Yeah, I think so."

"Alright, lets get down there and get cranked up, and remember those things handle a little differently than a car."

In no time, Ryder and Butler were bouncing across the dunes with the buggies running flat out, following the dirt bikes tire tracks, which was leading them back to Sidi Slimane. When they came near the old base the sand turned into an asphalt runway making it no longer possible to follow the tire tracks but it no longer mattered because now Ryder knew where they led. Cautiously, Ryder and Butler circled the base a couple of times looking for some sign of the dirt bikes. Finding nothing, Ryder pulled up in front of the main hanger where he and Baronga had the shoot out with the Arabs the night before. Butler pulled up next to Ryder, shut of his engine and then asked, "What do you think Ryder?"

"I think that we'll go inside and have a look around, but keep your piece handy, Butler. These guys are as mean as rabid dogs."

"Don't worry Ryder, I've got your back."

The big hanger door was closed so they entered the hanger using the same door that Ryder had gone through the night before. They slowly and cautiously proceeded down the hallway, methodically checking each office as they went.

Coming to the end of the hallway Ryder found himself once again entering the big hanger bay. Ryder held up his left hand and motioned with his finger for Butler to go down the left side of the hanger wall while he would go right. They had gone no more than about twelve feet from the hallway when two Arabs came running out of a room on the far side of the hanger. They started screaming something about, "Allah is great," and opened up with AK-47s.

The AK rounds immediately chewed up the wall behind Ryder. He wanted prisoners for interrogation but not at the expense of getting killed for them. He opened up with the Ruger and the Arab closest to him, pitched forward and crumpled to the floor with a nine millimeter round through his forehead. A second later his companion also went to meet Allah with two rounds in his chest.

Meanwhile Butler had allowed a tinge of panic to overcome him and he was shooting up the place, hitting everything except the Arabs. After empting three clips in quick secession Butler quit shooting and went about the business of trying to mentally get a grip on himself."

Ryder walked over to him and asked, "Are you alright?"

"A long way from it, but I'm not hit if that's what you mean? Ryder, I've only been in two gunfights since joining the CIA. That one back on the dune and this one here."

Ryder smiled and said, "Well, Butler, you did pretty good for your first time out. These guys must have been a couple we missed last night and they probably followed us to the office to get a little payback. We're not going to get anything out of them so we might as well head on back."

"You're right Ryder. Thanks to you, they look pretty damn' incapacitated to me."

"Butler, all this bouncing around in the buggy has caused my shoulder to start acting up some, so let's slow it down a little going back."

They arrived back at the office four hours later and went in and carefully went about the business of gathering up the rest of the explosives and loaded them into the buggies. Ryder's shoulder was a bit sore but he had decided to finish neutralizing the drones so there would be no chance of them falling into the wrong hands. He would have plenty of time to rest when he got back to Beirut.

The thought of waiting for the OMNI command section to figure out what they wanted him to do next didn't set well with Ryder, but he wasn't going to deliberate too much on what Harold had told him. When he got back he'd call Dante in Frankfurt and find out the current situation.

Ryder watched as Butler put the last of the Symtex plastic explosives into his buggy then said, "Butler are you ready to go on up to the drone launch complex?"

"As a matter of fact I am kind of curious to see what these drones look like before we blow them up."

"OK saddle up." Ryder said as he gingerly climb into his buggy and started the engine. They drove the relative short distance to the drone launchers and parked next to the camo net covering. Ryder got and walked over to where the opening in the net was located and motioned for Butler to follow him. Once inside Butler was awed by the sight of the drones and said, "Ryder how fast do these things fly?"

Ryder stepped over to the alpha drone and replied, "They have an estimated top speed of one point two mach which means they fly at about –"

"Yeah, I know that's around seven hundred and fifty miles per hour. I was a navy fighter pilot for four years before I got into the CIA. As a mater of fact I still fly P-2 Orions for the CIA once in a while when they decide to do communications surveillance."

Ryder was impressed and curious as he asked, "Fighter pilot ... so what did you fly in the navy?"

"F-14 Tomcats most of the time. I've logged a thousand hours in that bird. I was also checked out in the F-18

Hornet and I have around three hundred hours flight time in it. A hundred hours of that are nighttime instrument carrier landings. And last but not least, I was loaned out to the Air Force through an inter-service TDY, and I have seventy hours in the air force F-15 Eagle, plus some check rides in the F-16 Falcon."

Ryder grinned and said, "Here I am working with one of the navy's finest and I didn't even know it. Well if you're finished looking over the hardware let's put a match to it."

"It's a shame to do it Ryder. There's a lot of expensive electronic equipment sitting here."

"That's the way it goes. Let's go back out and get the firecrackers and put these drones out of their misery."

It took them twenty minutes to unload the explosives and start attaching them to the launchers. Ryder glanced over the equipment looking to find the most strategic positions where a charge would cause the most destruction as he said, "We have three squibs so lets assign one to each drone launcher and one to the control panel. Divide the comp-4 into roughly three packages and place one on each launcher at about the drone's middle, making it half way between the nose and tail fins; that's where the drone's fuel tanks are located. Lets attach the third package to the console near the control stick. Do you have any questions or suggestions about how we are going to set it up?"

"It sounds good to me Ryder. Besides this is your show." The two agents spent the next hour attaching the Comp-4 and inserting the squibs. When it was ready, Ryder tied all three electric primer wires together and then ran the single lead outside. He continued feeding the wire off the wire-reel as he walked toward his dune buggy. Butler followed him out and watched as Ryder climbed into his buggy, and then he went over and got into his own vehicle. Ryder drove slowly away from the launch complex trailing wire as he went with Butler following to one side in order to avoid driving over the detonation cord. At about one hundred yards the detonation cord ran out and Ryder stopped his vehicle. Butler also stopped, got out of his buggy and walked over to where Ryder had dismounted and was in the process of attaching the end of the cord to the ignition batteries.

Butler spoke casually, "Ryder, we are only about three hundred feet from the launcher and there's a lot of C-4 attached to those rails."

"I know, Butler. Way too much to be setting it off at this distance, but this is all of the det cord that we have. I want you to take your vehicle and go back to the office and wait for me there. If this thing goes south, take Baronga's Chevy and go back to Casablanca like we planned."

"Ryder, you had better think about this because you may be committing suicide. Why don't we go back and search the office again, maybe we can find more detonation cord"

Butler, We don't have time for long conversations or going back and looking for more cord, now get in your buggy and get hell out of here."

"OK Ryder. I'm not going to argue with you." Butler went to his vehicle, got into it and drove off toward the office. When he was out of sight, Ryder finished attaching the wire as he walked over to a little dune and sat down in a position that put the dune between him and the launcher. He sat the battery down and tore a couple of small pieces of cloth from his shirt. He balled them up, put them in his ears and picked up the batteries. He leaned as close to the dune as he could, closed his eyes and closed the detonator switch. The explosion that followed was something that Ryder could not have imagined. The noise, even with the makeshift ear protection, was deafening as a fireball rose up sending debris in every direction. Almost instantly drone and launcher pieces started raining down. Part of a tail fin bounced off of the dune buggy, destroying the remote console that was mounted on top. The metal hailstorm lasted for another two minutes more or less and then Ryder started believing that he was actually going to survive it. He got up, walked over to the buggy and got in. He started the vehicle and went back to the drone complex to assess the damage. Was the buggy running a lot quieter than usual or was it just his imagination. When he arrived at the drone site the first thing that he discovered was that there was no site. What had replaced the drone complex was a large black crater. It appeared that about half the comp-4 would have done the job. *What the hell,* Ryder thought, *I'm not an explosives expert. How was I supposed I know that many explosives would blow up half of Morocco?* He put the buggy into gear and was about to start back when Butler drove up next to him and stopped. He looked at Butler and noticed something odd. Butler's mouth was moving but he could hear no words coming out. He leaned closer and said Butler speak up I can't hear you. Again Butler's mouth began moving and his facial expression seemed very intense but still to Ryder it seemed that Butler was just mouthing words with no sound. Then it occurred to Ryder that there was a loud ringing in his ears but he couldn't hear anything. He pointed to his ears and said, "I can't hear anything. Follow me back to the parking garage. When they arrived Ryder parked and got out. Butler pulled up next to his vehicle, got out and walked over next to Ryder and yelled, "Can you hear anything now?"

Ryder heard him say it. The words sounded faint and far away but he did hear them. Ryder said, "Lets pull the Chevy and the Mercedes out of the building and put the buggies inside."

They proceeded to move the vehicles around until all the cars were where they were supposed to be. Butler once again walked over next to Ryder and yelled, "Has your hearing improved?"

Ryder stepped back and said, "You don't have to scream Butler, I can hear you."

Butler grinned and replied, "Woman scream, Ryder. I yell."

Ryder allowed a little smile to play across his face as he said, "OK then, just stop your damn' yelling. I saw a five gallon gas can in the parking garage part of the office. Get it and pore the gas all over everything."

Butler replied, "Roger Ryder." He went in and retrieved the gas can and proceeded to wet the interior of the place down. When he had finished he tossed the empty can on the floor, stepped outside and said, "I guess we're done."

Ryder said, "Not quite," and with those words stepped to the door and flipped a lit match though it. In a matter of seconds the place was engulfed in flame.

Ryder and Butler shook hands, said good-by, then got into their vehicles and drove off toward Casablanca.

Chapter 11

Kansi awoke the following morning around eight a.m. after a fitful night of horrible dreams. Then it all came rushing back to him. The events of the last twenty-four hours. But most of all he was thinking about the woman down in the lobby who had checked him in and ordered his clothes. *But why her,* he thought. *I have never been that interested in women so why do I want her so badly?* His lust for the woman was almost over whelming. He saw thoughts in his mind of him ripping her clothes from her body and then sexually ravishing her over and over. Then it dawned on him that it just wasn't the woman downstairs it would be any woman he came in contact with. For some unknown reason his sexual appetite was becoming voracious. Did it have something to do with the voice that had invaded his mind— yes he was sure of it.

And then conformation came at that moment as the voice in his mind said, "Go forth Kansi, for the old one must have a soul and I must have my lust quelled."

Kansi pleaded, "I cannot do as you asked. People are after me and I am on a mission for Allah. I must go to the bank and draw from my accounts and then go to America and carry out my part of the plan. Do you not see that I –"

"Quiet you son of a low bred pig. I will tell you what you must do. We will carry out your plan but all in good time. But first things first, and fear not, just go with your feelings and all will happen with Ogar." Then once again the voice became silent.

As the day went by Amal Kansi became more restless. He couldn't understand his craving - the hunger that was constantly with him. He left the hotel, caught a cab downtown, and now found himself walking the red light districts of Lisbon. His sexual appetite had also increased—at times almost to the point of being insatiable. After cruising the streets of Portugal's capitol he entered one of the little hole in the walls that passed for taverns and looked around. It was a typical Portuguese hangout, dark, with a crude wooden bar and a jukebox in the corner playing an instrumental version of 'Stairway to Heaven. Some of the ladies of the night sat at tables drinking the local wine, while others danced with American and European tourists who's tastes ran to the more base side of life.

Amal Kansi, not wanting to attract attention, walked over to the bar, ordered a glass of dark wine, and looked around, sizing the place up. He had in his entire life never entered a place like this until this evening. Seeing a secluded spot, he went over and sat down in a booth and took a pull from his wine and instantly scowled at the bad taste. As an Arab, he had never before experienced the sharp taste and flavor of alcohol. He looked up as a young, good-looking woman approached his table.

She wore a short, Spanish style; tight-fitting low cut colorful dress and high heels. He figured she was about twenty-three years old. She also wore a lot of make-up but that didn't hide the fact that she had a beautifully tanned face and an even better figure. Even in the dim light her jet-black hair shined and her moist sanguine lips presented an image to drive men crazy. To Kansi, her facial features appeared to be that of Spanish ancestry and she was a woman that every man would contemplate killing for, but instead, wound up settling for someone far less appealing.

She smiled sweetly. "Good evening, my name is Juanita. Would you care to buy me drink? I am very lovely and you must know that you are a very lucky man."

"Yes my sweet one, I think that you are very lovely. Come and share a beverage in my company."

She sat down next to him, placing her hand on his forearm and letting her leg brush lightly against his.

He had an almost uncontrollable urge to rip her clothes off and take her right there in that dark dingy little tavern.

Fighting to regain his composure, he motioned for a waitress to bring them a couple of drinks.

Juanita looked up at him, all the time her smile still in place. "You're a big Arab man. I like big men." She let her hand slide slowly down and come to rest on his crotch. Her voice became husky. "Hombre, you are a big man. What is your name?"

"I am called Kansi, Amal Kansi." From the moment she had sat down and touched him, Kansi's voice had become raspy and dry. He drank down the balance of his wine, emptying the glass.

The waitress returned with a robust smile and set their drinks on the table.

Kansi handed her a couple of bills and she quickly left.

Juanita picked up her drink and took a sip. "Mmmm, I like to drink. It takes my mind to pleasant times back in Madrid and that makes me feel good. Amal, do you want go home with me tonight and enjoy my beautiful body?" she teased.

It seemed to Kansi that Juanita was very sure of herself and why not, she was probably the most desirable woman this city had seen in a decade.

"Yes my princess, I want to go home with you tonight."

"Okay Amal, that's good, but first I would like to dance. Do you like to dance?" She got up and Kansi followed her onto the dance floor, taking her into his arms and pulling her in close. Kansi had no experience with dancing but decided to wing it as they did a few turns on the floor. Her perfume and womanly smell filled his nostrils. Finally he could take it no longer. Looking down at her, he said in a low, harsh voice, "We must go to your home. Now."

"But Amal, you just got here. Can't we just party a little before we go?"

His voice was an urgent whisper as he felt the Zombeast rising within him. "No. We must leave right away."

She tilted her head up and looked into his eyes. Abruptly, she took a step back and broke physical contact. But she could not take her eyes away from his unearthly orbs, which had begun to change from blue to a dark indigo. As it happened, she began to experience a strong sexual desire for him. This man was something she hadn't encountered in all the time she'd been on the streets. She'd been a prostitute for the last five years, and in that time had slept with more American and European men than she cared to keep a record. In all that time she had felt nothing. It had been just a job. She had been sixteen when she was first introduced to sex, and was a hooker by the time she was eighteen.

As they gazed into each other's eyes she realized that for the first time she wasn't the one calling the shots. She wasn't deciding how much money or how long. His steady stare was binding her to him and her instincts told her he was dangerous but she couldn't look away.

He reached out and touched her hand and it startled her. It was like a small current of electricity running up her arm. She felt like her whole body was now mildly vibrating and her blood had started to run hot.

Wanting to feel more she stepped forward and pressed her body against him. She reached out and put her arm around his waist, never taking her eyes off his, she said, "Okay, Amal, we'll go now." As they left the dance floor she picked up her purse and they walked out.

They arrived at one of Lisbon's older, rundown, four story hotels'. She keyed open one of the rooms on the third floor and they stepped inside, going directly to the bedroom. Amal grabbed the shoulder straps of her dress, ripped them in two, and then tore the dress from her body.

"Amal, please don't tear my damn' dress. It cost me two thousand lira."

"Do not worry about the dress my precious one. I will buy you new dresses."

She lay back on the bed, slightly spreading her well-shaped legs while watching Amal as he started removing his clothes. She massaged herself softly and sensually, and then called, "Hurry, Amal, hurry." He had instilled a feeling in her that she couldn't explain and all she knew was she had to have him inside her.

Amal mounted her with the intensity of a desert predator attacking a young lamb.

The suddenness with which he entered her, coupled with the size of his abnormally large penis, forced her to cry out in both pain and pleasure. So intense was her anticipation and hunger that within minutes her hips arched upward and she threw her head back. Mouth wide open, she screamed passionately. Her muscles were drawn tight and her body shook slightly as her fingernails bit deep into his shoulders, drawing blood. The sexual release was so fulfilling and so complete she continued to moan loudly as tears flowed from her eyes. The climaxes continued to come, over and over like the hot winds of a sirocco washing across the Sahara Desert.

She couldn't believe what Amal was doing to her and couldn't understand how a mortal man could make a woman feel this way. There was no question about the fact that she was totally under his control. He was like an opiate, but there was an old rule, the better the drug the higher the price.

Amal now felt the Zombeast inside, voicing his satisfaction. It was almost as if he and not Amal were ravishing the woman.

As the hours went by, Juanita experienced sexual pleasures she had never felt before. Her mind was focused, her legs were locked tightly around Amal's thighs and every muscle and fiber of her body was taut with lust and wanting. She was wet with perspiration, her eyes and cheeks damp with tears and she could hear the low and deep guttural sounds rising from her own throat.

Amal also moaned with animalistic sounds of passion throughout the night as his back and shoulders progressively became shinier with scarlet wetness.

Each time he ejaculated into her she had the feeling he was not making love to her, but using her, destroying her, as he sucked in her mind and soul. She could feel it killing her but because of the ceaseless overwhelming waves of pleasure there was nothing she could do. It was a tradeoff. The climaxes were wonderfully beyond anything she had ever felt before and she was proportionally giving up a piece of her life for every one. Worse yet, because the feeling was so incredibly intense, she was willing to even die for it. Through the night, hour-by-hour she alternately moaned her pleasures and screamed with pain, not knowing which was which, but wanting it all and more as he stole her mind and soul while ravaging her body.

Amal sensed something different in this woman. She was not like him in most ways but there was a common mindset in the area of sex that they both shared. He wondered for a fleeting second how he knew, and then decided it didn't matter … he just did. His sexual stamina also surprised him. How was he able to engage in vigorous, heated sex for hours on end and then still want more? He looked down at her passionate expression, and then without really knowing why, growled, "Bitch, in time, when I have completed copulating with thee, and sucking in and tasting all thy sweet juices, thy soul will be mine. And thy beautiful body will be as the ice of winter. For behold, my sexual needs are great and will require more then one mortal female to quell them."

Weakly raising her hand to rub his perspiring cheek she looked up at him as though in a trance and replied, "Yes. If it will satisfy your lust, take all that I have to give."

Toward morning, Juanita's body became progressively colder as her life was drawn from first her fingertips, then her hands, then arms and legs. Her life force was being pulled to the area where the two sexes joined to create new life, and then sucked into the Zombeast by her unearthly lover.

She felt herself growing weaker as Amal grew stronger, feeding on her life force. In the far reaches of her mind she realized the end would come soon, but she was too caught up in the pleasure Amal had opened up to her. She could still feel him inside, pleasuring her as he took the last vestiges of her life and soul. Slowly she started to lose consciousness.

She looked up into Amal's eyes for the last time and thought she must be hallucinating because they were no longer indigo, but somehow had become bright and translucent as she looked into them and saw her future. She saw them glowing with the burning crimson of a thousand fires then she left this world. She had taken her ride with the Zombeast and she had paid the price. Even to the very end, her last fleeting words were, "Please, Amal, I want more ... I need more."

She had begun this strange ritual with greed and an abnormal craving for money, and had received much more, and lost much, much more. She had given in to an unnatural lust; an unknown desire and it had taken her life.

The morning sun filtered through the dirty hotel window as Amal sat on the bed quietly looking at Juanita. Her skin was a pale gray, her body cold and shrunken and there was a hole in her upper abdomen. A testament to Kansi have taken her heart and eaten it. A cavity now existed where her heart once beat and her dimmed, sightless eyes, now resting in hollow sockets, stared at the hotel ceiling. But somewhere else in an unfamiliar place her mind and soul watched as the one in black armor thundered across pitiless dark skies.

Amal pulled the folding knife from his pocket once more and leaned over her as he carved the letters "LAMA" into her forehead.

He took a long hot shower, got dressed and sang little praises to his maker as he stepped out onto the streets of Lisbon to hail a cab. It was a beautiful day and Amal felt good and soon he would be going to America to make the Westerners pay with their lives.

He repeated this carnivorous bloodlust four more times in the following four nights with an all too willing prostitute, before returning to the El Cabaletta Hotel. With each encounter he had visions of himself striking fear into the hearts of the infidels and coming one step closer to immortality and being with Allah. For this, he was sure that he would have the seventy-two virgins upon his final demise.

Chapter 12

On the trip back to Casablanca Ryder kept turning the events of the last couple of days over in his mind trying to separate out what was fact and what was conjecture. There wasn't much doubt about the men that he and Baronga had encountered were bad people and probably deserved to die. They were up to something real bad on a global scale and everybody was convinced that it was a bomb that would make Hiroshima look like a firecracker.

The CIA and OMNI also were convinced that the terrorist either had the bomb or were making the bomb. It was just a matter of time before Kansi and company reveled themselves by issuing an ultimatum or just going ahead and blowing up a city. Maybe Ryder was convinced too. At least now there was some tangible evidence that he had recently uncovered to prove something was going on. But with all of that, there was still something in the back of his mind that told him to keep that little ace in the hole; and that ace was the right to change his mind.

The Casablanca traffic getting back into the city was just as bad as getting out. He finally arrived back at the Marrakesh Hotel and parked the Mercedes in front next to the main lobby. He turned off the ignition and sat there for a moment longer mulling over his situation then got out and walked the short distance to his room to get cleaned up. After a quick shower and change of clothes he felt better and decided to call Rose. He left his room and went to the downstairs lobby to see if he could locate a phone. He found two public phones near the check in counter. He picked up the receiver and asked the operator to ring long distance. A moment later he heard, "Do you speak French, English, or Arabic?"

"All three to some degree, but for the sake of simplicity let's stick to English."

"Yes sir. This is long distance, how may I help you?"

"Please ring Mid East Oil in Beirut." Ryder requested.

"Very good sir." said the operator.

Another minute passed and a man answered, "Mid East, Bronson here. How can I help you?"

"Yes. My name is Ryder and I'm trying to get in touch with Lisa Anne Nickels. She's one of your pilots,"

"That's correct, but she is not in Beirut. She took one of the new 727s to Heidelberg; shuttling some oil friendly politicians on a junket of some sort. She should be back tomorrow or the next day."

Will you tell her that I called? My name is Lance Ryder. I'm in Casablanca but I'll be back at the El Kadeem Hotel in Beirut tomorrow. She knows the number there. Would you please ask her to call me when she gets back from Germany?"

"I sure will."

"Thank you." Ryder hung up and decided to call the Casablanca International airport to see if they were able to track Kansi's plane. After a couple of attempts he was able to speak with one of the controllers that had been assigned to track Kansi's airplane.

"Jamul Wahadee, here, how may I help you Mr. Ryder?"

"Mr. Wahadee I'm calling to find out if you were able to maintain a radar track on the light plane that you picked up from our radar near Sidi Slimane."

"Mr. Ryder, we tracked your aircraft on a 270 degree heading for over four hundred kilometers before he dropped off of our screen. He is a light aircraft and based on the amount of fuel that he could carry, the fuel consumption rate, and his heading, it is almost a certainty that he could not have exceeded the Lisbon airport."

"You say almost a certainty. Is there somewhere he could have landed short of there?"

"Of course. There are small dirt strips here and there he could have landed on in an emergency. However getting fuel to fly out may be a problem and not a likely scenario. His biggest problem would occur if after he left the coast, he encountered mechanical problems and was forced to ditch in the Strait of Gibraltar. His airplane would sink and unless he had a life raft and a beeper it's not likely we would ever hear from him again. However, no one has picked up a distress call. No Mr. Ryder, we are sure that he went to Lisbon."

"Were you able to get his call letters from a radio transmission or from his transponder squawk?"

"No. He was flying completely silent with everything turned off. If he landed at Lisbon he would have had to turn his radio on as he neared the airport for a landing clearance but that would be out of our range especially if he were using a low wattage transmitter."

"Thank you mister Wahadee." Ryder dropped the phone back in the cradle and thought, *after that drawn out conversation I'm not sure if he helped me or just confused the situation.* Ryder picked up the phone once more and asked the long distance operator to connect him to the American Embassy in Frankfurt. After a brief wait a voice on the other end said, "American Embassy, Molder speaking. How can I help you?"

"Do you have a guy named Earl Duke still in residence there?

"Yes we do. He is the assistant congressional diplomatic liaison. Would you care to speak to him?"

"Yes." Ryder replied.

"You are in luck. Mr. Duke has just returned from playing a round at the newly opened Eisenhower golf course. I'll ring his office."

After a few rings a voice finally answered. "Earl Duke, congressional liaison. How may I be of service?"

"Duke, this is Ryder, do you have an echo scrambler handy?"

"Yes." Duke said.

"Slap it on the phone." Ryder said as he reached into his pocket and pulled out a small black device and put it over the receiver. He put the phone back to his ear and said, "Do you understand me?"

Hot Sand & Cold Blood

"Yes." came Dukes reply.

"Duke for the last few days I've been in Morocco with a CIA guy named Baronga. I'm going to call you back in an hour and brief you on what's happened so far but first I want you to get somebody in the state department and have them contact the base commander at Ramstein Air Force Base and have him dispatch a C-130 cargo plane to Sidi Slimane Morocco. It's an old American military base that was closed down in —"

"I've heard of the base, but we can't fly in there our military agreements with the Moroccan Government have expired."

"You don't have to land, just have the pilot fly to that point and then have him chart a direct route from there to the Lisbon International Airport. Have him fly the route at no higher than five hundred feet where the terrain will allow. Take two spotters along with long-range field glasses. I want them to look for small dirt landing strips and they will also be looking for a small airplane that may have landed. Additionally I want the pilot to fly a serpentine criss-crossing pattern. When the C-130 flies into Moroccan airspace have the pilot tell their tower that they are on an emergency resupply mission to Istanbul, Turkey. If you find a small plane, mark the position and dispatch an H-53 Jolly Green helicopter to fly out and land approximately one mile from the target and run surveillance on it. If there's a small Cessna out there, I want to know where it goes."

"What's going on Ryder?" Duke asked.

"I've firmly identified a target named Amal Kansi who has since flown out of Sidi and it appears that he's headed for Lisbon. I believe that's where he is now but I have to cover all possibilities, that's why I'm calling for the C-130. If you come up with anything call Dante. He's high enough on the food chain to coordinate almost all OMNI activity." Ryder instructed.

"What's your next move?" asked Duke.

"I'm going back to Beirut, and since Dove is dead, I'm going to wait for Dante to call with further instructions. If I don't hear anything from Dante within four days I'll proceed to Lisbon to see if I can pick up Kansi's trail."

"I'll contact Dante with this info and I'll talk to you again within an hour."

"One hour from now." Ryder dropped the phone back in the cradle and stood pondering his next move. He left the hotel and drove the Mercedes back to the rental service. After checking the car back in to the service, he returned to the hotel and asked the desk clerk if he had any messages. The clerk gave him a negative reply and Ryder went to his room.

After keying open the door and entering the room the OMNI agent reached into his pocket and pulled out the scraps of paper he'd taken from Kansi's office. He sat down on the old sofa to study the information in an attempt to glean every possible meaning from the words. Again, the only thing that stood out was, Company, Western States, and gas. If Kansi was referring to, the company as the CIA, then he should build his investigation around the area of Langley Virginia. On the other hand, another thought occurred to him about the area, New York City was bigger. Would it not make more since to explode a devise in a more densely populated part of the country. He tossed the papers into the table and decided that he just couldn't reach a definite conclusion until he had more pieces of the puzzle. He looked at his watch; it was time to call Earl Duke and brief him on the latest events. He went down stairs and upon reaching the lobby, saw that both phones were busy. He drank a soft drink while he waited and went over Kansi's papers in his mind. When one of the phones was available Ryder called Earl Duke and briefed him on everything that had happened.

"Alright Ryder, I'll brief Headquarters and I think that Dante will be calling you after you return to Beirut. He'll come up with a game plan and pass it on to you. He may also have some Intel that you can use. I called the air force and they have already dispatched a C-130 to Morocco. Those boys are always looking for an excuse to fly so it didn't take much convincing. If they come up with something I'll call you in Beirut with it. Do you have anything else?"

No, I guess that about covers it. I'm catching a plane out in the morning and should be there by tomorrow afternoon. Talk to you later."

"Yeah, Ryder. Later." Duke said.

The OMNI spy hung up the phone and then called the airport ticket counter. The phone rang several times and then a voice said, "Casablanca International, El Moroccan Airways. May I help you?"

"Yeah, my name is Lance Ryder and I want to book a flight out to Beirut the first thing in the morning."

"Very good Mr. Ryder. The first flight out will be at nine-fifteen a.m. on flight 786. Will that be soon enough, Mr. Ryder?"

"That will be fine, thank you" Ryder replied.

"Thank you for flying El Moroccan Airways Mr. Ryder."

Ryder dropped the phone in the cradle and went into the hotel bar to drink a beer and think about his own game plan before the next segment of this enigma unfolded.

The sun predictably rose to another hot and dry day. With bags packed, Ryder ambled into the hotel dining area and took a seat at one of the tables. A waiter approached his table with a cup of thick Arab coffee and said "A fine morning to you Sadeki Ryder. How about a well roasted side of camel, with eggs?"

Ryder glanced up at the tired looking Arab and said, "Fine, bring what ever you have." The blond spy ate in silence, trying to decide whether to go straight to Lisbon while the trail was hot or follow OMNI's instructions and continue to back to Beirut. He thought that under different circumstances he would have ignored OMNI and followed the trail; but then there was Lisa. There was also the possibility that Dante may have come up with new information. He thought about Lisa and wondered what she was doing at this moment. After finishing his breakfast he went to the hotel lobby, picked up a phone and called a taxi. A little over fifteen minutes later he was on his way to the airport. As the Volkswagen taxi bounced along Ryder's mind once again drifted back to thoughts of Lisa. His hopes were that she would soon be back in Beirut because he really wanted to see her before he left for Lisbon. He wasn't going to kid himself, part of the reason was for the sex, but it went much deeper than that; he was falling in love with her or at least it occurred to him that it was feasible. Then he seriously wondered if that were really possible so soon after losing his wife? And if it were true, he reasoned for a moment, then what about the ramifications of the change in lifestyles. If he married her, and that was a big if, he would likely have to quit OMNI and get a regular job, maybe as a cop. And what about Rose, would she want to continue to fly? Surely she would have to stop flying for Mid East and get a job with a domestic commuter airline in the States. The more he thought about the situation the more problematic it became in his mind. He reached a point where he decided that there were just too many unknowns to think about in the relationship and decided to just let the future take care of itself.

The driver pulled up in front of the airport terminal, looked back at Ryder, and announced, "We have arrived Sadeki. That will be fifty francs if you please. Can I help you with your bags?"

"No thanks," Ryder replied as he paid the driver and exited the cab. As he stepped onto the sidewalk he immediately drew a small crowd of street urchins, all begging for coins. Ryder took a hand full of change from his pocket and tossed it to one side in order to clear a path. It was a short walk to the El Moroccan Airways counter to pick up his ticket and check his bags. The overhead fans worked tirelessly but in vain to overcome the sweltering heat. Ryder looked at his boarding pass for a gate number. He shuffled along in the crowd until he reached gate seven and took a chair in the boarding area. He looked out through the large dirty window toward the tarmac and spotted the old DC-6 four-engine antique that was to fly him and the other unfortunates to Beirut. The DC-6, equipped with piston driven engines and propellers, was also known as the C-54 when it was used in World War II. American and European carriers had long since quit using them in favor of jet airliners.

Ryder looked at his watch and was just about to assume that the plane was going to be delayed by mechanical trouble or some other problem, when a tinny sounding PA system announced his flight. He stood, got into line and shuffled along with the rest of the sheep until he entered the aircraft and took his seat.

The plane was also warm and smelled of sweat. After a brief period the ground crew plugged in a power cart in preparation for engine start and the air conditioning started, offering a measure of relief from the heat and smell of the cabin. The pilot cranked the engines and taxied out to the runway. Ryder looked out through his window and detected an inordinate amount of smoke coming off the cowling of the number two engine. It was also running rough. *Great,* he thought, *now I'll bet we taxi back to the ramp so a mechanic can have a look at the number two engine and delay us in this heat for an hour or two.* To Ryder's surprise, the captain ran the engines' power up, released the brakes and started his take-off roll. The plane got airborne and turned east. Ryder watched the troubled engine for an hour and noticed that a small stream of oil was starting to leak out of the engine cowling and pour off of the trailing edge of the wing. He called to the flight attendant about the same time the seat belt light came on. He buckled his belt and once more looked out through his window just in time to see the troubled engine burst into flame. The aircraft's nose pitched down slightly and it felt like the plane was picking up speed. The abrupt shift in aircraft direction generated screams from women and children, and then general pandemonium erupted. The aircraft rocked around the skies causing carry-on luggage to be tossed about adding to the fear and confusion. The Arab woman seated next to Ryder was out of her mind with fear. Her eyes were wide with panic and her screams were relentless.

He reached over, put his arms around her and held her as tight as possible. At the rate the plane was dropping he knew that they were too far from the airport to make it back.

F. Washington Brown

Ryder couldn't tell exactly how long it took but it seemed like the pilot managed to level the aircraft some and it appeared that he was trying to turn back toward Casablanca. A quick look through the window told Ryder that it would be anybody's guess as to how long they would remain aloft. They were still losing altitude but less rapidly, then it occurred to Ryder that the pilot was trying to slow as much as possible to get the plane in position for a wheels up belly landing. Once more he glanced through the window and saw sand dunes coming up fast. *If he can find a flat stretch of desert,* Ryder thought, *we might not have any casualties.*

The airplane hit a dune and once again became airborne. The second contact with the desert was a little smoother. After four bounces the aircraft just simply careened along the smooth sandy floor until it slid to a stop. The woman next to him was no longer making a sound; her mind had taken her passed that point and now she sat in a quiet state of shock. Ryder looked out and except for the bent propellers; the airplane seemed to be intact. He had a minor abrasion on his left cheek, but other than that he was unhurt. He looked at the woman next to him and she seemed all right. He unbuckled his belt and went about the business of checking the other passengers for injuries. The situation was nothing short of a minor miracle. An old man sitting up front close to the exit door had a broken leg and as it turned out his injury was the worst suffered by anyone. The flight attendants were helping people back into their seats clearing the isles of luggage and other obstacles.

The cockpit door opened and the captain entered the passenger cabin. He took the mike from the hook on the forward bulkhead and said, "Ladies and gentlemen, please be calm and remain in your seats. If you are injured try not to move around. We are down about one hundred and ten miles from the nearest airport with rescue aircraft. I radioed our location before we landed and received an acknowledgement from Ben Gurion Airport and they relayed the SOS. We should have help arriving before sundown. I'm going to open all passenger doors to try and get fresh air into the plane. If you decide to leave the aircraft, remain in the immediate vicinity. The pilot then repeated the information in Arabic.

Chapter 13

The helicopter pilot maneuvered the English built rescue chopper in as close as possible, blowing clouds of dust into the air as he did. With a bit of effort, got the helo settled on the desert floor and shut off power to the engine. He exited the helo and approached the airlines captain who was waiting near the left wing of the downed DC-6. After a short discussion they started directing passengers to begin boarding the rescue chopper with the standard procedure of women and children first. Before long four more rescue birds arrived and within a span of five hours the choppers had made enough round trips to evacuate all of the passengers. Ryder was among the last to leave.

Upon arrival at the little airport everyone was directed to what appeared to be a large waiting room and one by one were checked for internal injury. Once cleared by the physician everyone was released to a room that passed for a dinning area. While the passengers were getting a snack and trying to regain some normality in their lives, the airport manager radioed the El Moroccan Airlines to find out when the replacement aircraft would arrive. The airport was not designed for commercial air traffic and the runway would just barely be long enough to allow the DC-6 to land and take off.

After a rough night of trying to catnap on a wooden floor, Ryder stood outside the waiting room the following morning, eating an Italian roll and wondering how this episode would impact his schedule. He looked into the distance and saw a speck in the sky that slowly turned into a DC-4, which is a seven-foot shorter version of the DC-6. Ryder watched as the pilot made a couple of circles around the field to check for wind direction, lined the plane up for final approach and extend full flaps to slow the plane as much as possible. He touched down as close to the overrun as possible to give himself more runway to stop the aircraft. Ryder could hear the brakes squealing as the pilot tried getting the plane to slow and stop. Just as he reached the far overrun the bird came to a halt. *Damn'*, Ryder thought, *and that was empty. He's going to have a real job getting that bird off the ground loaded with people.* The pilot turned the big plane and taxied back to the terminal.

The passengers were directed to board the aircraft, buckle up and place their heads in a lowered position.

The pilot taxied back out to the runway almost to the marker lights. Ryder peered intently out through the window and spotted a windsock in the distance. The aircraft was going to take off into a headwind, which would help. Ryder felt the plane shutter as the pilot ran the engines up to full power for over two minutes and then released the brakes. With the full load of people the plane was slow to get rolling. It started picking up speed but too slowly. At the halfway point Ryder estimated the ground speed to be around sixty knots and for a safe take off it should have been around ninety. The giant bird continued lumbering along picking up speed but the runway in front was disappearing fast. Then Ryder saw the overrun, which meant that they were out of runway and the ride was starting to get rough. At that moment the pilot must have eased back on the yoke because Ryder felt the noise rise a little and the ride smoothed out. Little by little the aircraft gained altitude. Before long he felt the DC-4 level off and figured that they were at cruise altitude. He looked at the lady next to him and remarked; "Now that's one hell of a pilot."

She looked back at him and smiled, not understanding a word he had just said, but glad to be on her way once more.

The balance of the flight to Lebanon was uneventful. Even the landing at the Beirut International was as smooth as glass. As the aircraft taxied to the terminal Ryder wondered if anything had transpired either with Lisa or OMNI. He deplaned and walked through the terminal. Reaching the street, he hailed a cab and directed the driver to the El Kadeem Hotel. On the way to the hotel Ryder gave more thought to Kansi's operation at Sidi and again wondered why he and Baronga had found no bomb making equipment. It was just one of those little details that kept eating at him. Even if Kansi's boys had completed and moved the bomb, wouldn't there be any residual material left. Logically it seemed like there would be some pieces of wiring or implosive material left behind or something, but he and Baronga had come up dry.

The driver pulled up in front of the El Kadeem then turned to face Ryder with a big grin and sat patiently waiting to be paid. A nostalgic thought went through Ryder's mind that made him smile. His current driver in some ways reminded him of the last driver he'd had in Casablanca. As he pulled out some money to pay the man he said, "Excuse me, what is your name?"

The swarthy little man in the front hesitated for a moment as if trying to remember how to form the words in English and then replied, "Yusef Merwan. Four dollars American please."

"I know a driver by the name of Mohammad Kaleed in Casablanca that could be your brother? He has a big toothy smile and he wants to take all the foreigners on the tour."

"Thank you sir. I am glad that the thought gives you pleasure"

Suddenly the thought was swept from Ryder's mind. He paid the driver, got out and collected his luggage. Climbing the steps to the lobby doors, Ryder wondered if his old room would be vacant – the room where he and Lisa had spent so many happy hours. Pushing through the double doors he went into the hotel and directly to the check in counter.

A medium built Arab man wearing herringbone pants and a short-sleeved shirt stood behind the counter with the facial expression of a freshly buried cadaver. With matching enthusiasm the Arab asked, "May I help you with a room?"

Ryder dropped his bags on the floor and replied, "Yes. I want a room. I was here some time ago and was given room two-eighteen. I know that this may sound a bit strange but it has some sentimental value and I would like to know if it is available?"

The Arab looked at his book and after a moment said, "Yes it is, but sir, it was only vacated this morning and is being cleaned. The cleaning woman will need a little more time."

"That's fine, I'll go to the lounge and have some refreshment. Will an hour be enough time for the woman to finish?"

"Yes. That should be more than sufficient."

Ryder signed the book, picked up his bags and shuffled into the lounge. He went to the table were Lisa had been sitting when he'd first approached her. He pulled out the same chair, sat down, and signaled the waitress for a beer. He ran his hand across the wood grain of the polished table as he let his mind drift back to that night. *Damn'* he thought, *what I'd give to have her sitting across from me now.*

A different waitress ambled up, set a Heineken on the table and said, "That'll be a buck, my blond Nordic one."

Ryder had been lost in thought but now looked up and upon seeing a familiar face, smiled and exclaimed, "Margaret, well I'll be damned, been awhile since we talked. How's business?"

"Good, good. So where is the girlfriend?"

"Oh, you mean Lisa. I think that she's in Germany. As a matter of fact I was getting ready to drop my bags off in my room and give Mid East Oil a call and find out if she's still in Europe or on her way back."

"She is a cute lady as I recall."

"Yeah, she sure is and I really miss her." Ryder said

"Well listen, business is staring to pick up so I had better get back behind the bar." She hesitated for a moment as if trying to articulate something but not quite sure if she should. Finally she said, "Before I go, have to be honest and let you know that I came over to tell you that I get off work at twelve. I was also going to ask if you wanted to see me home, but the look on your face when you talk about Lisa, tells me that inviting you home is probably a bad idea."

Suddenly Ryder was very serious. "I'm flattered that you feel that way – but you're right, it probably is not a good idea. You are a very attractive woman and I would be very lucky to have you, hell, any man would be lucky to have you, but Lisa and I have developed a relationship that I want to pursue." Attempting to lighten the mood Ryder smiled and added, "Hey, I'll tell you one thing and that is you are the best lady bartender in Beirut. You are also very good at dealing with some of the obnoxious people that come into your establishment."

She smiled and said, "Thanks, Lance Ryder. Don't forget to drop by now and then."

"I will, Margaret."

Still smiling, she turned and went back to her duties.

Ryder for a time reflected on what had just happened and then his thoughts returned to Lisa. He checked his watch and figured that the cleaning woman should be finished with the room. He stood, picked up his bags and went back to the check in counter. The clerk gave him the key and he went to the room to drop off his things. He keyed open the door, entered the room and all the memories came flooding back. After hanging his clothes he went back to the lobby, picked up the house-phone and asked the operator to put him through to Mid East Oil. After a couple of rings a female voice said, "Mid East, Mr. Wintermans office."

"Hello, my name is Lance Ryder. I'm trying to find one of your pilots. Her name is Lisa Nickels."

"Mr. Ryder I'm not in travel scheduling but I think Ms. Nickels is due back in Beirut tomorrow afternoon sometime. Is there somewhere you can be reached in case I see her?"

"Yes, I'm staying at the El Kadeem room two-eighteen."

"Thank you Mr. Ryder. If I see her I'll deliver the message. Will that be all?"

"Yeah, that's it, and thank you." Ryder hung up the phone and stood for moment thinking about the last time that he and Lisa had spoken. He'd been pretty rough on her and the parting had not been easy for either of them. He decided that he would take the time to make it up to her. He'd take her to the finest restaurant in Beirut. He'd take her on some kind of a vacation, maybe a two-day trek to Southern Italy.

The OMNI spy stood on the little balcony off his room once more looking at the street scene below. He'd gotten a good night of sleep and had spent most of the day lounging and eating. It was now late evening and Ryder was drinking a martini and trying to make up his mind as to whether or not to call Mid East Oil. If the Mid East employ was right Lisa should have been back by now. He didn't want to appear desperate but he did want to know if she were back. Then the thought occurred to him. Maybe she didn't want to see him after the way he had abruptly dismissed her in Morocco. Yeah that was a possibility and he couldn't blame her if she declined to see him again. After all, he'd just kissed her, put her on the plane and sent her on her way. Well to hell with all of that, maybe it was possible she no longer cared for him but a least she was going to have to tell him to his face. He wasn't going to call Mid East, he was going to go to their offices and find Lisa ... to explain to her that he loved and wanted her. He stepped into the room from the balcony and set his glass on the coffee table. He started toward the door and noticed that someone was jiggling the doorknob. *Damn'*, he thought, *some of Kansi's guys have tracked me back to Beirut and I'm in trouble because my P-89 is on the dresser and there's no time to get it.*

The door swung open and Ryder went limp with relief.

Lisa was standing there with a smile and looking better than he remembered. She walked into the room, dropping her purse on the floor as she came and slid her arms around his waist. Ryder threw his arms around her and he was so happy he was just speechless. She looked up at him with those beautiful green eyes glistening on the verge of tears and he kissed her hard and long. Ryder couldn't get enough of her, nor she of him and the whole scene just became weird with all of the, nibbling, kissing, licking, biting, unbuttoning and unzipping of cloths. Stumbling around and finally falling, they luckily managed to hit the bed at which time they proceeded to remove the last of their clothing. The rest of the night was filled with noises that little children shouldn't be subjected to and Lisa making demands of Ryder that he wasn't totally sure he had the stamina to fulfill. Lisa rolled over on her back, spreading her beautiful long legs as she did. Ryder kissed her breast and stomach sliding his tongue in small circles around her belly button.

She put her hands on top of his head, pushing him down as she said, "Go on down lap dog, you know what I want."

Ryder's tongue swept her insides for an eternity and finally she tensed up and moaned loudly as her body trembled slightly with a climax so overwhelming that she wondered if it would ever end and hoped that it wouldn't. Finally it subsided and she was wet with perspiration and felt a little weak. Her vagina was so sensitive she almost could no longer handle the touch of his tongue. She put her hands on his chest and pushed him over onto his back and kissed his hairy chest. She continued working her way down until she took him into her mouth She tried to take his whole shaft into her mouth but it was too big. She ran her tongue around it and then slipped her lips over the head and milked it until she felt him tense up. He mumbled something about if she didn't stop he wouldn't be able to stop. Then she felt and tasted the warm sticky substance squirt across her tongue. By the volume she was sure he had not been with another woman since they had last saw each other.

Ryder being young recovered quickly and in five minutes was again ridged. He reached down, took her by the waist and turned her over on her back and slipped in between he legs.

Lisa moaned as he buried his shaft in her and in a husky voice he said, "Alright Rose, now that we have the foreplay out of the way we are going to do some serious fucking."

Her eyes were half closed passionate slits as she looked up at him and mumbled, "You just do what a mans gotta do, and after you're done then you're gonna do what I want you to do. You think that you're the stud in charge here, but before the night is over you will be whimpering for mercy. "

Her challenge just made Ryder's penis harder as he slammed it into her over and over and the sweat ran in rivers. Around four in the morning they ran out of steam and just before they drifted off to sleep, Ryder said. "I love you baby."

"I know you do, Lance, and I love you too. Just don't ever send me away again."

Chapter 14

Kansi awoke in his room at the El Cabaletta, and even now after a night of debauchery he had thoughts of the young woman who worked downstairs as a desk clerk. He wanted her more than ever. However there was something else on his mind. It was the American he had encountered back as Sidi Slimane. Would this American be coming after him, Kansi wondered. What were the possibilities? *Maybe the foreigner will think that he has killed me,* Kansi thought, *but then he would wonder where my body had gone.* However, Kansi never saw him come back, maybe the American was killed in the firefight that he had heard before he left. And what if the foreigner did think he was still alive, *how would he know where I have gone*, Kansi thought. He finally came to the conclusion that he was safe for now and he could take a little breather and indulge his new found hobby, but he should not become too comfortable. If for no other reason than just his business in America, his stay in Lisbon would have to be limited, just long enough to get this strange new sexual bloodlust out of his system. True there were women in America but when he got to America he would have to have this fascination behind him. His mind would have to be devoted to the business at hand and he could afford no distractions. He knew that if it weren't for the women, especially the one downstairs he would clean out his bank accounts and catch a Delta flight for New York. Yes he would let Ogar feast another few days and then depart. There was really no worry, his passport was in order, and he could leave on a moments notice.

To be on the safe side, he got dressed and took the elevator down to the dinning room. After a big breakfast of lambs eyes, grapes, and Italian bread, he left the hotel and hailed a cab. The old Audi taxi pulled up to the curb belching smoke from the tailpipe and Kansi got into the back. The cabbie said, "Where to sir?"

"The Lisbon Ban'co de Internation'al and be quick."

The driver headed for the Lisbon banking district and as soon as they arrived at the requested bank. Kansi said, "Remain parked here, I will return shortly."

The driver replied, "Very good sir."

Kansi entered the bank and went to one of the cashier cages. He dropped a bank draft on the counter and said, "I would like very much to withdraw all the funds in this account."

The teller looked at the draft and her eyes became wide and she stammered. "But sir, this draft is for two hundred thousand dollars; you will have to see a bank officer for a release of these funds."

"Fine. Where is he?"

"In the back. Go through the second door there and see Mr. Mahoote," she was pointing toward a mahogany door about twenty feet away.

Kansi said "Thank you." then got up and walked through the doorway.

A large round Indian looking man wearing a turban was seated behind a big wooden desk reading what appeared to be stock reports. He was also smoking a hand rolled Cuban. He looked up when Kansi entered the room and said. "What can I do for you sir?"

Kansi took a chair and replied, "It is my desire to cash in this bank draft."

The banker leaned forward as far as his bulk would allow, stretched out a hand and said, "Let me see what you have."

Kansi handed him the draft and said, "I would like all of that in American and all but fifty thousand in large bills."

The banker looked at the draft and whistled. After careful scrutiny he said, "You are Kansi? Alright Mr. Kansi, produce two identifications please." He pressed a button on his desk and shortly a woman appeared in the doorway and said, "Yes Mr. Mahoote."

F. Washington Brown

The banker glanced at her and said, "Bring two hundred thousand American, fifty thousand of it in small bills."

Soon the transaction was complete and Kansi was once again in the taxi heading for the El Cabaletta Hotel. After deliberating and vacillating back and forth on the issue he finally decided that he would take the time to get this sexual hunger out of his system once and for all. That way he could focus and devote his complete attention to the task at hand when he left for America.

Kansi paced the room contemplating his dilemma. Earlier he had called a colleague in New York and had found out that the time was quickly approaching when Kansi's presents would be required. He'd stalled his collaborator by telling him that he had financial business in Lisbon that would require two or three days.

He walked to the window and looked down on the city lights of Lisbon. By now he knew most of the sleaze joints where the prostitutes plied their business. He glanced at his watch. It was nine a.m. and time to catch a cab. He felt the Zombeast stirring in the back of his mind; making his impatient presence known. Kansi took an elevator down to the lobby and was walking toward the front doors when he looked over and saw her behind the counter. He hesitated for a moment, and then walked over with a friendly smile and said, "I wanted to thank you for the quick service in ordering my clothes."

It was no problem Mr. Kansi, that's just part of our duties and I was happy to help you. *Here I go again,* she thought, *why do I get these feelings when I look into his eyes. It's not like me to want to take my cloths off in front of a man that I hardly know.* With a smile, she said, "Is there anything else I can do for you Mr. Kansi?"

He studied her phenomenal beauty for a moment and replied, "Uh, well you have me at a disadvantage. You know my name but I don't know yours, and by the way, just call me Amal ... Mr. Kansi is too formal."

"Very well, Amal. My name is Katerina and I'm originally from Bulgaria." she obligingly replied.

"Katerina," he said slowly and softly, letting it roll off his tongue. "It is a beautiful name. Perhaps you would let me buy you dinner one evening before I leave?"

Her knees became a little weak as she replied, "We'll see, Amal. I don't have a lot of free time but Friday I'm off duty; maybe then."

"That sounds promising. Until then, Katerina," he said as he turned and left the hotel. His lust for her was becoming too great for him to risk further conversation.

Kansi was careful not to patronize the same tavern more than once because the women that he left with never came back. However it was not a problem because Lisbon's east side had an abundance of back-street pubs and brothels; and the women who haunted these places rarely aroused suspicion if they disappeared. The police usually figured that they just decided to move on. If a body turned up now and then, it was assumed they had a disagreement with a John, or maybe a drug overdose. Kansi was starting to generate a few bodies here and there but he decided that by the time the police realized they had a mass murderer on their hands, he would be gone.

He instructed the cab driver to pull up in front a particularly grungy looking place. After departing the cab he quickly entered the joint; Ogar was impatient to get started. He look over the prospects on his way to bar. He ordered a glass of wine, which by now he was starting to acquire a taste for, and continued visually scouting for an attractive lady of the night. He saw a bleached blonde sitting alone at a table and decided she would be Ogar's sacrifice tonight. He slowly ambled over to her table and with a personable smile said, "Good evening, I am new to the city. I saw you alone and thought that maybe I could join you for a drink. May I sit down?"

She glanced up at him and said, "Yes, please have a chair. My name is Marie and who might you be my tall one?"

"I am Kansi, Amal Kansi."

Kansi slid into a seat and bought a round of drinks and took the opportunity to scrutinize her looks a bit more closely. She wasn't as attractive as some of the women he'd had on pervious evenings but at this point beauty was not a prerequisite. He wanted sex and lots of it. He wanted it rough and Ogar wanted her soul. They talked and drank for a while then Kansi decided that the wine he'd been putting away needed an outlet. "He said excuse me I haven't been here before. Can you tell me where the benjo is?"

She laughed, pointed a finger toward the rear, and said, "All the way in the back and the men's is on the right."

Kansi stood and proceeded to the rear, entered the latrine and began to relieve himself. He smiled and thought, *my penis is ridged and I haven't even gotten her into the room yet.* He was in the process of buttoning his trousers when he felt something hard touch his back and heard a gravely voice behind him.

"Alright, easy and don't even twitch mate. Hand me over the ol' money purse and be quick about it. I knows that a well dressed dandy of your station must 'ave a tidy swag."

Without thinking, Kansi, with lighting quick speed wheeled and grabbed the would-be robber by the gun hand and squeezed until he dropped the revolver and squealed with pain, "Please mate I was only jokin' I was. Please let me go and I'll be on me way."

Kansi was pleasantly surprised at how he had reacted. Now he would make the most of this situation. Looking around, he saw a closed door that appeared to lead still further to the rear, *maybe to the ally.* He thought. He hit the man in the face with such force that his neck snapped and he went limp. Kansi opened the door and dragged him into what appeared to be a storage room. He closed the door behind him and dropped the man behind a stack of storage bins. He had a strong desire to rip the man's heart out and eat it right there and then, but he had no time. He left the room, closing the door behind him and figured it would be morning before someone found the robber. Kansi went back into the main bar as if nothing had happened.

She was smiling as he approached their table and motioned for him to sit as she said, "We need more wine."

As he sat down he reached over, took her hand and placed it squarely on his crotch. Through his pants she could feel of his huge erect penis and reacted as if someone had touched her with a cattle prod and then her mood changed as she looked into his eyes.

Continuing to hold her hand on his penis he said, "Do you have a room or and apartment?"

"Yes," she weakly replied as her vagina became wet.

"Let's go," he growled.

"Come with me, " she said, and feeling as if she were in another world, she stood and moved toward the front door.

Kansi slowly walked along looking at the row of suits, trying to decide what to wear for the upcoming evening with Katerina.

The salesman remarked, "Now here is our latest line direct from Italy. This is a double-breasted gabardine guaranteed to make you irresistible to your lady. Kansi look it over and felt the material. Finally he said, "Yes, this will do. I'll take it."

Kansi paid for the garments while the salesman dropped a plastic cover over them. He took the suit and left the store. As he walked along he remembered the conversation that he'd had with Katrina yesterday. He'd thought it would be easy to get her to go out with him but when it came right down to actually picking the day and time she turned out to be somewhat reluctant. She'd said it had something to do with family custom to get to know a man better before going out alone with him. However with some reservation she finally agreed to dinner the following Friday night. Kansi felt good. Katrina was not just another tavern whore to be sacrificed, this was a real lady. A lady that he was totally going to enjoy serving up to Ogar. He pulled the piece of scrap paper from his pocket that she had written her address on: 1501 Matador Street. While not in the most affluent part of Lisbon it was in the better section of town,

He stepped through the hotel doors and went to his room to get ready to pick up Katrina. He looked at his image in the mirror as he put the finishing touches on the new dark blue silk tie. *There,* he thought, *what a smart suit. I'm sure she will like it.* At that moment Ogar came to the forefront of Kansi's mind and murmured, "I'm sure that you are right Kansi. I'm sure that she will like it right up to the moment she dies." Ogar chuckled and became silent.

Kansi finished dressing then took the stairs down to the lobby to help break-in the new patent leathers. Reaching the pavement he decided that he had plenty of time so he would walk part of the way before he caught a cab. After all he had an hour to kill before it was time to collect her. Walking along gave him time to think about his opponent. It would help to know how smart this American was that had shot him. He was sure that the American suspected him in a plot; and why not, Kansi had planned it that way. He had put out the rumors through the underground about a hydrogen bomb trigger being smuggled into the Middle East from England. It was just pure coincidence that one had actually come up missing from Lakenheath. There was no hydrogen bomb, there never had been. It was all a red herring to throw the CIA off the scent. A diversion to keep the real plan of mass destruction from being discovered and it had worked. The American at Sidi Slimane was proof of that.

The shoes were a little tight so Kansi decided it was time to give his feet a rest. He signaled a cab and gave the driver the address. As the Mercedes pulled away from the curb, Kansi made up his mind that he would rent a car when he got to New York.

The taxi stopped at 1501 Matador and Kansi said, "Wait, I will return in a few minutes. He stepped onto the curb and looked around. The area was well cared for with the manicured lawns and tall Italian cypress trees. The apartments were snow white with red Spanish tile roofs. He went to the door and rang the bell. After a fashionable wait,

Hot Sand & Cold Blood

Katerina opened the door with a pleasant smile and said, "Come in, I'm almost ready."

He stepped in, closed the door and asked, "You have a beautiful place. Do you share with anyone – a roommate or mother perhaps?"

"No just me," she replied as she slid the earring stud through her left ear. "There," she said, "I'm all ready." Katerina locked the door behind her and they leisurely walked to the cab and got in.

As the driver smoothly navigated the streets, Kansi asked, "So my most lovely one, where would you like to dine this evening?"

"If you don't mind I would very much enjoy, 'The Buccaneer'. It is a favorite of mine," she happily replied.

"The Buccaneer, it is then." He leaned forward and said, "Cabbie, The Buccaneer please."

The Buccaneer was a nice restaurant but not lavish. Kansi amusingly figured she'd brought him here so as not to strain his wallet. He held the door for her as she preceded him into the establishment. She chose a booth near the windows' overlooking the street and they leaned back into the soft cushion back rests and relaxed. They made small talk until the food came and then the conversation subsided a bit while they ate. All the conversation on Kansi's part was obviously made up lies because if he had told her the truth about himself she probably would have screamed and left. He told her that his father was an oil rich member of the Saudi Royal Family and he was in Lisbon to close a deal with Shell Oil. Also that his business trip would take him to New York and quite possibly to California.

Katrina said, "I'm very impressed but I'm afraid that my family is just ordinary people for what there is left of them. My father was killed in an auto accident and my mother lives five blocks from me. I was married for three years but we got a divorce and he went back to England. I stayed because my mother likes it here."

Finally the dinner was over and as Kansi paid the check he asked, "Katrina is there was something more you would like to do ... a movie perhaps?"

F. Washington Brown

"I don't know Amal, I have not given it much thought," she said. As she had begun to get to know him she was starting to get mixed thoughts about the man. On one hand there was something about him that scared her, but on the other there was something that made him very sexually attractive. She had to admit to herself that she had not been with a man in a long time and she felt that maybe it was right that now might be an appropriate time. "Amal I am a bit tired and I do have to work tomorrow. If you don't mind maybe we could just end the evening by going back to my apartment and watch television for awhile."

"I understand Katrina and I too have business tomorrow." He once again flagged a taxi and they got in.

Kansi had restrained himself to this point but he was rapidly reaching a peak mentally where he wanted to pull her clothes off and he could feel Ogar beginning to stir with anticipation. After the time they had spent together Kansi could tell that Katrina was interested but wondered why she was not becoming visibly hot with passion. Then the clarity of the situation came to him. The whores he had killed were evil, wanton, and sluts and would readily welcome an unholy sexual encounter, but Katrina was different. She obviously lived a clean, honest life and would not be influenced by Ogar, or at least not as much. Kansi did not understand how he knew, he just did.

They reached the apartment and she keyed open the door and they walked into the living area. She said, "Amal, why don't you recline on the sofa while I hang up my coat?"

Obligingly Kansi started for the sofa knowing that his restraint was almost gone. Any moment Ogar would have his way and Katrina, and in the span of the next six hours she would become nothing more than a cold used up shell of a woman. Amal's lust would be fulfilled and the old one would have another soul.

Starting for the closet to hang up her coat, Katrina caught Kansi's reflection in the hall mirror and almost screamed because what she saw was not Kansi. Thinking her eyes were playing tricks she looked back at Kansi, who by this time was seated on the sofa. She noticed that there seemed to be a change in the color of his eyes from an azure blue to a sort of indigo but that could be due to the room lighting. Other than that, the guy on her sofa was Kansi. Then she looked back at his reflection and saw what appeared to be a bulbous hairy gray shimmering being with a single large indigo eye. It also appeared to have tail encrusted with course hair.

She was choking on panic and started to tremble and loose control but had presents of mind to know that if she were going to live she must maintain a normal appearance at least until she could get into the bathroom. Walking normally as possible she entered the bathroom and immediately closed and locked the door. Fortunately for her current situation, the apartments were designed for two tenants to share a single bathroom. She went over and tried the door leading into the other apartment and it was locked. She knocked lightly and momentarily the handle turned and the door opened. Relieved, Katrina rushed into the apartment and the neighboring couple just stood there with a surprised expression.

On the verge of hysteria and not waiting to explain she just simply said, "Close and lock the door."

The neighbor lady said, "My dear you look like you've just seen a ghost. Why don't you come over here and have a seat. I'll get you some water."

Exasperated that they didn't grasp the situation she growled. "Shut and lock that fucking door if you want to live."

That they understood. The couple, as if shocked, rapidly stepped over each other getting to the door. After almost slamming it closed and sliding the bolt, they turned and the neighbor lady said, "Now, tell us—"

The woman quickly discovered that she was talking to herself, because Katrina was nowhere in site.

As fast as her feet would carry her Katrina went down the back steps, through an ally and down the street. She flew like the wind and didn't stop until she reached her mother's house. She had not given Kansi the address so she felt safe for the time being.

Chapter 15

Ryder slapped Lisa lightly on her well sculptured buttocks and mentally thanked her mother and father for putting her together with such precision as he said, "It's morning woman. Today I will take you out and show you the wonders of the Middle East."

She rolled over onto her back and looked at him with the hint of a smile playing at the corners of her mouth and replied, "Not today. I've seen enough of the crude camel meat markets. Today we will take a company jet and fly to Athens for a feast of mutton and oranges, or whatever. The cuisine in Greece is so much more civilized."

Ryder was a little taken aback by her statement and queried, "Let me get this straight, we are going to take a Mid East Lear jet and fly the European Continent for a day, on non-official business and the company is not going to fire you."

"Listen, Mister Lance 'macho' Ryder, I may be a woman but I'm also the chief pilot for Mid East. Hell, I can do anything that I want with those planes."

Taking a passive posture Ryder grinned and replied, "All right lady, what ever you say. Lets get those engines cranked up and spend the day drilling holes in the sky at Mid East's expense."

After a quick tryst to get their blood pumping, they had a leisurely shower, got dressed and headed for the airport.

The twin jet engines could be heard quietly purring in the background as Ryder comfortably relaxed in the cockpit's co-pilot's seat and peered out at the cool looking blue water below. The Mediterranean Sea was special to Ryder. He'd spent a good deal of time lying on its sandy beaches.

In an exceptionally good mood, Lisa smiled at Ryder and teasingly said, "The right seat that you're sitting in is for the co-pilot. In other words it's for the captain wanna-be."

Ryder lazily glanced over at her and said, "Really Lisa, it's for the captain wanna-be? Well that still makes him or her some sort of a pilot doesn't it?"

"You're right my exalted sex provider, him or her is a pilot, just not THE pilot," she teased.

Sitting up straight, he said, "Lisa, do you mind if I take the controls for a moment?"

She considered his request for a brief period, and then said, "I suppose, Lance. We're not in a traffic pattern so I guess that it's safe enough. Now remember, take the wheel, put your feet on the rudder pedals and just keep it straight and level."

"Oh, Lisa, you are too kind to me," he said with grin. Ryder took the wheel, slipped his feet onto the rudder pedals and checked his air speed. It was around two hundred and twenty knots. Remembering back to flight manuals that he'd read, he knew that this model of Lear could handle about three hundred and sixty knots before the wings and airframe became stressed. He reached over and pushed the throttles up. The bird quickly accelerated to three ten at which time he pulled back on the yoke bringing the nose up. When the airplane's pitch-up indicator reached eighty degrees he cranked the wheel right in six increments, putting the bird through a perfect six-point barrel roll. Next he pushed the yoke forward until the elevator caused the nose to pitched down slightly, input full left rudder and left wing down aileron, putting the plane into a tight descending left turn. When the airplane had completed a full 360-degree turn, he reversed the controls for a respectful butterfly figure eight. At this point, he leveled the plane, pulled the throttles back to two hundred and twenty knots, and corrected the course back to a straight and level 270 degrees where Lisa had been flying before Ryder had taken the controls. He said, "The airplane is yours my lady," and then he took his hands off the wheel.

Almost in shock, and with her eyes wide as silver dollars, Lisa took control of the Lear. It took her a moment to regain her composer then she said, "You son of a bitch, don't you ever do that again. You could have killed us."

"I don't think so Lisa. I've logged hours in planes with a higher performance rating than a Lear, although I've got to admit that it handles like a dream. I'm sorry but I guess it goes back to my Marine Corps days when I flew F-4 Phantom fighter jets. It seems like that every time I get behind the controls my fangs come out." He settled back in his seat and relaxed with a big grin. "Oh, by the way Lisa can you switch frequencies on that radio and get some music."

"Why don't you do it, dipshit, since you know so much about airplanes', and while you're at it, go back and get me a cup of coffee."

Amusingly, Ryder thought, *no doubt about it, Lisa is trying to reestablish herself as the alpha pilot.* He said, "Would you like cream and sugar, baby?"

"Don't be so condescending, you know that I only take cream in my coffee, and it'll take a hell of a lot more than calling me, 'baby' to get back on my good side."

"Yes dear. Will that be all? " Ryder couldn't stifle his smile so he got up and went to the rear for coffee.

By the time they had landed at the Athens airport Lisa was once more in a good mood. They decided on the Marina Del Sol restaurant for a lunch of rich tasty shrimp, crab, a little sea bass and chef salad; all topped off with a bottle of light Chablis and a scenic view of large and small sailing craft moving in and out of the harbor. Afterward, Lance rented a small two mast sloop and they put to sea for a trip around Patra Island.

Lisa sit next to Lance as he expertly guided the beautiful sleek craft through the smooth azure waters. There was just enough wind to billow the sails and send salt water spray cascading along the sides of the hull. She put her hand on his shoulder and said, "I suppose now you're going to tell me that you are a professional sailor."

Hot Sand & Cold Blood

As the boat plowed forth cutting a frothy white wake, he leaned over nibbled on her ear and replied, "No, but if you really want to know what I'm an expert at, I'll lash this wheel in place and take you below into the bunk compartment and give you a demonstration."

"My, my," she said, "aren't you modest. If you're so good at sex on the high seas, why don't we just do it on the deck. There's no one around to critique your technique except me, Popeye."

"Popeye?" he chortled.

"Yeah, Popeye the sailor man, get it?"

"That does it lady. You're the one that's going to get it," he laughed as he untied and removed the top to her skimpy two-piece swimming attire, adding, "I don't know why you bother to wear this thing because when it's wet I can see right through it."

"Lucky you," she retorted as she hungrily pulled at his swimming trunks, and soon they were at each other like two dolphins in heat.

Late in the evening, Ryder pulled the boat into an aesthetically appealing and private little cove and tied up for the night. They took a couple of deck loungers ashore and sat on the beach, drinking a glass of France's finest while listening to the sounds of critters that dwelled on the island.

Lisa said, "Lance tell me about yourself and I don't mean the bullshit about working as a consultant for Mid East. What do you really do, where did you learned to fly. Why so much secrecy. Do you work for the CIA or FBI or some other cloak and dagger Mickey Mouse organization?"

"Lisa we're having a pleasant time. I don't know why we should ruin it by bringing that up."

"We need to talk about it. You seem to have a habit of leaving on a moments notice and sending me away in the process. I love you or at least I'm pretty sure that I do. Would you give up your weird job and do something more conventional to be with me?" she asked.

F. Washington Brown

He replied to her question with a question. "Would you quit flying for Mid East and take a job with a commuter airline in the States to be with me?" he asked.

Her reply was to say nothing, and for an hour there was almost silence save for the birds in the trees. At around midnight they picked up their deck loungers and went onboard the boat. They made love to the gentle rocking of the boat and afterward drifted off to sleep listening to the surf rolling across the beach.

The sun snuck up on the sleeping couple and it was almost noon before they awoke and got the sails rigged and ready to continue around the island. They enjoyed the journey and it was welcome relaxation for both of them. Lance carefully steered the boat around some large shoals that jutted out a mile or so from the island while Lisa stretched out on the bow. She lay on her stomach with her arms hanging over the side dangling a rope in the water. She was playing with three dolphins that were majestically gliding along next to the boat. After some period of time she become tired of the game, and went to the stern to join Lance. "Honey," she said, "I'm sorry that we had words and I hope that it doesn't effect our relationship."

"I feel the same way, Sweetheart. I don't want to loose you. I love making love to you more than anything, but it goes much deeper than that. I get lonely when you're not with me and there is a need that only you can satisfy."

"I know Darling and I feel the same way. The other day when I took that shuttle flight to Heidelberg, the whole day was hell. I thought about you all the way there and back. I called Connie while I was there and I told her about you. She was devastated by the news and begged me to fly to Frankfurt to see her. I felt that a phone call wasn't the proper way to say goodbye after all that we had been to each other so I juggled the schedule a little and went to see her for five hours. I have to admit that I went to bed with her one final time, but I swear Lance, it wasn't for me it was for her. I just couldn't leave her cold like that. I hope you can understand. When I got back to Beirut I received a call from her. She was bitter and called me a two timing bitch. I listened to everything she had to say without hanging up. I felt that I owed her that much."

Ryder was silent for a while. He had just gotten a whole lot of information to process. Finally he said, "Yeah, Lisa I agree. You probably handled it the best way you could have under the circumstances."

The balance of the trip was fun and uneventful. Before entering the harbor Lance and Lisa dropped and secured the fore and main sails. He used the small diesel engine to maneuver the boat into the slip. They secured the sloop fore and aft with ropes and then retrieved their belongings, after which they merrily hopped over the side and shuffled up the gangplank.

Ryder stopped briefly to pay the rental on the sloop and then they went on a tour of the city. The ride was twofold; first they wanted to see the Greek Acropolis as well as other interesting parts of the city, and two, they needed to find a hotel. There were many things to see in Athens. It had been the land of untold battles during pre-roman times. The round-outs with cascading fountain statues depicting cherubs holding bows and arrows while urinating on lily pads. Large angels stood watch over monumental cathedrals. The tour was both educational and entertaining, but the day was drawing to a close. It was time to find a place for the night. They decided on one of the older hotels in the center of the city.

Ryder signed the book and the clerk gave him a key for room four-fourteen. They took the elevator up and Ryder keyed open the door. Walking into the room, they looked it over and were impressed. It was like stepping back a hundred years in time. It had the elegance of the Sistine Chapel only on a smaller scale.

After giving the room a visual inspection they showered and went down stairs for dinner. They took a table near the window and shortly a balding middle-aged waiter with a double chin approached wearing a white coat, black pants and a towel draped over his left arm.

Looking at them with an expression of aloofness, he asked, "Pardon me, but is the lady and gentleman ready to order?"

Ryder said, "I think so. We'll have a bottle of chilled Dom Perinnome, followed by Peking duck with honey sauce, a nice salad with lots of dark greens, and a side of melon."

"Very good sir," the waiter replied as he haughtily turned and walked away.

Ryder looked at Lisa who was also almost ready to burst out laughing, and said, "Somebody needs to buy that guy a personality."

"Honey, now that is the truth, the whole truth, and nothing but the truth," she said. Then suddenly getting serious, she added, "You know Lance, sooner or later we're going to have to address those issues."

"And what issues might those be?"

"Don't evade the subject. I'm talking about the issues we discussed on the beach last night and you know it."

"Oh, those issues. Lisa I'm enjoying you and I'm enjoying this time we're having together. I don't want to ruin it by discussing things that doesn't require resolution at this time. There may come a time when we may have to make some hard decisions in order to be together. I prefer to wait until then to address those issues, as you prefer to call them. I'm not trying to be difficult I just want our time together here and now to be a fond memory in the future."

"I suppose that you do have a point. Alright if that's the way you want to conduct the relationship from your point of view, then we'll just proceed and let the future take care of it's self."

Ryder detected an odd voice inflection in her response to his opinion of how they should handle the future, but he assumed that it was just a woman's nature to get into the nesting mode fairly early in a relationship.

The waiter returned with the food and it turned out to be an extremely tasty meal. As they ate Ryder pondered life's little dilemmas. Man and woman relationships seemed to always be balanced with the positive and negative aspects just like the dichotomy of good and evil. Was it because of a need for symmetry in as much as a person could not accurately gage the degree of good without equal amounts of evil for comparison? That, Ryder understood because there were good people and bad people in the world. However, it seemed that relationships were different. There were no good and evil properties involved yet they suffered a similar predicament. Lisa was not a bad person and Ryder didn't consider himself to be a bad person, but here they were headed for this train-wreck full of negative consequences and neither one seemed to be willing to take the steps to stop it. How could they be so equally and completely immersed in love and happiness with one another with complete knowledge of what was at stake and still allow the relationship to stand on the abyss of total disaster. Maybe mutual ego was the culprit. Could it be that simple? Then there was the rationalization that was a part of the equation. Ryder saw his profession as noble and necessary. He was the force that kept the world from becoming a sewer. Obviously he could not see exactly how Lisa viewed herself, but he envisioned that it must be something in a similar vain. She had put in many long and arduous hours, days, months and years to achieve her current status and position. How could he ask her to sacrifice that? Even with all that, it was painfully obvious that something or someone was going to have to give if this fledgling romance was to have a future. The situation hadn't as yet burst into open verbal warfare between them but they weren't stupid people. Very few words needed to be exchanged in order to convey all of the unspoken pitfalls that could derail their future together. The prospect wasn't pleasant and Ryder tried to get his mind on something else.

"How was the duck," he asked, not so much a desire to find out what she thought of the food but more as a catalyst to jump start the conversation.

"Honey, I think the food here is five star. I'd recommend it to anyone," she replied with a grin.

"Baby, you took the words right out of my mouth," he said. It was small talk to put the real issues behind them, and for the time being it was working. After dinner they attended a movie and went for a walk around the plaza. It was a warm clear night with a comfortable breeze that made for end of a beautiful day. They once again entered the hotel and went directly to their room. Tomorrow they would have to rise early and go to the airport. Besides the body contact of holding hands during the walk had caused both to start getting the urge. Lance opened the door and followed Lisa into the room. Without a word they both went straight to the bed and started undressing. Kicking off her shoes, Lisa said, "Honey, its getting to the point where I can't go for more than about a day without having you in me. It's going to be rough when I have to fly back to Germany."

By now they were both naked and Ryder scooped her up and dropped her on the bed. Then leaning down to where his face was about ten inches from her stomach he said, "Do you remember that you wouldn't let me do that the first time we were alone together."

Breathless by now with anticipation she passionately spat out, "Enough talking just shut up and fuck me. And if you want to use that tongue, use it for something besides talking." Just before finishing her sentence, she reached up and put her hand on the back of his head and pulled him down until his face was firmly buried in her muff, then she added, "You are not going to quit until the beaver is happy."

Ryder was sitting on the bed tying his shoes as he called out to Lisa, "Sweetheart, do you want to get breakfast in the hotel or grab a snack at the airport?"

She spat toothpaste into the bathroom sink and replied, "I don't care, maybe a continental breakfast before we leave the hotel." She finished dressing and they walked down to the hotel dinning room. She ordered the continental and Ryder had coffee with orange marmalade on toast. With the exception of one other couple they had the place to themselves. Swallowing the last of his coffee, Ryder got up and went over to pay the cashier while Lisa waited for him by the front door.

Out on the street, Ryder flagged a cab and followed Lisa into the back of it. She glanced at him, smiled and said, "You'll have to admit Admiral Ryder, going for a boat ride was a lot more fun than mulling around Beirut."

He put his hand on her leg and said, "Yes I admit it. I also notice that you get this smug little look on your face when you're right."

Her smile broadened a little as she said, "I don't think I can say the same because for a good part of last night I didn't even see your face."

They walked across the tarmac and boarded the Lear. Lisa went through the checklist and then lit the engines. After bringing the RPM to 100% she throttled back to idle and taxied out to the end of the runway and applied the brakes. She pick up the UHF radio mike and keyed the button, "Athens tower this is Lear 731alpha 46 bravo. I'm requesting a clearance to take-off on runway 23, over.

"Lear731alpha46bravo, you are cleared to take-off on runway 23. Expedite your exit from traffic pattern, we have a heavy inbound from Dublin International. Your assigned cruise altitude is angels ten, over and out."

"Roger tower." She rolled onto the runway, put the nose on the centerline and pushed up the throttles. As they passed the six thousand foot marker, she pulled back on the yoke and the nose came up. She quickly climbed to five hundred and rolled the aircraft hard right to clear the traffic pattern. She continued climbing until she reached the ten thousand foot assigned cruise altitude."

Ryder said, "I think that was the smoothest departure I have ever seen."

"Why thank you, Darling. That's the first compliment you've paid me today, I hope that it's not the last." she said.

Ryder glanced at her with a playful grin and replied, "Sweetheart, with your accomplishments you don't need compliments."

Wistfully she said, "Maybe so, honey, but I'm a woman and I need them, just like the flowers need the rain, or so the song goes."

They chatted and traded the flying back and forth until Beirut airport could be seen over the horizon. She called the tower for a landing clearance and then looked at Lance. "Alright honey, the airplane is all yours."

Ryder took the wheel and banked right to line up for a final approach. He pulled the throttles back to forty percent, dropped the flaps fifty degrees and asked, "What's the roll out speed for this plane?"

"Seventy knots, Honey." she purred.

As the airplane descended he held the nose up and watched the airspeed indicator bleed off. As he rolled out on final he dropped full flaps and throttled back to twenty percent. He flared the bird as the nose passed over the outer marker lights. When he felt the wheels make contact with the runway he looked at the airspeed indicator; the plane was rolling at exactly seventy knots. He pushed the throttles to idle, applied a little pressure on the brakes and initiated reverse engine thrusters. He taxied over to Mid East's reserved parking and gave the Lear back to Lisa. She taxied the bird into its slot and set the parking brake. After shutting down the engines she looked at him with a scintillating expression of admiration and said, "Honey, is there anything you can't do?"

He smiled back and replied, "Well I may not be able to survive if you keep making these harsh sexual demands of me."

She screwed up her face in mock sympathy and said, "Oh, you poor, poor baby. Just for complaining, I will require twice as much from you tonight and I know that a pagan sex god like you can handle it."

They exited the airplane and entered the terminal. As they made their way across the lobby Lisa said, "I have to call the Mid East head office and find out what's on the agenda then we'll grab a cab and go to your hotel. Why don't you wait for me at the front door, I'll only be a minute."

"Alright Sweetheart, go ahead, the phones are over there to the right."

She walked toward the bank of phones and Ryder headed for the front door the hail a cab.

Picking what looked like the cleanest taxi in the line up, Ryder threw the bags in and waited for Lisa.

Ten minutes later he saw her emerge, looking a little less content than when he last saw her. She walked up to him and said, "Lance I've got bad news. There's an oil cartel meeting in Riyadh and they have to have a rep from Mid East. That rep has to be there by this evening for an early morning meeting."

Lance said, "Have another pilot take him."

"There are no other pilots, I'm it. I'll have to fly him, but it's only for two days. I'll be back Wednesday."

"Damn' Lisa, I guess if you have to go, you have to go, but try and get back as soon as possible. Here, take this cab. I'll get another one, just let me get my clothes out of the trunk." He kissed her and then retrieved his things while Lisa got into the vehicle. She looked through the back seat open window with a forlorn expression and said, "I love you Honey. Kiss me to last a couple of days."

He leaned down and kissed her through the window and then watched as the driver took her away. He caught another cab and went back to the El Kadeem. He was crossing the lobby when he heard someone call his name. He looked over and saw the clerk waving his arms in an attempt to get the OMNI spy's attention. Ryder walked over to see what he wanted.

"Mister Ryder, I have an urgent message for you. A man called and left a number and said for you to call as soon as I give it to you."

Ryder took the paper and read the number but it didn't ring any bells. "Did the guy give you a name?"

"No Mister Ryder, just a number."

Ryder reached into his pocket and gave the clerk ten francs and said, "Thanks." He walked over to the counter, picked up a phone and asked the operator to put him through to the number. He heard the phone ring twice and then a man's voice said, "Speak."

Ryder hesitated a second then said, "I was given this number and told to call."

The man asked, "Are you Proteus?"

"That's right." Ryder replied.

"Proteus, it's February five," the voice said

"You should buy your wife Jade green." Ryder replied. The code identified the voice as Dante.

"Proteus, is your scrambler handy?"

Ryder had already discreetly slipped the little device over the phone. "It's in place, do you read me?"

"Affirmative, Proteus you are green lighted to proceed without delay. CIA confirms target is most likely in Lisbon. If his destination is the U.S. we want him terminated before he leaves Portugal."

A little irritated, Ryder said, "There's been a lot of time lost. If you had put this call through two days ago our chances would be much better. I'm working with a cold trail."

"Couldn't be helped Proteus, red tape and all that. An Air Force T-38 jet trainer landed at Beirut three hours ago with the pilot on stand by. I've had a man calling you every hour since seven a.m. this morning. I want you out of Beirut no later than one hour."

I'll need to call ... hello, hello." Ryder hung up because there was no point in talking to a dead line. He pondered the call for a minute then once more picked up the phone. "Operator, Put me through to Mid East Oil's main office." Shortly he heard a pleasant female voice.

"Good Afternoon. Mid East, may I help you?" said the employ.

"This is an emergency." Ryder said. "I need to speak with Lisa Nickels."

"I'm sorry sir, but Captain Nickels is in the process of flying an executive to Riyadh, Saudi Arabia for a meeting.

As a mater of fact you only missed her by about twenty minutes. I would guess that she is taking off about now. Is there anything that I can help you with?"

"Damn'." Ryder said.

"Sir, I'm sorry."

"I apologize, I wasn't talking to you Miss," Ryder replied then added, "Listen when you see her tell her that I had to leave on short notice. There's nothing that I can do. Tell her that I'll call as soon as I can."

"I will Mr. Ryder. Is there anything else?"

"Tell her that I love her." Ryder said.

"I think she already knows that, Mr. Ryder. Good bye."

"Good bye," he said and hung up. *Damn* he thought, *this day is not going well at all.* Well it was back to packing a gun, playtime was over. He went up to his room, started to key open his door and noticed a couple of scratches around the keyhole that looked new. He tried the door and found it locked but loose. He carefully and quietly keyed it open and slipped inside. He closed it behind him and scanned the living area and saw nothing. He started slowly down the hall and into the bedroom. He continued toward the nightstand that had his P-89 Ruger taped underneath. He was within a few feet of it when the louvered closet door shattered open and Brad Hymen emerged holding a revolver in both hands. He was livid with rage, which made him dangerous, it also made him careless.

He growled, "Ryder, you sorry bastard, you cost me my job. I worked for that stinking company fifteen years. I could have retired after twenty, but you fucked it up. I could have shot you when you first came in the bedroom but I want you to know and see it coming. Turn and face me so I can feed you a lead pellet."

Ryder judged his distance to be about seven feet, in the ballpark for a counterclockwise round kick. If Hymen wanted him to turn then turn, then turn he would. Ryder wheeled and pivoted on his left foot while bringing his right leg up and straight out, cleanly knocking the gun out of Hymen's hand. In one continuous fluid movement he dived for the nightstand. Sliding his hand under the stand he ripped the P-89 loose and came up with it pointed at Hymen's head.

Hymen meanwhile was hysterically scratching around for his weapon.

Ryder watched his pathetic attempts for a second and knew that he could subdue Hymen without killing him. Ryder didn't have to kill this dirt bag – yes he did, and squeezed the trigger over and over until Hymen quit twitching and the gun's slide action slammed back and locked indicating that it was empty. Smoke curled off the barrel and for a moment Ryder felt disappointment because the Ruger's clip only held fifteen rounds. Hymen's child molesting days were over.

Chapter 16

Kansi thought that he saw Katrina enter the bathroom and decided that if she were not out in two minutes he would go in and get her. Ogar was making his desires abundantly known. A few seconds went by and able to stand it no longer Kansi got up from the sofa and walked to the bathroom door. He tapped lightly and said, "Katrina, I'm a little worried. Are you alright?" He tapped again and tried the door and discovered that it was locked. Now becoming angry he said, "If you don't open the door I'm going to break it down." and still there was no answer. Kansi grabbed the handle while at the same time slamming his shoulder against the door, shattering it open. The door would have normally required more than one assault but Ogar had increased his strength immensely. Seeing no one, he cursed loudly.

The neighbors on the other side of the second bathroom door listened to the cursing while they cowered in a corner and dialed the police. They could have sworn that the sounds coming through the wall and door reverberated like something half human and half animal.

In a foul mood, Kansi quick searched the apartment and left the building. He went straight to the red light district and entered one of the local haunts. Before long he was escorting a prostitute from the establishment. Kansi looked at her with insatiable lust and loathing and thought, *bitch; you will pay for Katrina's treachery and deceit. I will take your sex until you have perished and then I will take your soul and eat your heart.* As they entered her rundown room, Kansi thought, *you will be my last feast in Lisbon.*

F. Washington Brown

The taxi pulled up next to the airport terminal while Kansi fumed in the back seat with worry and nervousness. He paid the driver, collected his bags, and quickly entered the building.

Soon after he'd killed the prostitute the previous night, he had gone back to the hotel to make a flight reservation, retrieve his things, and check out. There was no doubt in his mind that Katrina had somehow figured out what he was up to and he thought that she might go to the police. However, what would she tell them and besides he wasn't afraid of the police per se'. Nonetheless, to be detained for questioning would interfere with his plans in America and that was his concern. To be on the safe side Kansi had decided to leave Lisbon immediately.

Using one of a couple of fake passports listing his name as Mohammad Kansi, he handed it to the ticket agent and bought his ticket. The agent took the cash and handed back a ticket and boarding pass. The terrorist checked his bags and went straight to the gate twenty waiting area. He took a seat and hoped that Delta flight 240 would not be delayed. He fretted as the time slowly ticked off, but finally he heard the PA system come to life and announce that flight Delta flight 240 was to start boarding. Allah was apparently in a good mood and flight 240 left Lisbon on time. Soon Kansi was slipping through the skies at thirty thousand feet, sitting in first class, sipping a glass of French burgundy. He'd acquired a taste for it but he reasoned that it was probably more Ogar's doing than his own. Ogar was diversified in his desires. He relished the sex, debauchery, killing, blood letting, eating of the victims hearts, wine, taking of souls, and the general swath of terror they had left behind. *Yes*, Kansi thought, *it was the right time to have left Lisbon.* The bodies had started turning up and the police presents on the street had become more pronounced. There was little doubt that the Lisbon authorities were starting on a hunt for some sort of a Jack-the-Ripper.

Kansi smiled and thought, *who knows, when I am in America I may take a few of the infidel's women to meet Allah.* Kansi looked at the woman sitting next to him and noticed that she was about thirty-five years old and quite pretty as he asked, "Excuse me but are you American?"

She returned his smile and said, "No I'm from England, and I'm just visiting my sister, Pauline, and her husband, Ray, who live in Racine, Wisconsin. My husband, John, had to work but he and my son Jeffery will join me at Pauline and Ray's house in one week. Do you live in the United States?" she asked.

"Oh, no," Kansi replied, "I'm going to new York and then on to California on business. My family is in oil. By the way," Kansi added as he extended his hand, "I'm Kansi, Mohammad Kansi, and might I ask your name?"

She gave him her hand and replied, "My name is Susan McCarthy. I'm please to meet you Mr. Kansi." As Kansi took her hand she noticed a kind of tingling feeling at his touch, a feeling that she liked very much. She held the handshake a little longer than she normally would have as she gazed into his eyes. She felt an inward embarrassment because she didn't even know the man to whom she was speaking; yet with just his touch he was making her loins wet. She pulled her hand back and momentarily averted her eyes. She suddenly felt ashamed, shocked, and confused because she normally did not think of herself as a loose woman except with her husband. Nonetheless, this man had just made it clear to her that she was. Her husband John was the only man that she had ever slept with in her entire life and she was happy with her marriage, but now she felt herself wanting this complete stranger. *What has gotten into me,* She thought?

Kansi looked at her obvious embarrassment as a victory. Mentally he had just taken this straight arrow of a faithful little wife and mother and turned her into a wanton slut. He knew that if they were alone, in a matter of minutes she would be begging him to have sex with her. It was abundantly clear that at this moment she was stunned, and humiliated at finding out whom she really was. However, Kansi could sense that she would soon get over the feeling due to her mounting desire to feel him inside her, and shame would be replaced by lust. Turning on the charm, Kansi said, "You look too young to have children. How many have you?"

Still off balance and trying to collect her thoughts, she stammered, "Uh, I ... I have just the one, uh Jeffery. He will be ten in May. Slowly she was starting to get back on track.

Kansi, as if to comfort her, placed his hand on her shoulder and said, "That's wonderful, a ten year old boy." The woman was love starved and Kansi knew she would be easy. Just some kind words and a touch here and there and she would be his. He looked into her eyes and moved his hand from her shoulder and placed it on her leg.

She didn't protest and made no move to stop him. Her eyes were locked with his and she was at a total loss as to what was happening to her. All she knew at this moment was that she wanted him. She started to say something then hesitated and then started again. "Mohammad ... do you mind if I call you Mohammad?"

"By all means," Kansi said with a pleasant smile, "please call me Mohammad."

"Mohammad," she said, "I don't quite understand why, and this has never happened to me before in such a short period, but I like you very much. I hope you don't think that I'm being too forward. What I mean to say is that you seem like a nice man."

"Not at all. I don't think that you're being too forward," he said as he leaned over and kissed her. He heard her emit a faint moan as her tongue hungrily snaked into his mouth.

They deep kissed for about five minutes then breathlessly she said, "Mohammad, I want you. What can we do? What I mean to say is, there is no privacy. Do you have any ideas?"

Being a pilot, Kansi was familiar with a variety of airplanes. Of course he'd never flown a Boeing 747 but he'd read extensively about them. An absurd thought had occurred to him that a plane the size of a 747 could be used to crash into a building like a bomb. But of course no one would ever be insane enough to do something like that. He had even mentioned the idea to some of his fellow collaborators and they had all laughed at the concept. All with the exception of one young man who had been listening. His name was Osama Bin Laden.

He replied, "Yes, Susan, I have an idea but I'm not sure that you would be willing to do it."

With eagerness showing in her voice she said, "Anything, I'll do anything that you want. Just tell me."

"Alright, first of all we can't use the restrooms because there is too much traffic in and out of them. However, I have a second idea but you may think that it's weird and extreme. In the area below us is where they carry the luggage and cargo. It's pressurized because they also carry passenger's pets in pet carriers. Toward the rear of the plane in an area where people rarely go, there is an access panel on the floor with drop down steps. This is for the crew to get into the cargo hold in case there is mechanical trouble while the aircraft is in flight. If we quietly slipped back there we could have privacy for almost the complete trip. What do you think?"

Almost pleading she said, "Oh yes, Mohammad, Lets go now. Just show me where."

"Alright, I'm going to get up and walk to the rear as if I'm going to the bathroom. So as not to draw attention you wait two minutes and follow me back. I'll wait for you on the other side of the galley. After you join me in the narrow passageway I'll show you where the access panel is. Do you fully understand what you are to do?"

"Yes," she replied.

Kansi looked around, then stood and started for the rear of the aircraft. As he slowly and inconspicuously walked to the rear, he thought, *it's true my dear that there is a way to gain access to the cargo hold. However, I didn't tell you about the compartment that's below the cargo hold. It's called the NOSE GEAR WHEEL WELL and when the bottom doors for that compartment opens to lower the nose gear for landing, there is nothing but open sky below.*

Kansi walked passed the galley, entered the narrow passageway and stopped to wait for his eager soon to be lover. He didn't have to wait long for within two minutes she was standing next to him. She was excited by what she perceived to be an adventure and started to say something, but Kansi put his index finger to her lips and mouthed the word, "Quiet."

He took her hand and led her further toward the rear of the aircraft. The light was dim so Kansi was forced to go slow and almost feel his way along. After they'd walked about twenty feet Kansi stopped and started feeling around on the floor. He located the panel and the recessed latch that secured it. He flipped the latch up, twisted it counterclockwise and pulled up on the panel. The panel opened and the steps below slid down allowing them access. Kansi entered the cargo hold first then helped Susan down. Once she was inside, Kansi reached up and closed the panel. He felt around on the bulkhead until he found a light switch. He flipped it on and said, "The light is dim but enough for us to move around without falling over things.

She turned and slipped her arms around his waist while pressing tightly against him. She felt his erection and said, "Hurry Mohammad and get your clothes off." She started to unbutton her blouse but he grabbed her hand and said, "Wait for a moment longer and come forward with me. He took her hand and walked toward the front of the airplane, passing electronic boxes and weird machinery as they went. As they walked he spotted a thick cloth cargo covering that could serve as something comfortable for her to lie on. He picked it up and they walked on. Then ten feet in front of him Kansi saw the access plate that covered the nose gear wheel well. He stopped just short of it and spread the cloth covering on the floor.

Susan, without a word, started removing her clothes. When they were both totally naked they dropped onto the cargo cover and Susan rolled over on her back and spread her legs. Kansi didn't want any foreplay plus Ogar's hunger was too great to allow it. He quickly slid in between her legs and plunged his large erect penis completely into her, burying it with the first stroke. She was well lubricated because of her lust and wanting but she was totally unprepared for Ogar. She screamed uncontrollably with pain as Kansi (aka)

Hot Sand & Cold Blood

Ogar ripped into her privates. With no pause, Kansi, out of pure unnatural lust, slammed his large penis into her over and over with absolutely no consideration for her or anything save getting himself sexually satisfied and ultimately taking her soul.

Soon her vagina adjusted to the size of his huge organ and her screams of pain turned into cries of passion. At first the pain had been excruciating but she also found it desirable, and then she realized that there was a very thin line between pain and pleasure, especially in these circumstances. She lifted her legs and wrapped them around his buttocks and with pure lust in her voice she hissed, "Come inside me Mohammad. That's right, shoot your Jizz Load in me you sadistic bastard ... just keep fuckin' me. Oh, please let me suck your big wanker. I want it in my mouth. You can fuck me ... all you want ... Oh God, I can't get enough! I want all of your big wanker and I went it deep ... that's right you fuckin' stud ... bring it on!" Then she began to feel to feel the biggest climax of her life welling up inside her. It started like a slow rolling wave and then started to build until finally it reached the gargantuan proportions of a surreal tidal wave as it rolled over her like a giant tsunami sending shockwaves of pure indescribable pleasure through absolutely every fiber of her body. She didn't think that her mind was going to be able to handle it but slowly the climax subsided only to have another and another come rolling through her mind and body in its wake. The experience was just overwhelming.

Kansi continued stroking her as he matched her climaxes one after another. He knew she could feel his penis pulsing each time he ejaculated into her. He was sweating; breathing heavy and grunting like a wild bore in rutting season each time he climaxed into her. Finally he raised up on his knees while at the same time grabbing the back of her neck and pulled her up into sitting position. She anticipated what he wanted and shifted her legs around so that she could comfortably go down on him. He shoved her head down onto his crotch as he slid his penis into her mouth and said, "Alright you fuckin' hose beast, take all of my cock in your mouth and down your throat. I want you to suck it until I come and then you swallow it. If you waste a drop I'll beat your ass."

She needed no encouragement as she eagerly took his penis into her mouth. She sucked it with the gusto of a hungry hound dog vacuuming up Alpo.

Almost in no time Kansi felt a huge climax building. He became ridged and quivered slightly as he felt his juice surge forth from his penis. He held her head tightly against his crotch and he could feel her jaw and throat muscles working as she hungrily drank his creamy sperm. She run her tongue all around the head to make sure she got every drop. Kansi relaxed his grip on her and let his hand fall to her shoulder. She looked up at him with half closed eyes and a lustful smile. Her lips and chin were glistening wet with semen and Kansi could tell by her expression that she was a happy satisfied woman. They had engaged in hard sex for three hours and still Kansi needed a little more. He slipped his hands around her waist and flipped her over onto her hands and knees. He positioned himself behind her, and like the Star Trek movie, went where no man had gone before.

She screamed with pain like she had never felt before and almost passed out. Slowly as before, the pain subsided and she begun to feel comfortable with what Kansi was doing to her. She even reached a point where it felt good and she thought she would come. Finally she felt him tense up and heard his growl as he pumped his load into her.

Kansi pulled out and cleaned up with some rags he found lying around on the crates of cargo, making a mental note to visit the washroom upon returning to the passenger cabin. Kansi was also starting to have a mental struggle with Ogar. He could hear Ogar in his mind saying, "Let me take her soul Kansi. Kill her and drop her into the nose gear wheel well. When the pilot opens the doors to put down the wheels she will fall out and drop into the ocean just short of Atlantic Beach near New York City. I can read your mind, remember. I know what you are planning so let's do it"

Mentally and without spoken words, Kansi said, "Please, Ogar, be quiet and let me think. You are too impatient. I will handle it." Kansi looked around, found his pants and slipped them on, then looked over and saw Susan sitting on the floor putting on her shoes. He walked back over and stood behind her for a moment, then he said, "Susan, do you like the sex with me?"

"Oh, I love the sex with you Mohammad."

He dropped to his knees behind her, putting one hand on her shoulder and with the other he brushed her hair to one side so he could kiss the back of her neck.

She sighed and softly said, "Mohammad you are such a man. Where did you learn to make love?"

Kansi replied, "It's the woman that I make love with that makes all the difference." As he spoke, he removed his hand from her shoulder and placed it loosely around her neck. Then suddenly he took her neck firmly with both hands and applied enough pressure to stop her from breathing. She reached up grabbed his hands and tried to pull them loose but it was no contest. He loosened his grip just before she slid into unconsciousness then laid her down on her back. Next he quickly ripped off her panties and unzipped his fly. He hastily slipped his penis deep into her vagina and slowly began having intercourse with her. He opened her mouth and placed his open mouth over hers, slipping his tongue in as he did. He was in a hurry because the ritual had to be done and the plane would be landing soon. Gradually, Kansi could feel her spirit being pulled out as Ogar started sucking in her life force and soul. Kansi felt her essence adding strength to his own as they combined. At last Ogar, with a little chuckle signaled that he was finished. Even though she was dead, Kansi continued having sex until he felt himself ejaculating into her. *Necrophilia,* he thought, *what a pleasant feeling.*

Kansi pulled his mouth away from her cold shriveled lips and looked at her shrunken cold gray face. At this point what he was looking at in no way or form resembled the Susan that he had come down into the hold with. Kansi slipped the rest of her clothes on her, but not out of respect for her dignity. He simple didn't want them getting caught and remaining in the wheel well when the doors opened. He stepped over to the nose gear wheel well access cover, leaned down and turned the latches. Next he grabbed the handles and pulled the cover off and dropped it next to the entrance. He lowered Susan's body into the wheel well feet first. He guided her body down and around the big tires. When she was completely in the wheel well he let go of her hands and she fell ten feet, landing on the lower doors. When the pilot lowered the landing gear over Atlantic Beach; poof, she would become shark food. Kansi closed the access cover and headed for the steps that would take him back up into the passenger cabin. After replacing and closing the latches on the cargo hold access cover he walked back passed the galley and discreetly slid into a washroom. A few moments later he stepped out and walked back up the isle.

As he relaxed back into his chair he signaled a passing flight attendant and ordered a glass of dark wine. Kansi knew that Susan would not be missed until her husband went to pick her up at the Racine airport. The airlines would just list her as a no show.

Chapter 17

Ryder went downstairs and placed a call the authorities, along with a second call to OMNI HQ advising them as to what happened with Brad Hymen. He hung up and then went back to his room to pack all his belongings. He got back downstairs about the time the authorities arrived. Ryder explained to the police sergeant in charge that Brad had been waiting for him and what had happened after that. After a quick investigation the police decided to take Ryder to the Beirut station for questioning. They were putting him into what passed as a squad car when one of police radios buzzed and a patrolman answered it. He said no more than a couple of words then quickly handed the radio to the police sergeant. The sergeant exchanged a few words and then walked over and addressed the driver of the car they had put Ryder into. In Arabic, the sergeant said, "Take this man to the airport immediately."

Twenty-five minutes later Ryder was stepping out of the car and walking toward the airport terminal entrance. Once inside he looked around and started for the ticket counter. He was just about there when a young guy wearing a U.S. Air force flight suit approached and said, "I assume that you are my passenger since you're the only American looking individual in the place."

Ryder stopped and asked, "Are you my ride to Lisbon?"

The airman said, "That's right. I'm Captain Simmons and I drive a T-38 Talon Air Force jet two-seat trainer. I was sent down here from Ramstein Air Base to pick you up and fly you to Portugal. Are you ready to go?"

Ryder shook hands with the pilot and said, "Let's go fire up that T-38."

Ryder was having little trouble keeping his oxygen mask adjusted. It was because the flight helmet he was wearing was not his and hadn't been custom fitted for his head. But it mattered little because he was once again airborne and twenty minutes into a flight that would put him closer to Kansi. However, he did have a big regret that kept gnawing at him ... that was not being able to tell Lisa in person that he'd had to leave the country. The thing that she had said about asking him to, never leave her again kept going through his mind. He had a feeling that going to Portugal without being able to tell her that he was leaving would prove to be pivotal and come back to haunt him. It was problematic in his mind but he couldn't worry about it now. It was a fifty-minute flight from Beirut to Lisbon by way of T-38 Talon. They were flying at thirty thousand feet when Ryder heard Captain Simmons key his radio and ask the Lisbon tower for let down and landing instructions. "Lisbon tower, this is U.S. Air Force Talon, alpha, fox, tango, 8-6-4-2-9er, call sign, Blue Eagle 6, requesting let down instructions and permission to enter your traffic pattern. My altitude and position is angels three-zero, on heading 270 degrees, over." The Captain released the button to wait for a response from the tower.

Ryder remembered from his marine corps flying days that, 'angels three-zero' meant 30,000 feet.

Shortly Ryder heard the Lisbon tower respond with, "U.S. Air Force Talon, confirm that your transponder is squawking on frequency 175.5, over."

"That's affirmative Lisbon tower, over."

"Blue Eagle, we have you on radar. Descend to 1500 feet and enter pattern on heading 350 degrees. Land on runway 21 left. Please expedite, Blue Eagle; we have multiple heavies inbound. Do you copy, over?"

"Copy tower, Blue Eagle will expedite."

Ten minutes later the jet trainer was taxing toward the parking ramp designated for cross-country aircraft. The Captain slid the canopy open as he maneuvered the jet into a space and shut down the two, centerline thrust J-79 General Electric engines.

They exited the plane and walked toward the terminal. As they entered the building, Ryder turned to the pilot and said, "I appreciate the ride Captain Simmons."

Smiling, the pilot said, "It was my pleasure to give you guys in the CIA a little help. I'm going to the cafeteria for a bite, and then I'll call transit maintenance for fuel. Hell, I'll be back in Germany in two hours, ready to do some serious flying."

Ryder replied, "Uh, I'm not CIA, but you're close. Have a good flight." Ryder shook the officer's hand and left the terminal. Hailing a cab, he hopped in and said, "Take me to the Sheridan Hotel."

The cabbie acknowledged the request and sped away from the terminal. After checking into the hotel, Ryder stepped over to the bank of house phones and put in a call to OMNI. He wanted to let them know that he'd arrived and to find out if were any developments in the case. As the phone rang, Ryder slipped a pocket scrambler over the mouthpiece because only a squeal could be heard on the number that he'd dialed without one. On the third ring he heard a woman's voice, "OMNI, give me your code ID."

Ryder said, "This is Proteus, January 5 ruby red."

The woman replied, "Alright Proteus, you're are valid. What can I help you with?"

"Let me speak to Dante," Ryder said.

"He's not in at the moment and I can't transfer you. I'm Charlene and I have current data, reference, your case. Are you ready to copy?"

"Roger, Charlene." Ryder said

Charlene cleared her throat, "Lisbon International Airport indicates that a light single engine aircraft, make Cessna 172 landed approximately five days ago and then was apparently abandoned. No one to date has come forward to initiate paperwork and forms or pay parking rental fees. Aircraft is registered to one Amal Kansi. No confirmation that Kansi arrived in the aircraft. The only identification the Lisbon airport tower received was the call sign when pilot requested landing instructions. We have no further leads on Kansi. The standard inquiry to the CIA came back with no more than what we have on the case. In other areas of standard inquires, the feelers to the local law enforcement in Lisbon reveled little except for the Lisbon police homicide division reports a higher number of killings than usual for this time of year. Our best assessment is that Kansi has gone to ground or possibly doubled back to the Middle East."

"Has OMNI or CIA queried the State Department passport section at the American Embassy in Lisbon to find out if there has been any requests for a passport or passport renewal for an Amal Kansi?"

"We are in the process of doing that but we have gotten no call backs on our requests."

Ryder cursed under his breath, "Goddamn' incompetent civil servants over at the State Department, always on coffee break."

"Did you say something sir?"

"No, I was just mumbling to myself. Call me at the Sheridan as soon you get something back from the passport division."

"We'll do that Proteus. Is there anything else?"

"Yeah, for the low degree of Intel sophistication that we're dealing with here, let's drop my Proteus code ID and refer to me by my name. It will simplify our communication and I can't believe this band of radicals is taking the time, nor do I believe that they have the skills to run surveillance on us."

"Roger, Proteus, uh, I mean, Agent Ryder."

Ryder hung up the phone and then called the downtown cop station. He knew that he was probably wasting his time, because of standard police policy almost all around the world; they rarely give out information on the phone. However, he might get lucky and save himself a trip to the Station. On the second ring he got an answer, only the guy answered in Portuguese. After the cop rattled off a few words in Portuguese that Ryder assumed was the cop identifying himself, Ryder said, "Do you speak English?"

Hot Sand & Cold Blood

There was a pause and then the policeman said, "I, uh, am speak little ... wait, you wait."

Ryder heard the receiver drop onto a desk or table, and then after a moment someone picked and said, "One thirty fourth precinct, Lisbon Police. I am Captain Fernandez, the prefect on duty. How can I help you?"

"Yes, Captain Fernandez, my name is Lance Ryder. I'm an agent working for an International security organization affiliated with Interpol, and I need a little information on the increased homicide rate that Lisbon is currently experiencing."

"Mr. Ryder, I cannot give you that information on the telephone. Please come down to the Policia Headquarters, identify yourself, and we will be, 'how do you say', happy to work with you."

"Right, thank you. I'll be right down." Ryder hung up and thought, *well so much for the short cut.*

The ride to the station gave the OMNI spy some time to contemplate the reasons why Lisbon was in a killing season. Could be the hot weather had people stirred up or maybe rash of bank robberies that had gone wrong. At any rate he would know something shortly. The hack pulled over in front of a large stone building that displayed two big round glass globes out in front. The white glass balls were supported by tall ornate metal poles that stood on either side of the wide steps that led up to the doors of the station house. On the globes was written: Policia.

Ryder paid the driver and ascended the steps. Once inside he couldn't believe the pandemonium. It reminded him of being in a New York City cop shop. To the left of the cop on the desk was another policeman trying to get a drunken prostitute to sit down so he could book her. She kept yelling at him and putting her hand in his face. Apparently with patience running low, he grabbed her and slammed her into the chair, whereupon she became somewhat less noisy.

Ryder made his way to the desk and said to the policeman, "Excuse me, but I'm looking for the Prefect."

The man gave him a blank stare and then said, "No comprendo, yo no comprendo." Then he smiled and his eyes lit up. "Oh! Prefect, El Prefecto. Uno momento." He pointed toward a door to the left and said, "Mieda, mieda."

Ryder said, "Gracias," and headed for the door. He knocked on the green door and heard a man's voice say, "Ventae." Ryder opened the door and went in.

The man behind the worn desk looked to be around fifty with salt and pepper hair and a mustache. He leaned back in his swivel chair and said, "Have a chair and be comfortable. You look American. Are you the law investigator that called me earlier?"

"Yes, that's correct. I actually work for OMNI."

"I think that I have heard of that. Is it not like the CIA?" asked the Prefect somewhat quizzically.

"Yes, except that I work for more than one country." Ryder said.

"Ah yes but of course. Do you have some identification Agent Ryder?"

"Yes. But it doesn't identify me as Lance Ryder or as an OMNI agent for obvious reasons when we are on a case. However for verification, call the American Embassy in Frankfurt using your operator and a number that you obtain. That way you will be sure that you are actually contacting the embassy. Ask for a man named Earl Duke. He's my contact for the time being and he will confirm my identity."

After a couple of calls with Ryder and the Prefect trading the phone back and forth, the Prefect was convinced. He finally said, "Alright Agent Ryder, with what can I help you?"

"I understand that you've had a string of murders. Can I ask you about the circumstances and something about the victims?

The Lisbon cop eyed Ryder for a second and then said, "Except for a couple of men the victims have all been woman, prostitutes to be more precise. We have been keeping the investigation as quiet as possible because of the way the women died."

"And how was that," Ryder interjected.

"A very mysterious thing, Agent Ryder. It is as if all the life was just sucked out of them."

"What?" Ryder said, somewhat taken aback.

"Yes, we find them in hotel rooms, and in back rooms of taverns with their hearts cut out and missing. And they have nothing left. The faces are dry, gray and bloodless. By their facial expressions they look as if the very soul was just taken away by some evil thing. We also find large amounts of semen and we believe that they engaged in long periods of sexual activity before they died."

At this point Ryder lost interest and said, "I don't think that this could be the guy that I'm after. It sounds to me like you are dealing with some kind of nut rapist or a Jack-the-ripper type of personality. Thank you for your time." He stood and headed for the door.

"Before you go Agent Ryder there was just one last thing, and I tell you this because you are an experienced investigator and I need help. First of all, the victims had letters carved on their foreheads. The letters spelled, LAMA. Does that mean anything to you?"

Ryder thought for a moment then said, "Well a lama is an animal with four legs that lives in the South American Andes. It's something like an Alpaca. However, it just doesn't ring any bells with me."

"Alright Agent Ryder we only have one other thing. We had a woman come in with a very strange story. If it were not for the killings we would dismiss her as a lunatic. But the situation says that we look at everything. This woman works at the El Cabalettas Hotel as a registrar. She says that a man came in with blood on his clothes and registered close to a week ago. She also said that three or four days later he asked her out on a date and she accepted. During the date he was a gentleman so she thought she could invite him home for a nightcap. Then the story gets weird. She says that when they got back to her apartment they went in and he sat down on the sofa. Meanwhile she went to hang a garment in the closet and that's when she caught a glimpse of his reflection in the mirror. She said the image was not human. She went on to say that it was grayish red with one large eye and generally speaking, ugly as hell. She became very fearful and managed to escaped through the bathroom."

At this point Ryder could not refrain from smiling as he said, "Sounds like the lady needs a little vacation. Sorry but I don't think that I can help you. Thank you again for seeing me. Good bye."

Looking a little resigned, the Prefect said, "Good bye to you, Agent Ryder."

Ryder left the police station and caught a taxi back to his hotel with the hope that maybe the Embassy had turned up something. He entered the hotel lobby and went to the guest phones and called the embassy and reached no one who would be able to help him. The night answering service said that Earl Duke should be available at around eight a.m. the following morning. Ryder hung up and went to his room. He was exhausted. He grabbed a shower and ordered a meal through room service. When the food arrived, Ryder turned on the television and collapsed into an overstuffed reclining chair. As he ate he fumbled with the TV trying to pick up an English speaking station. Stumbling across some sort of geographic explorer program he decided that he didn't need to understand the language to watch the jungle animals. He munched away on his tough sautéed steak while a heard of elephants trumpeted across the screen followed by a small group of zebras. *Zebras*, he thought, *they're a little like a lama, they both have four legs.* Then it hit him with the clarity of looking through a polished plate glass window. Lama spelled backwards was, Amal. Ryder dropped his plate on the coffee table and took the elevator back down to the lobby. He went to the phones and once more called the police station. When the desk sergeant answered Ryder asked for Prefect Fernandez.

"I'm sorry sir, but all the day shift has gone home. Prefect Fernandez will be here at seven thirty a.m. sharp. You are lucky I am working sir because no one else on this shift speaks English."

"Yes, thank you very much. I will call him first thing in the morning." Ryder hung up and went back to his room. *I need to speak with that hotel registrar first thing in the morning,* Ryder thought. He slumped back into the chair and his eyes drifted back to the screen but his mind was elsewhere. At this point his brain was stymied by what was rapidly turning into a convoluted situation. He understood the concept of Kansi being an assassin, a killer and terrorist, but why would he delay his escape. If he were the killer why would he invite this attention to himself? Maybe this was coincidence? Maybe Kansi had left the country. As he watched the Wild Kingdom parade across the screen his analytical mind puzzled over the development but it took him nowhere. Tomorrow he would speak to the witness and see what she had to say.

Chapter 18

Kansi was just finishing his second glass of sherry when he looked up and saw the, 'fasten seat belt light come on'. A flight attendant came along, took his glass and advised him that they were approaching New York City and that he should buckle up.

The Arab terrorist complied and a short time later he felt a slight bump as the aircraft's tires made contact with the runway. With a little smile playing across his face, Kansi thought, *good-bye Susan, I hope that you have a good swim.*

Kansi deplaned, collected his bags and headed for the car rental counter. After picking up a Ford four-door Galaxy and pulling onto the streets he felt some apprehension to be once again driving in New York City. He found the high-density traffic to be somewhat intimidating. As he drove, thoughts about his earlier experiences in the United States came to mind. He had illegally come to America with his parents when he was younger. They had enrolled him in a Boston school where he attended classes for close to a year and he had even obtained a drivers license. However the INS later ran an immigration status check on the Kansi family and they were deported back to the Middle East. Kansi thought about those days as he slowly navigated the big city traffic and conceded that the deportation could have even been the nexus that fed his ill will toward the United States. But now he was back with a vengeance and a plan designed to make the American Government pay. Indeed it would pay for all the perceived injustices. *But there is no point in dwelling on the past,* he thought. *I need to find a temporary place to stay.* Deciding on the Hampton Inn, he pulled into the parking lot and went in to register. He told the clerk that he'd like a room with a view facing the street. Feeling that he had surely put enough distance between himself and any would be pursuer; he registered as Amal Kansi and went to his room. He ordered a meal from room service and then called his contact in New York. The phone rang a few times and then someone picked up. "Salamalakim. United Arab Charities, may Allah be blessed. This is Abdul El Mohammad. How may I be of service?"

"Abdul, this is Amal Kansi. We have to meet to discuss the finalization of the plan. Are you ready to go to California?"

"Ah, Amal, is that truly you? May Allah be praised. But I thought that you were not to come until next week." Abdul said.

"That is true," Amal replied, "but the Americans are a little too close."

"Did you not spread the rumor about a fake bomb plot to get the Americans to go chasing their tails?" Abdul, asked unable to mask the slight dismay in his voice.

"Yes, but it did not work out as well as I had hoped. They found Sidi Slimane and now it may be possible that they may have found out more than we want them to know." Kansi said.

"So does this alter our plan?" Abdul asked.

"It means that we have to act sooner than we had planned. Once again I ask, are you ready to go to California?"

"Yes Amal. Everything is in place and we were just waiting for you to arrive, but we do have some problems. Our colleagues have gone to Texas, New Mexico, Arizona, and California as we planned. However, we had to change a few things because of security and other reasons." Abdul replied.

"Good, good. Abdul bring me the changes and we will discuss them. I'm staying at the downtown Hampton Inn. How long will it take you to get here?"

"One hour if the traffic is not too bad, otherwise maybe an hour and a half. Is there anything else that I should bring?"

"No, just the plans and the changes you have made."

F. Washington Brown

As Kansi ate he wondered about the changes in the plan that Abdul had mentioned and what he meant by the reasons for the changes. Whatever they were, Kansi didn't like the idea of somebody altering the plan without his approval.

Almost one hour and a half later to the minute, Kansi heard a knock at his door. He went to the door and opened it a crack to verify that it was Abdul. Upon seeing Abdul's round smiling face, Kansi stepped back and said, "Come in my friend."

Abdul entered the room and they embraced and kissed each other on both cheeks. Afterward, Kansi said, "Have a chair at the table and let's lay everything out so I can see what alterations have been made."

Eager to show Kansi the developments, Abdul quickly took a chair and sat down while spreading out a couple of maps and several sheets of paper. Kansi took a seat on the other side of the table and patiently waited for Abdul to explain the changes. Pointing to a town on a map that he had laid out, Abdul said, "The towns in Texas that we have targeted are Dumas, and El Paso. In New Mexico we will wire the pumping stations in Las Cruces, Deming and Lordsburg. In Arizona we have people in Tucson and Phoenix. And finally I have sent some of our brothers to Blythe, Los Angles, and San Francisco in California. Kansi, I am sorry to report that we have some problems."

"And what problems might those be my friend?" Kansi asked.

"As you know we contacted the American named Thomas Barns and paid him to obtain the long range transmitters."

Impatiently Kansi said, "Yes, yes, I know. The Thomas Barns that works as an electronics engineer at the White Sands Missile Range in New Mexico near Las Cruces. The agreement was that for two hundred thousand dollars he would deliver twenty long-range transmitters with directional antennas and delay timers. He also agreed to tune the transmitters to frequency 164.5 megahertz. Plus he was to calibrate them with the built-in twenty-minute delay timers

Hot Sand & Cold Blood

so that our brothers could activate them at the precise hour and still have time to leave the blast areas. So what is the problem? Did he fail to deliver the transmitters?"

Abdul hesitated for a moment and then replied, "No, he delivered some of them."

"How many?" Kansi asked, feeling anger because of this latest development.

"He delivered ten. He was to deliver the first ten and then wait two weeks so as to not raise suspicion and then deliver the last ten. He was stealing them from his own organization and he said it was very risky because the items are state of the art technology and expensive."

"What about the last ten," Kansi said?"

"He will not be delivering the last of the transmitters because he was killed in a car accident three days ago. However, we have found another technician named Ted Green who worked with Thomas Barns and has access to the transmitters. Our brother Mousawi has talked to him but as yet has not mentioned that he wants to buy electronic equipment. Mousawi has told Green that he is an exchange student studying electronics at New Mexico State University. We thought we would get to know something about this Ted Green before we offered him a deal. Mousawi says he has heard that Barns and Green were doing something illegal besides the transmitter deal but is not sure if what he heard is true. If we can confirm this then we can confront Green and force him to obtain the other ten transmitters that we need."

"Besides the transmitters, do we have all of the other things that we need?

"Yes, Amal, we have blocks of the high explosive Symtex comp-C, the squibs and everything necessary to set off the preliminary explosion. Of course the big fireworks will be provided by the Americans themselves." Abdul giggled.

"Is this information the last that you have heard from Mousawi?" Kansi asked.

"I called him yesterday evening and that is what he has told me. Mousawi hired a private investigator to track

Greens movements and check out his background, friends and whatever else he can find. As soon as we're sure we will confront him and force his cooperation."

"It sounds alright," Kansi said, "but we need to push to get this roadblock solved because we are running short on time."

"Yes I know, Amal, but we cannot go faster than circumstances will allow. I told Mousawi that I needed daily updates. I will call him again at eleven this evening to see if anything has developed."

"Alright Abdul, we will wait for his report and see what he has to say. Tomorrow one way or another I'm flying to San Francisco, California. That is where we will start the chain reaction. It will put their economy into disarray and plunge them into anarchy."

"Yes, Amal, we will bring the infidels to their knees. Amal if that is all, I will get back to the business. I must keep up appearances so as not to raise suspicion."

"Yes, Abdul that is good thinking, and call me if you find out anything." The two Arabs embraced once more and then Abdul started for the door. Before leaving he stopped, looked back and tossed a piece of paper on a small table near the door.

"What is that," Kansi asked?

"It is Mousawi's phone number," he said and then added, "Salamalakim, my brother."

After Abdul had left Amal thought about their meeting for a while and wasn't sure that he'd liked what he'd heard. The positive side was that their plot had not been discovered, but he didn't like the business about not having all the transmitters on hand. He let it slide for the moment and decided to get some fresh air and look the town over. After all it had been years since he had seen the big apple. The Arab terrorist got dressed and decided to cruise the East Side. He couldn't seem to get rid of the insatiable hunger inside. As he drove up one street and down the other he began to rationalize the situation. He knew that it was close to the time when he would execute his mission and he should keep his mind on that important business. Nonetheless how could he keep his mind on the business at hand when this need burned within him? He decided on a compromise. He would take a woman's soul in New York, but only one. Tomorrow he would leave and the city police would think it was just a coincidental big city murder. He reasoned that this would satisfy the Zombeast's lust for blood even if it were only for a little while. After the plot was executed and finished he would return to the Middle East and once more slip into Israel. There he would go on a blood trail of debauchery. He would rape, kill, take souls and plunder until Ogar was totally satisfied. However, tonight there would only be one. As he cruised the dance club section he spotted a hole-in-the-wall called, 'The Paper Steamboat'. There was a line of people waiting to get in. He drove around the block until he found a parking space and slipped the Ford into it. Stepping out of the car he headed toward the club. Kansi scanned the line until he saw a lone woman who looked to be around twenty-eight. She was wearing a mini skirt, which showed off her supple legs. She had dark brown hair and a pretty face. He put on an enthusiastic happy front, ambled up to her and said, "Hello Anna, I haven't seen you in a couple of years."

She looked at him and shot back, "Fuck off Jack. I can tell when some dipshit is trying to put the make on me."

He looked into her eyes and said, "I'm sorry but I must have gotten you mixed up with Anna." He smiled and added, "You sure do look like Anna."

She looked back into his eyes and her voice softened as she replied, "You have the wrong person, my name is Brenda ... Brenda Slone."

Attempting an embarrassed expression, he said, "I'm very sorry to have troubled you and I'll be on my way. Good bye." All the time they were talking he maintained eye contact with her. Now he broke eye contact and took a couple of steps as if to be walking away.

She hesitated for a second and then said, "Wait a minute man, maybe I was a little rough on you but I get a lot of guys hitting on me for just one thing. Maybe it's me that owes you the apology. Like I said my name is Brenda Slone, and who are you?"

He stopped, turned back to her and said, "My name is Amal Kansi. I haven't been in New York City for a couple of years. As a matter of fact I just got back in town today and don't know anybody. All my friends that I knew before have apparently moved. I was very happy when I saw you because I thought at last I had found one of my old friends."

Brenda said, "Look man, I mean Amal, I'm not with anyone tonight. Why don't you go to the club with me and we can keep each other company? If you have to go to the end of this line, you will be all night getting into the place."

His smile broadened as he said, "Thank you very much." He raised the rope that cordoned off the line and slid under it. The couple behind them grumbled for a minute or two about him being a line breaker but then went back to their conversation about the good times they'd had hanging out with rock stars. Before long Brenda and Kansi were conversing like they had known each other for years. Kansi wondered about the gift of gab he had received from Ogar. In the past Kansi had always been shy around women and stumbled over his words when making conversation with them. That all changed when the Zombeast melded with him. Now it seemed that everything he said to a woman was gold and something she wanted to hear. Kansi wondered how much was his ability and how much was Ogar's influence. After all Ogar's stake in their union was the taking of a human soul and his reward for presenting it to the Old One. They worked their way forward until they finally reached the front door and then into the club. The disco music was ear shattering loud and the flashing strobe and colored lights on stage was blinding. However the table area was fairly dark. They moved in and around the crowd until they found an empty table and sat down. Kansi glanced at his new friend Brenda and could tell that she was instantly into the scene. She was smiling and her shoulders and head were moving to the disco rhythms. He thought, *that's it infidel woman, have a good time with your last night on earth.*

She looked at him and said, "Come on Amal, let's go burn some floor. By the way, what kind of name is Amal?"

Speaking up over the crowd noise he said, "It's Arabic. I'm from Morocco. Why do you ask? Do you not like it?"

She laughed and stood as she said, "Hell man, a name is a name, it's OK with me. Let's go." She dropped her sweater over the back of her chair and danced onto the floor.

Kansi was apprehensive as he followed her out. He had never danced to this type of music before, but until the Lisbon Taverns he had never danced at all. Once on the floor, he was amazed at how he danced. He looked around at the best dancer on the floor and was soon copying the guy's moves perfectly. Then he started to innovate moves of his own. When the music ended they walked back to their table and sat down. He had actually enjoyed it and wondered if this was more of Ogar's implementation. He looked at Brenda and she was looking back at him with an expression of amazement as she said, "Really, just who are you and where in hell did you learn to dance like that? We have to enter the dance contest. Hell, man, we can win it hands down."

Kansi thought about it for a moment and wondered if it was too high profile. After all he didn't want anybody remembering him from this place. Then he heard Ogar stir and send the words via telepathy, "Go forth Kansi and engage in mirth for I enjoy this also. As modern man would say, I live vicariously through you my friend." Kansi ordered drinks and he felt no further inhibitions. They danced every dance until the contest was announced. They hit the floor with their best moves and Brenda was right. They walked away with the trophy and a hundred bucks.

Once again they returned to their table and Kansi ordered another round. After the waitress left with the order Brenda said, "It took me some time to pick up your style and sync up my steps to yours but once we started to click it was like fuckin' magic. Amal, nobody out there can touch us. You and me are going to become regulars here. What do you say?"

Kansi looked at her with a sinewy little smile and said, "That's right baby, you and I are going to become like one." They danced until the place closed and as they were leaving Kansi asked, "Do you have a car?"

She looked at him somewhat calculatingly and replied, "No I came in a cab."

"Would you give me the pleasure of letting me drive you home?" he asked.

She was silent for a moment obviously thinking about the ramifications. Finally she said, "Ordinarily I would tell you to piss off because I don't know you, but there is something about you that I like. Sure you can give me a ride home. Hell, who knows, I might even take you upstairs for a ride."

They stepped out onto the street to a light rain, actually more like a mist, made a little dash for Kansi's car and hopped in. Kansi started the rental and pulled away from the curb. Once into mainstream traffic, he said, "Where do you live?"

She slid over next to him and replied, "One Hundred and Ninety Sixth Street. I'll give you the apartment number when we get there." She kissed him lightly on the cheek as she dropped her left hand on his leg and whispered, "Tell me Amal, does this bother you."

Kansi was becoming increasingly aroused and knew that Ogar would welcome another soul. Yes tonight Kansi relished the thought of making another infidel pay the supreme price. "If you must know Brenda, I would have to be a fool for it not to bother me."

She laughed as she turned around in her seat and placed an arm on the dash to get a better look at his face. She studied his features for a moment then said, "Amal, your eyes look like they have changed color. It must be the city lights that are doing it but they appear to have a dark indigo-like cast to them. They look almost black. Has anyone ever told you that before?"

At this point Kansi was so sexually stimulated that he was forced to chose his words carefully and put effort into maintaining his light playful demeanor as he replied, "What

Hot Sand & Cold Blood

ever do you mean about my eyes? No one has ever commented on my eyes. You must have drank too many daiquiris tonight my sweet."

"Maybe so," she said, "but you are one dancing son-of-a-bitch, I'll give you that. You never did tell me where you learned to dance."

"Oh, just here and there." Kansi said. They moved along smoothly on the darkened wet city streets exchanging small talk until finally Kansi said, "OK baby we're at one hundred and ninety sixth, what apartment complex."

Brenda had been relaxed with her eyes closed. She sleepily looked around getting her bearings and then she said, "There up ahead on the left. It's the Queen Ann Apartments. Pull around back into the parking garage."

"Yes, I see it." Kansi replied as the pulled the car onto parking area she had indicated. *Sure she is interested,* Kansi thought, *but she is not hungry for me like the women in Lisbon.* He reasoned that it might be the difference in cultures and that could be the reason she is not so easily impressed. He parked the car and then leaned over and kissed her. Brenda slid her tongue into his mouth and emitted a little sigh. She moved her head back slightly to look at his face and with a grin said, "If you can fuck like you can dance I may adopt you. Come on let's get to the bedroom. Grabbing her purse, she opened the door and stepped out.

Wasting no time, Kansi followed her up the stairs and into the apartment. As they entered, Amal was impressed with the fancy interior. The decor was done in all eggshell white modern with austere white pipe stair banisters and railings. Ogar was now making it abundantly clear that he wanted to be inside his latest prey. Once in the bedroom Kansi took Brenda into his arms and roughly unzipped her jeans.

With an edge to her voice Brenda said, "Whoa, Amal, I want to fuck you too but take a little slower."

"Brenda can we turn out the lights?" Kansi asked.

"Amal, I have a little fetish about leaving a couple of small black lights on so I can see my lover's face while I'm fuckin' him."

F. Washington Brown

Brenda, now completely undressed and playfully feeling her liquor, spread her arms out and with a slight leap, fell backward onto the bed. With a smile of anticipation she lay there on her back with eyes closed, waiting for her lover. Her wait was not long for Kansi was immediately in between her legs. He plunged his penis into her with such a painful abruptness that it made her eyes fly open. Kansi began stroking her vigorously and what should have been a pleasurable experience for her immediately turned to disbelief. What she saw in the ceiling mirror made her scream with terror. For Brenda it was a sudden nightmare. Feeling him in her was good and except for his indigo eyes Kansi looked normal, but when she looked into the overhead mirror she saw this nasty horrible muscular looking creature humping her. The sickening grayish-red color of its body coupled with the large hideous horned head and one large indigo eye drove fear into her very core. A long scabrous hairy tail extended out from between the buttocks that resembled a snake as it darted about sampling the feel of her smooth legs. She tried to move but felt powerless to stop it. Its grip on her tightened as it became tense in anticipation of a looming climax. Accompanied by an unearthly wail it ejaculated into her and her vagina involuntary contracted with pleasure as she felt the creature's warm sperm being spewed into her. The whole scene was insane and spiraling out of control. Her eyes and mind were terrified but her body was feeling the pleasure of being pounded by this monster's rough sex and huge erect penis. She tried to command her body to stop but she couldn't keep the climax from rising within her. First she bit her lip to stop it and then an uncontrolled moan escaped her lips as a tremendous climax rippled throughout her body and mind. As it subsided something in her mind told her that she must find a way to stop this unnatural sex or she would die. In an attempt to totally divorce her mind and body from what was happening to her she waited until the Zombeast completed his third climax, at which point he momentarily relaxed his grip on her. Hoping that her judo classes had not been a waste of money, she put both hands on the right side of his chest and

Hot Sand & Cold Blood

with supreme effort quickly rolled the Zombeast a little to her right. He was so engrossed in the sex he had not expected this from her. Given this opportunity, she jabbed her index finger into his left eye.

The Zombeast rose up off her, put his hand over his eye and squealed like a wild wounded bore. With his attention distracted Brenda rolled off the bed to her left, grabbing her purse as she hit the floor. Quickly pulling the .32 Smith and Wesson from the handbag, she rapidly put five rounds into his chest.

The Zombeast roared in pain and fell back as Brenda leaped to her feet and rushed from the apartment and into the night.

Kansi was in great pain and thought that he was going to pass out and then Ogar spoke, "Fear not Kansi for you will not die. Even as I speak you have begun to heal."

It was true. Kansi looked at his chest and saw the wounds beginning to close and his strength was returning. Soon he felt well enough to hurriedly get dressed and leave which is precisely what he did.

Driving back to his hotel it occurred to him that some of these American women were proving to be more problematic than what he had encountered in the past. Because of this incident it also made him realize that he had better contact Abdul for any developments and the leave for San Francisco at first light. He figured that Brenda would go to the police but she had been drinking so that would be the end of her credibility. Still there was blood on her hands. Ten blocks from his hotel he glanced to his right and saw a furniture store on fire. The sight of the flames made him shudder with fear.

He drove on as the city fire trucks appeared in his rear view mirror, and ten blocks later pulled into Hampton customer's parking lot. As he stepped into his hotel room he once more looked at his chest and saw that it was completely healed and he felt invulnerable. He stepped over to the nightstand and picked the phone. He dialed Abdul's number after four rings he heard it pick up.

Abdul's sleep filled voice said, "Arab Charities, Abdul speaking."

"Abdul, this is Kansi. Have you heard anything from Mousawi about the transmitters?" Kansi asked.

"Yes. Mousawi says that since we were pressed for time he went ahead without waiting for the investigator's report and took a chance that the electronics technician Ted Green would cooperate. Mousawi propositioned him about the transmitters and Green said that he could get them but it will cost us four times as much as the original agreement with Thomas Barns," Abdul replied.

"Why has he raised the price?" Kansi asked.

"He claims since he was not part of the first agreement it is not binding and he can charge whatever he thinks they are worth."

"Does he have the transmitters now?"

"I don't think so, but he claims he can have them on one days notice when we come up with the money." Abdul replied.

"Call Mousawi back and tell him to tell Green that we have the money and we will hand it over when he gives us the transmitters. Tell him to set up a time and place for the exchange sometime day after tomorrow."

"But Kansi, we didn't plan to pay that much and with the expense of buying the other material and flying our people to the different places we do not have enough money to pay him," Abdul said with some dismay clearly showing in his voice.

"I will detour my trip though New Mexico on my way to San Francisco. We are not going to pay this Mr. Green. When he shows up with the transmitters, Abdul will meet him with a few thousand dollars in a briefcase. When Green opens the case to count the money, I will take him out with a scope and high powered rifle." Kansi said.

"What about the body and won't he be missed?" Abdul asked.

"It will be a few days before the police get serious about looking for him and by then it will be too late. As for the body, we will drop it in a canyon or lake. Even if they find him it will take time to investigate the case. Don't worry Abdul; I know what I'm doing. After I get off the phone I'm going to call the airport and book a flight out to Albuquerque, New Mexico. I will be there long before it's time to make the exchange. I'm changing your assignment. I want you to close your shop and fly to Dumas, Texas. You can help coordinate from there and also you will in a position to see the last big explosion in the attack on the American system." Kansi said.

"But Kansi who will run the charities? My wife is not trained."

"Book your wife on a flight back to Iraq because five days from now the United States will be dying of anarchy triggered by infrastructure failure. In less than a month the entire system will collapse. There will be no American branch for Middle Eastern Arab Charities and there will be no America." Amal was becoming emotional so he stopped speaking for a moment and in a calm voice he added, "Do you understand your instructions Abdul?"

"Yes Amal, I understand. I will call Mousawi right away and tell him what you have told me. Salamalakim"

"Salamalakim, Abdul."

"Salamalakim, my brother," Kansi replied and hung up the phone. He looked at his watch. It was three a.m. He picked up the phone and called the airport.

Chapter 19

Ryder rolled over in bed and looked at his watch. After getting dressed he hurried to the downstairs restaurant and got a quick bite before heading back downtown to the police station. He arrived at eight fifteen a.m. and went directly to Captain Fernandez's office and knocked on the Prefects door.

The Prefect called out, "Ventae, come in."

Ryder entered the Prefect's office and closed the door. "Good morning Captain. I think that I've figured out who murdered those women."

Looking a bit skeptical the Captain asked, "And just who do you think is responsible, Agent Ryder?"

I think that Amal Kansi did it, the very man that I'm investigating. We believe that he left Morocco and headed here. You told me that all the prostitutes had the word, lama cut into their foreheads. Is that correct?"

"That is correct Agent Ryder, but what are you getting at exactly?"

"Captain, the word, LAMA spelled backward is Kansi. This guy is more warped than I had previously thought." Ryder said.

The Captain considered Ryder's statement for a moment then said, "I see what you are saying about the word, lama. Does this man Kansi have a record for this kind of motes-operandi anywhere else?"

"Not as far as I know and that's what puzzles me and also threw me off because Kansi is suspected of totally different types of crimes." Ryder said.

With his interest piqued the Captain asked, "If I may ask, what sorts of crimes?"

"Well I can't get into much detail because it's a matter of the American national security, but it has to do with suspected sabotage. Captain, you mentioned a woman with a strange story about a man with blood on his cloths, coming into the El Cabalettas Hotel. I would like to speak with her because the time period she gave you dovetails with same time Kansi left Morocco and flew to Lisbon."

"Yes, the woman's name is Katerina something or another. I can have one of my people look it up. Better yet why don't we drive to the El Cabalettas and have a talk with the lady." The Captain tapped a buzzer on his desk and a moment later a detective appeared at the door and said, "Si' Capitan."

"Jorge, call the El Cabalettas and see if the woman we talked to about the killings is working. Katerina I believe is her name."

"Si Capitan." The man turned and walked away.

"Agent Ryder, I think that if there is nothing more to discuss here why don't we drive over and see our witness?"

"It sounds good to me," Ryder replied.

As they entered the complaint and booking room the cop named Jorge approached the Prefect and said, "Capitan, the woman you speak of is working today and has been told that you are coming to see her."

"Thank you Jorge." the Prefect replied.

They left the station and got into the Prefect's car. On the drive to the El Cabalettas they exchanged a bit of small talk. However Ryder's mind was preoccupied with an incident that had happened two years prior in Vietnam. He remembered that some minor peripheral data had cropped up while he was investigating a drug runner named Eddie Slade. While in the process of chasing Eddie, Ryder had spent time asking questions in various military police stations from Saigon to Bangkok, Thailand. He had heard vague rumors about some Saigon hookers being killed in a strange and gruesome fashion. He didn't remember details but it had something to do with cutting their hearts out and a letter or something carved on them. Initially he had not suspected Eddie of the killings because generally drug runners ran dope and didn't kill unless they were cornered. But just prior to Ryder killing Eddie, the dope runner displayed strange behavior that led Ryder to believe Eddie had a hand in killing the woman. Ryder said, "Captain, tell me something. I know this will sound crazy, but these women who were killed, they didn't by chance have their hearts cut out did they?"

The Prefect's face went white as he quickly pulled to the curb and slammed his foot on the brake. He pulled his revolver and placed it to Ryder's head. With caution permeating his voice he said, "Ryder, I will ask you a question and how you answer it will determine if I put the cuffs on you. Now, how did you know the hearts were cut from some the women?"

Now it was Ryder's turn to be alarmed because he hadn't expected the Prefect to affirm his question. Cautiously he said, "Captain, please put your gun back into its holster. I am as much shaken up by your answer to my question as you are by mine."

Curiously the Prefect asked, "What do you mean?" as he slowly pointed the gun away from Ryder's head.

"I mean that when I was in Vietnam a similar thing happened and I believe that the man responsible was killed in a fire."

"Agent Ryder, I purposely told all of my people and the medical personnel to not leak that information because I didn't want a lot of people confessing to the crime. You know what I mean, if someone comes in and confesses we ask what he did to the body. If he can't say, we eliminate him as a suspect. But you, Ryder, that's a different story. Either that was a lucky guess or you just went to the top of my list."

"Trust me Captain it was coincidence and a lucky guess, but now that I know what happen, it puts a new spin on my investigation."

"And what would that be," the Captain asked?

"Captain it's just to freaky and I am not sure you would believe me."

"Tell me Agent Ryder and let me be the judge."

For the remainder of the ride, Ryder explained what he knew and his opinions of Eddie Slade. As they pulled up in front of the El Cabalettas the Captain said, "You are right, that is a freaky story. If it wasn't so unbelievable I would probably arrest you because not even a guilty man could make up that crazy story."

As they entered the hotel Fernandez nodded toward the woman behind the counter and said, "That's her.

The two lawmen approached the check-in counter and Fernandez said, "Excuse me please Senorita, but we met the other day. I am Captain Fernandez and you are Katerina ..."

The woman smiled and finished his sentence, "Katerina Linguine, and yes I remember you Captain. It was about that horrible experience that I had. I am still having nightmares about it. Did you catch him, it, or whatever?"

"No, Senorita Linguine we did not but that is why we are here," the Prefect replied. This is Agent Lance Ryder from the United States and he thinks that he may be looking for the same person."

With some consternation showing on her pretty face she said, "Well, you are too late. He came back to the hotel and checked out the same night he scared me. One of the other clerks said he left around four a.m. I was so afraid I did not come to work for two days."

Ryder asked, "What name did he register under?"

She glanced at the OMNI agent and replied, "Kansi, Amal Kansi."

Ryder's face lit up, "Miss why didn't you tell the police his name?"

With a surprised look she said, "I did tell one of the policemen Kansi's name but after I told him that I had seen a monster he asked me if I had been drinking. I don't think he believed anything I said."

The Prefect said, "That explains why the word didn't get passed along."

Ryder said, "Miss, I understand from the Captain that you went out to dinner with Kansi."

"Yes we went to dinner and had a relaxing evening until I saw that thing in the mirror." She seemed to be getting nervous and unsettled and being reminded of Kansi.

Ryder said, "Miss I know this is tough but try to remain calm. In the course of talking to him did he say much about himself, like where he came from, where he was going? Did he mention his family or background? Some men talk or brag when trying to impress a lady."

She squinted her eyes thoughtfully at the ceiling for a moment and said, "Well, he mentioned that his family was in oil and that he was in Lisbon on business. Let's see, oh yes, he also said when left here he was going to New York, and even said something about California or maybe it was Texas. I can't be sure, I don't know much about the United States."

Ryder felt that she was providing valuable information but couldn't understand why Kansi had been so candid with her. The only thing that explained it he reasoned was that Kansi had no knowledge of the drone tracking radar that he and Baronga had used to track his plane. He must believe that he has gotten completely away with no trace. If this were the case and it appeared that it was, it would make tracking the terrorist much simpler. After hearing her statement, two things were clear. The first was that Ryder had conformation Kansi had been here, and the second was, after the high profile situation he had created locally he was no longer in Lisbon. He had gone to New York City, or according to the hotel clerk, maybe even further west. Ryder understood Kansi's desire to get to New York City. It was high-density population and an ideal place to explode a hydrogen bomb, and Langley being even better. So why would Kansi go to California or Texas? Maybe Katrina had misunderstood what Kansi had told her. At any rate it seemed like his business in Lisbon was close to being wrapped up. "Miss Katrina," Ryder said, "I don't want to seem like that I'm pressing an issue but I need you to be as sure as you can about Kansi's statement to you about having business in California or Texas."

"Well, Senor Ryder I would not swear to it but I am sure I heard him mention those states." she said rather defensively.

Ryder looked at Captain Fernandez and said, "Prefect, that is all I have. Do you have any ideas or questions for the lady?"

"No, Agent Ryder, I think you have covered the situation very well." He looked at the clerk and said, "Senorita Katrina, we thank you for your cooperation and Sleep well I don't think you will be seeing Mister Kansi again."

With a visible expression of relief she replied, "Thank you Captain Fernandez. It is a great burden lifted from my mind."

The Prefect smiled and added, "Maybe later Senorita Katrina, you and I can get together over a cup of coffee and discuss any little details that we might have missed. Oh, by the way call me Juan."

She smiled back at him and replied, "Yes Juan, that sounds fine. Call me."

The Prefect turned to Ryder and said, "Agent Ryder if you are ready we shall be off."

Ryder replied, "I'm ready Prefect." It was all the OMNI spy could do to keep from grinning at the Prefect's obvious pass at Katrina. *Well more power to him if he can take her out to coffee,* Ryder thought.

The two men left the El Cabalettas and Captain Fernandez dropped Ryder off at his hotel. As the Captain pulled to the curb he asked, "Agent Ryder what are you going to do now?"

"I think that I am done here Captain. It seems pretty obvious the Kansi has caught a plane for the States and that fits with what we think he is trying to do. You've been a great help Captain," and with a grin, Ryder added, "Good luck with your business."

With a knowing look the Prefect asked, "And what business would that be, Agent Ryder?"

"The business with Miss Katrina," Ryder said maintaining his smile.

"Oh, that business," the Prefect replied. "Good luck Agent Ryder and have a good trip."

Ryder got out and closed the car door. Then he leaned down and looking through the open window said, "Good luck to you also Prefect and good hunting."

The Captain put the car into gear and drove away.

The OMNI agent entered the hotel and stopped at the counter to make a call. He picked up the phone and when the operator answered he said, "Put me through to Mid East Oil in Beirut."

The phone rang several times before a secretary picked up. "Mid East Oil."

Ryder said, "Let me speak to Lisa Nickels please."

"I'm sorry sir, Captain Nickels is currently in Europe. Are you Lance Ryder?"

"Yes I'm Ryder. Did she leave me a message?"

"Sir, Captain Nickels tried to call you several times when she returned but apparently you didn't return her calls. Then she was told by the hotel registry that you had checked out. She has since taken another flight back to Europe and she didn't say when she would be back. It's none of my affair sir, but I believe that she is very unhappy with you. I'm not sure that she would take your call if you were here."

Suddenly feeling A slight bout of depression Ryder said, "Thank you Miss. When she gets back would you tell her that I called? Tell her that I'm sorry and I will try to contact her as soon as I get to New York."

"I'll give her your message sir. Will that be all?"

"Yes." Ryder said and then he hung up. He picked up the phone again and called the airport.

A ticket agent picked up and said, "Lisbon International flight reservations."

Ryder said, "I want the first flight to New York City."

"What airlines would you like to book with sir?"

"It doesn't matter I just want the next flight out."

"That will be flight 235 with British European Airways sir. It departs Lisbon at six p.m."

"Fine," Ryder said, "I'll take it. The name is Lance Ryder and I'll be paying with American Express."

"Thank you sir. That will be two hundred and fifty dollars one way."

"Thank you," he said and hung up. Feeling a bit morose Ryder trudged to his room to pack his things. With three hours to kill he figured that he might as well do it in the airport lounge drinking scotch to take the edge off of his depression. He also wanted to have a talk with the chief of airport security to find out the names of everyone who had flown to New York in the last two or three days. He figured that Kansi would have used a fake name and passport when he bought his ticket. However, so far, either his ego or stupidity had prevented him from doing that.

Ryder arrived at the airport and went directly to the ticket counter and paid for his ticket. After the ticket agent had tagged his bags, Ryder said, "I need to speak with your security chief."

With a tired expression and even less enthusiasm in his voice the ticket seller said, "If it's official business, come on back."

Ryder followed the man to a back office and introduced him to head of security.

"My name's Agent Ryder and I'm affiliated with Interpol. I need to look at your passenger list on all flights to the States in the last three days."

"Mister Ryder that would require me to reassign people to do this and how do I know that you are legitimate?"

"Call Captain Fernandez the downtown Prefect." Ryder replied.

With a resigned expression the security chief said, "Never mind." He looked at the ticket agent and added, "Rodriquez, put two people on this." Then glancing back at Ryder he said, "Give Rodriquez the name."

After thirty minutes of looking, one of the employees said, "The closest name I find to Amal Kansi is, Mohammad Kansi."

That's it, Ryder thought. *Well I was wrong, Kansi is attempting to cover his tracks albeit in a somewhat of a sloppy manner.* It indicated that Kansi was slightly concerned but not worried. "Thank you for your help," Ryder

F. Washington Brown

said as he left the room. The OMNI spy reached the gate boarding area with ten minutes to spare.

Chapter 20

Ryder boarded the British built aircraft and took his assigned 20A window seat. Soon the four Rolls Royce jet engines were spooled up to 100% and the B.E.A. airliner was screaming down the runway. The nose came up and moments later Ryder looked out to see Lisbon disappearing under the wing just to be gradually replaced by the azure Atlantic Ocean.

The stewardess came by dispensing liquor and Ryder requested a scotch and soda with a twist. He relaxed back into his seat and let his mind wander over past events and how they might relate to his current situation. It occurred to him that he might be overly pragmatic to the point of eliminating pertinent facts. In order to see the whole picture he would have to entertain the spiritual side of events that had transpired in the distant and more recent past. Two things stood out in his mind. Two years ago he had cornered a drug runner named Eddie Slade in an aircraft hanger full of drums containing gasoline. The confrontation ended with Ryder emptying two full Mac-10 magazines into Eddie's chest without killing or even slowing the drug runner. In the process of shooting Eddie, Ryder's bullets had accidentally pierced the gas drums, setting the hanger on fire, which brought about Eddie's demise. Still weirder was that after Ryder had ran a safe distance from of the hanger to escape the flames he had looked back. What he had seen almost derailed his mind. Eddie had been slowly exiting the hanger completely on fire from head to toe. Ryder remembered that Eddie had walked toward him for a short distance and then stopped. As Eddie had burned he'd started to melt and become a blackened pool. Then the real mind bender happened. Out of the burning molten pool rose a frighteningly heinous being wearing a suit of black armor. It grew to a height of around twelve feet at which point it released an ear splitting forlorn scream and then disappeared. Ryder had tried to put it out of his mind and had managed to do it until recently. For obvious reasons he had never mentioned the experience to anyone. However, now he was forced to reexamine the issue. When he had shot Kansi two or three times back at Sidi Slimane only the have the terrorist get up and walk away ... well that presented too much of a coincidence. He could hardly bring his mind to think the unthinkable. However, if there were some sort of evil stocking him in the form of various people of questionable backgrounds, he must think of ways to counter the threat. At present the only one that came to mind was fire. It had killed Eddie Slade when nothing else would. If that were true why would only fire and not bullets be the Achilles heel for this evil? Could it be that was the reason evil was contained within the fires of hell? The possibilities were becoming too bizarre for Ryder to contemplate further. However, when he caught up with Kansi again the OMNI agent would keep fire in mind no matter how ridicules it seemed to his rational side.

No longer able to entertain these alien thoughts of the supernatural Ryder's mind turned to Lisa. He knew that he was digging himself into a hole with her. These latest developments had really put him in the doghouse but he was sure that once he saw her again he could straighten it all out.

The flight attendant brought another round and the blond spy began to fantasize the things he would do with Lisa once they were back together. The fantasizing turned to dreams and the next thing he knew someone was shaking him. He drowsily looked up and saw the flight attendant.

"Sir, please fasten your seatbelt. We are getting ready to land." she said then continued down the isle to rear of the plane. Ryder groped around until he found the belt and snapped it together. The pilot made a flawless landing and by the time passengers started disembarking Ryder was fully alert. After picking up his bags he went to the Hertz counter and rented a red two door Ford. He headed downtown and checked into the nearest Hilton. After getting cleaned up he thought about putting in a call to OMNI headquarters in Brussels and then decided against it. Instead he put a call through to the local New York City OMNI branch office. The phone rang twice then a woman picked up.

"OMNI, New York regional. May I help you sir," she asked?

"Ryder here, I want to speak with Agent Dante if he is available."

"I'm sorry sir, but the agent in question is currently in Europe. Commander "Alex Power is available. Would you like to speak with him?"

Damn, Ryder thought. *Alex is still on the job. I thought that he retired more than a year ago.* "Yes, put him on please."

There was a delay and then an aging male voice answered. "Commander Power speaking."

"Commander Power this is Lance Ryder. How are you sir?"

"Lance," the old commander exclaimed, "I'm fine, it's good to hear your voice. Where are you?" By his voice inflection it was obvious he was pleased to be hearing from the young investigator.

"I'm in New York, commander, working a case. Have you spoken with Dante recently?" Ryder asked.

"Yes I have and I believe that he is still somewhere in Europe bird-dogging an investigation dealing with a bomb threat." Power answered.

Becoming serious, Ryder asked, "Commander do you have a phone scrambler handy and if so, would you slip it on the phone?"

"Yeah, Lance I have one and I'm putting it on as we speak. Now what's on your mind?" the old agent asked.

Ryder fitted his security device over the phone and said, "Commander I'm not going to be very specific, but I'm doing the investigation and field work on that case. At this point I'm fairly certain that what ever the terrorists are up to, New York is not the target, which is what we were led to believe at the outset."

"Dante did tell me that He thought that New York was targeted for a nuke threat but didn't elaborate," Power said.

"Commander, I need some help. I believe an Arab named Amal Kansi is behind this threat or at least one of the major players. I also believe that he's in Yew York. I tracked him from Morocco, to Lisbon and now to New York. My problem is that the big apple is a big town and he could be anywhere. I want you to use OMNI communications resources to trace down all phone calls in the city's Arab community from seven days ago to the present. I want phone records on all Arab businesses, residence, charities, etc,. I want to know about all calls in and out of the state. I have a feeling that their operation extends from coast to coast," Ryder said.

"Lad, do you think that this group of Arab terrorists is going to set off more than one bomb?" Power asked.

"I'm not sure commander, but I believe that whatever it is, it's not confined to Yew York City. How soon do you think that you can have that data?" Ryder asked.

"Well I'd have to check with the communications and wiretap department but from past experiences I think that we could have that info by late this evening or early tomorrow. Probably couldn't get it any sooner because they have to coordinate with the local and long distance phone companies" Power replied.

"Good I'll call you later this evening. It's good to hear your voice again Commander Power."

"Same here, Lance. Good bye."

"I'll talk to you later Commander Power," the Omni spy said and then hung up.

Ryder smiled and thought about the day when Power had brought him into the organization. At the time Ryder had been a Major with ten years service in the Marine Corps. He had spent his first two years as a fighter pilot flying F-4 Phantoms off the deck of the USS Enterprise. His eyes had became less than 20-20 so the corps had transferred him into military intelligence. A little later he caught Power's attention because of a couple of tough cases he had solved, and subsequently Power had him transferred to

Hot Sand & Cold Blood

OMNI. He remained on the Marine Corps active duty roles the first three years while working for OMNI. However, because of chain-of- command problems the Marine Corps released him to work for OMNI full time.

Putting the thoughts behind him for the time being, he left the hotel and drove to the downtown tourist office. He entered the office and looked around to see if he could find state and interstate literature that might help him. He walked over to the maps and books section and scrounged around until he found maps of Texas and California that detailed places of interest. He studied the maps in depth but was drawing a blank.

A young woman employ stepped around from behind a counter and approached him. With a cheerful smile she said may I help you sir?"

Ryder looked up from the map he was eyeballing and said, "Well I'm not sure."

"And why would that be sir," she asked still maintaining her smile?

With a little exasperation in his voice he said, "Well, because I'm really not sure of what I'm looking for, myself."

"Excuse me," she said a little quizzically.

"Miss, I'm looking for maps or literature that contains things or places of interest that a state chamber of commerce might want to show off to attract tourists. I need this information primarily for Texas and California. I think that I'm looking for things that are man-made and big. Let's say something like the Golden gate Bridge. More to the point what I'm looking for would be something that if it were to suddenly disappear, grave economic or security issues would result."

She looked at him thoughtfully for a moment then said, "Sir that sounds like a strange request. Why do you want to know that?"

Ryder glanced at the young woman's apprehensive expression and grinned to put her at ease. "I can assure you," he said, "that there is nothing clandestine in my request. I'm employed by a state agency to compile data on worst-case scenarios on the possible destruction of national treasures by, lets say, acts of god. We want to know how this would affect the tourist trade."

"Oh," she remarked," as her face brightened. "Well let's see first we need to get you better maps. What you're looking at is for tourists. We have detailed atlases, state planning, and building guides and diagrams that details everything in every state even all the infrastructure." Her demeanor was starting to assume an air of authority as she added, "Come with me mister …"

"Johnson, my name is William Johnson," Ryder said, barely concealing a chuckle. He added, "And you are …?"

"Patricia Ellis," she answered. "Well, come with me Mister Johnson." she said as she led him through a door and into a well lighted office.

Ryder followed and watched as she commenced opening drawers and file cabinets, pulling out every imaginable kind of maps and diagrams.

"Now Mister Johnson –"

Ryder interupted, "Just call me William; Mister Johnson is bit too formal."

She smiled with just a hint of coyness as she replied, "OK, William. I have collected everything from California and Texas for you. See, now for instance in Santa Cruz there are a couple of fairly large oil storage facilities where tankers come in from Alaska."

Ryder looked at the detailed map of the facility and concluded that it serviced a local area and was small potatoes. Nothing there big enough to attract a terrorist group. They continued pouring over first the California information and then the Texas literature. Ryder studied the Galveston area oil storage complexes and thought that it may be a possibility. However that still left California out and according to everything that he'd found out to date, California was included as part of Kansi's grand plan. Finally he said, "Miss Ellis –"

"Oh, look who's being formal now, William. Call me Patricia," she said.

"Uh, alright, Patricia, I don't see anything here that strikes me as being in particularly vulnerable to a natural catastrophic event. However I haven't taken the time to look over everything. I know that I'm really going out on a limb here, but I'd like to borrow all this material overnight to give it further scrutiny. I promise to have it back no later than, oh, say four p.m. tomorrow."

She considered his request for a moment and then said, "Well I don't know, William, I can't let those valuable documents go out the door with just anybody ... at least not without some sort of a quid pro quo."

"Alright," Ryder said with a grin, "and what would the lady like in return?"

She returned his smile and said, "I think the least you could do is buy me dinner at a nice restaurant ... maybe like the, Lands Inn."

"Lands Inn, it is then. What time shall I pick you up?" he asked.

"I live at 740 west 53rd apt 320, Carlisle Arms apartments, say around sevenish" she replied.

"Sounds good to me," Ryder said as he gathered up the arms full of material.

Patricia helped and soon Ryder was on his way back to the hotel to do some micro document searching. He entered his room and threw the documents on the bed. He threw a couple of pillows up against the headboard, kicked off his shoes and stretched out. He began going over every heavily populated area in detail. He checked every oil storage location. California politicians and Ecological groups had become very environmentally aware and as a result, big oil refineries and storage facilities had for the most part been banned. He checked everything from amusement parks and multinational corporate headquarters to national monuments. In the final analysis he simply just couldn't find anything in his estimation that would warrant or attract a terrorist organization strongly enough to want to destroy it. Maybe the target really was New York.

At a quarter after six he put the documents aside and got ready to pick up Patricia. Leaving the hotel, he got into the Ford and checked his watch. It was twenty until seven; he would be a few minutes late but he was sure that she would let it slide. As he drove along his mind dwelled on Patricia for a few moments. She was an attractive woman with blonde hair and a petite body. And if it were not for Lisa he could almost imagine himself spending some serious time with her. With her use of body language she had certainly let him know that she was available. The thought made him smile as he recalled how she was a bit less than sophisticated with her overt overtures. He kept a check on the street numbers a short while later, rolled up in front of the Carlisle Arms. He eased the Ford into a tight spot between two parked cars and got out. Ryder ascended the steps and went through the large fancy front door. He found himself in a large lobby done up in Early American, with ultra high ceilings and a hallway leading straight back from the center of it. He walked across the lobby and down the hallway. He checked the numbering and saw that first apartment started with 100, which meant he was going to have to climb stairs or find an elevator. Walking a bit further he spotted elevator doors on the right. He stepped inside and punched 3rd floor. In no time he was ringing Patricia's doorbell.

The door opened and there she stood with a hundred dollar smile and dressed to make strong men grovel with desire. Stepping back to allow him entry, her smile turned to a mock frown as she lamented, "You're fifteen minutes late. We've barely met and already the man is taking me for granted."

Grinning at her antics, Ryder stepped into the apartment and said, "Pat, uh, may I call you Pat?"

"I was wondering when you would get around to that. Yes, call me, Pat; everybody does." she answered.

"Good, well I guess I owe you an apology. I became engrossed in the maps and forgot about the time?"

"I thought it might be something like that, but don't think twice about it. Would you like a drink before we go?"

He knew what a drink could lead to and replied, "If it's all the same to you, I don't care to drink on an empty stomach, maybe after dinner."

"Fine, I'll get my purse and we'll be on our way," she said.

As they got into traffic, she slid over next to Ryder and gave him directions to the Lands Inn. As they drove, Patricia did the usual picking of the imaginary lint from Ryder's coat, and other little things that women do to let the man know they're interested. The small talk rolled along at about the same pace as the car and soon they were cruising the Lands Inn's parking lot looking for a place to plant the Ford. Ryder found a spot, and then did the gentleman thing by opening her door.

They had a nice dinner with a couple of drinks after. Ryder could tell that Patricia was having a pleasant time, and he too, was relaxed and enjoying the ambiance. Ryder's mind was divided between the attractive woman he was with and wondering how much time he had left to stop Kansi from blowing up the world, or at least part of the United States. His preoccupied thinking about Kansi must have affected his behavior because Patricia said, "William are you OK? You've gotten quiet and hardly spoken a word in ten minutes or so."

"Oh, I'm sorry," he said, "I guess that I'm kind of a workaholic and I'm afraid that I've just become a little sidetracked. It was rude and I won't do it again."

"That's alright," she said cheerily, "sometimes it happens to me."

Ryder made a point to keep his mind off of Kansi for the remainder of the evening. The balance of the date went smoothly and somewhere around one-thirty a.m. Ryder found himself pointing the nose of the Ford into the Carlisle Arms parking lot with Patricia's head resting on his shoulder. He slid the car into a space and turned off the engine.

"William, I had the most wonderful evening," she mused. "How about you, did you enjoy yourself?"

"Yes, Pat I had a great time and the food was delicious"

Ryder realized that he had come to a time when it was fish or cut bait. He regretted entering into the dinner date arrangement because somewhere in the back of his mind he had known it would reach this point; it always did in these situations. He wondered where Lisa was and what she was doing? Sure she was angry with him but she would get over it; women always did. Now he was painted into a corner because of this dinner date with Patricia in exchange for use of the maps. He knew that the next thing on the agenda would be her inviting him to spend the night. He didn't want to hurt her feelings by not excepting and on the other hand he didn't want the guilt he'd feel if he did accept. The answer was clear, he'd just tell her that he had enjoyed her company but there was someone else in his life. Yeah, she'd feel disappointed for a day, but with her looks it would be only a day.

She looked into his eyes and said William would you like to come up for a nightcap?"

"I have an early day tomorrow so maybe I should just walk you to your apartment," he said while opening his door. He went around, opened her door and they entered the building. She keyed open her apartment and stepped inside and Ryder followed her in. She turned to face him and he extended his hand to shake with her as he said, "Thank you Pat, I had a great time."

"I did too William," she said, "but a handshake between a man and a woman seems so formal especially after they've been to dinner together. At least let me give you a little kiss on the cheek before you go." As she spoke she brought her arms up and put them around his neck while at the same time raised up on tiptoes and kissed him full on the mouth, slipping her tongue in between his lips as she did.

Ryder's hormones leaped into hyper drive and he knew that he was not going to be able to walk away. He raised his foot and gently tapped the door closed then reached around behind her and unzipped her skirt. He let it fall to the floor and then dropped to his knees and slipped his thumbs into the waistband of her panties and slid them down to her ankles.

She lifted one foot out of them and spread her legs while placing her hands on his shoulders.

Ryder buried his face in her crouch as his tongue explored her vagina. Ten minutes went by before he could even think of moving to phase-two foreplay. Finally he came to his feet and between kisses they quickly got undressed. He picked her up and carried her into the bedroom and dropped her onto the queen sized four-poster bed. She rose up and leaned forward taking his penis into her hand and then into her mouth. At some point he pushed her back onto the sheets and slid in between her legs. Tomorrow he would feel guilty as hell, but that was tomorrow.

Chapter 21

Kansi pulled into the rental car drop off area in front of the terminal and checked in his Ford. Entering the airport he went into the lounge and ordered a Budweiser; he had broadened his taste in liquor. With an hour to kill before his flight left he figured this was as good of a way as any. Kansi tipped the bottle up and let the cold intoxicating liquid run down the back of his throat. He decided that he must put together a plan for hijacking the transmitters. New York gun laws were tough and trying to get a firearm on an airplane, even here in the United States where security was lax was risky. No, he decided he would wait until he arrived in New Mexico to purchase the rifle and scope and then coordinate some plan with Mousawi. He empted his beer and motioned to the bartender to set up another. He contemplated one scenario after another for setting up a kill on Ted Green, but ultimately decided that he could firm up nothing until he saw the lay of the land. The beer was starting to blur his thinking as he checked his watch. It was close to boarding time and this was one flight he didn't want to miss. He left the lounge, headed toward gate seven and entered the passenger waiting area just as the PA system announced American Airlines flight 105 to Albuquerque. *Allah be praised,* he thought, *my timing is perfect.* He got into line and boarded the AA727 and noticed that the flight was about half booked. He took his seat and for the time being, gave no more thought to his business in New Mexico. He'd never been in New Mexico but he had heard that it was dry and sort of a desert much like his native country. *Good,* he thought, *I will feel right at home.* Except for a little turbulence the flight was uneventful and they arrived in Albuquerque at two-fifteen p.m. to a clear sky. He stepped off the plane and found Mousawi happily waiting for him. He waved and shouted, "Mousawi my brother how is life with you?"

Mousawi looked across, spotted Kansi and answered, "Allah has been good to me and how are you my friend?"

"Also good," Kansi replied as they came together. They hugged and kissed each other on the cheeks and then went to pick to baggage claim to pick up Kansi's luggage. "Mousawi have you any news on the transmitters," Kansi asked?

"Abdul called me last night and told me that you said to go ahead and set up a meeting to buy the equipment. I called the technician Ted Green but got no answer. I was going to call again this afternoon."

"It is good that you have not contacted him as yet. We must first get prepared. Lets find a gun shop and purchase a weapon."

"I know of a gun shop on the southwest side of town that stocks many guns. That is where I bought my .44 Smith and Wesson." Mousawi said with a confident smile.

"Good," Kansi said, "lets go there now."

"I must warn you, Kansi, there is a three day waiting period."

"What!" Kansi exclaimed. "Three days is going to hamper our schedule. Do you know of a private owner who might sell one today?"

"I know of no one, Kansi. I think that we should go to the store right away and pay for the gun and wait the three days. That is not such a long time."

"Perhaps you are right, Mousawi, but I do not like it." Kansi said as they left the airport terminal and started across the street. Walking down a narrow entrance between two rows of parked cars Mousawi pointed and said, "There you see the black Chevy suburban, that's our car."

Kansi looked the vehicle over as he approached and then tossed his things on the back seat. The two terrorists got into the front and Mousawi cranked the Chevy and drove away. The gun store that Mousawi had referred to was a twenty-minute drive. They entered the store and Kansi immediately spotted a rack of deer rifles on the back wall. He went to the rear with Mousawi in tow. Kansi walked down the row of rifles carefully inspecting each as he walked by. He spotted a .306 Remington with a scope already mounted. He pulled it off of the rack and slammed the bolt back to check the action. He closed the bolt, then shouldered the weapon and looked through the scope. Finally he said, "Yes, Mousawi, my brother, this will do Allah's work."

"Yes," Mousawi said, "and what is even better, we will use the American pig's own weapon the bring about his demise." Both men displayed smug expressions at Mousawi's remark as they walked over to the cashier's counter to purchase the gun.

A young woman clerk stepped up to the register with a smile and said, "How may I help you gentlemen?"

Kansi replied, "I would like to buy this fine bolt action hunting rifle and a fifty round box of .306 one hundred and twenty grain copper jacketed ammunition."

The clerk said, "Sir, I can sell you the bullets today but I'm afraid that you will have to wait for a three day background check on the rifle. That is federal law."

"OK, OK," Kansi, said, barely able to conceal his impatience's. "How much for everything?"

"Sir, you can pay when you pick up the gun. First I will need to see your driver's license or official I.D."

Kansi fished around in his back pocket until he produced a wallet. As he removed the license and handed it to her he said, "It's from New York, I hope that's alright."

"That's fine," she answered, "as long as it's valid." She took the license, filled out the forms then looked up and said, "Sir, that will four hundred and sixty dollars including tax."

Kansi handed her the money then collected his change and receipt. Not missing the fact that she was an attractive woman he eyed her with a casual smile he said, "Thank you Miss." At this point, Ogar rumbled, letting Kansi know that this woman would make an excellent sacrifice.

"Thank you, Sir, and come again." she replied.

"I shall make a point of doing just that," he said. Turning to Mousawi, he added, "Let's be on our way my friend." They left the store and headed to Mousawi's apartment to solidify a plan for getting the transmitter from Ted Green. They arrived at Mousawi's dingy little two-bedroom apartment and wasting no time, Kansi pulled a stack of documents from his briefcase and tossed them on the table. "Mousawi," he said, "when you left Cairo you were given only the preliminary information and instructions for Allah's great work. What you see here are the complete plans and blueprints for the destruction of the United States. But first we must put those aside and concentrate on a small piece of the puzzle that has become a thorn in our side; and that is Green. First I want to know where this White Sands Missile Range is located and where Green lives. Also how is the area; is it well populated like Albuquerque, or is there a small number of people with a lot of open land like the Middle East?"

Mousawi considered the questions for a moment and then said, "There is a city called Las Cruces that is smaller than Albuquerque and it's a little over two hundred miles south of here; that is where Ted Green lives. White Sands Missile Range is twenty-five miles due east of there. There is a mountain range between Las Cruces and White Sands, and at the top of this mountain is a tiny town called Organ. I thought maybe we could meet him there for the exchange."

"No, no towns!" Kansi exclaimed. How about the road from Las Cruces to this White Sands, is there any open land?"

Mousawi once again considered Kansi's words then finally said, "Yes there is a place and I think that it would be perfect because it is back off of the main road. Between Organ and White Sands there is a picnic area called Aguirre Springs. The place is hardly used this time of year. It's about a mile off the highway and you can only get there by a small dirt road. It would be perfect because it's about half way up the mountain. We could get there early giving you time to get into position and hide in one of the large crevasses a little above the picnic area. It would provide you with an excellent view of the entire area."

Kansi pondered this and replied, "Do you think that this Ted Green would be afraid of meeting us at such a deserted place?"

"White Sands can be seen from this location. I think that would give him a sense of security, besides I don't think that he would even consider such a venture if he were a coward. As yet we have not discussed a meeting place for the exchange, so I will call and ask him."

"If we are that close to White Sands do you not think that people will hear the rifle shot when I kill him?"

"Kansi," Mousawi said, "this is the West, and people shoot guns here all the time especially during Oryx hunting season.

"Ok, so what are the routes for getting there," Kansi asked?

"We take a freeway called Interstate 25 south to Las Cruces and then turn east onto a four lane state road called 70." Mousawi said.

"We have three days to plan, so I think that we should go to Aguirre Springs and decide exactly what it looks like and where I will sit in wait." Kansi stated in a matter of fact way.

Mousawi's face brightened as he said, "An excellent idea, Kansi. Then you like my plan, yes?"

"It sounds good so far, Mousawi. I will have to make further decisions when we get there. On the other hand I might see something on the way there that looks better. Are you hungry?"

"A little," Mousawi replied, "but this American food is not fit to feed a desert scavenger. I wish for even one bowl of, Kus-Kus made with camel and lamb."

With a knowing smile Kansi said, "Come, Mousawi, let us dine on this raunchy American Cuisine; it is a small price to pay for Allah's work."

They left the apartment and went to a local Mexican restaurant and had a meal of tacos, frijoles, flautas, tamales and rice. After washing it all down with a couple of Tacate

Hot Sand & Cold Blood

beers, Kansi paid the check and the two terrorists headed for Aguirre Springs.

As Mousawi took the off ramp to highway 70, Kansi glanced sideways at him and said, "Because of the three day wait for the gun you must call Green and tell him that we are having trouble getting the money and that we will arrange the meeting for Monday. That is four days from now. Try to make it in the evening just as the sun is going down that way it will give us a little more cover."

"An excellent idea, my friend," Mousawi said.

They drove for a time in silence with Kansi carefully scrutinizing the countryside. As they started the climb toward Organ Kansi asked, "How much further?"

Mousawi replied, "We are almost to Organ and the springs is four miles beyond that." The Chevy labored up the side of the mountain and through the little community of Organ. Reaching the apex of the peak the vehicle started it's decent down the other side. Approaching a sign on the right that read, 'Aguirre Springs picnic area one mile', with an arrow pointing south, Kansi made a right turn onto the dirt road and proceeded up a narrow winding path. Presently the narrow side road leveled out and the came to wide flat area with picnic tables and fire circles made of rock. Mousawi stopped the vehicle and they got out and looked around. Mousawi pointed farther up the mountain and said, "The road ends here but the mountain continues sharply up. There is where you will be, behind one of those boulders."

"It looks good to me Mousawi," Kansi said, "This is where we will do it. Then we will put his body back in his car and push it into that ravine to the left over there."

"Arroyo," Mousawi corrected.

"What did you say," Kansi asked?

"Arroyo, "Mousawi repeated. "Out here in New Mexico, they call the crevices Arroyos."

"I won't quibble. If there is nothing more to see then let's get back to Albuquerque and you can make your phone call to Green and set this thing up." On the drive back to Albuquerque the two exchange little conversation except how the operation would be executed. Mousawi keyed open his apartment and entered, followed by his fellow conspirator. He picked up the phone and dialed Green's number. As he sat down at the kitchen table he said, "Uh, hello ... yes, is this Ted Green? Mousawi here... yes of course, but I was not expecting to pay quite that much for the items. It will take about three days to have the money sent ...you know the Aguirre Springs picnic grounds ... OK, why don't we meet there on Monday at around six p.m. for the exchange? ... Yes, I understand ...but it is perfect, no one will see the exchange so there will be no witness to see us together ... right, I knew you would see the benefit of this plan ... Yes I will have all of the money. OK, Monday then. Good-bye." Mousawi hung up the phone and smiled at Kansi.

Impatient for the verdict, Kansi spat out, "Well just don't stand there looking like a castrated camel, what did the man say?"

"Everything is set and he will do it just like we asked." Mousawi replied maintaining his wide grin."

"Allah be praised," Kansi chortled. The pair settled in to impatiently wait the three days

---

Mousawi followed Kansi into the gun shop and went straight to the gun counter.

A young man was stooped down, stacking boxes of ammunition in the glass display case next to the cash register. He stood when he saw the two men walk up and then he said, "May I help you?"

Kansi said, "Yes, I paid for a gun three days ago and I've come to pick it up."

"The name sir," the clerk politely asked?

"Kansi, Amal Kansi. It's a .306 hunting rifle."

The clerk looked through a stack of paper, pulled one out the stack and said, "Ah, here it is, and you are right. The receipt says it's been paid." The clerk reached back and lifted the rifle off the rack and then handed it and the sheet of paper to Kansi. "There you go sir, have a good hunting season."

The two left the gun store and went back to Mousawi's apartment where Kansi spent the remainder of the day looking and handling the rifle. The following day around two p.m. Kansi said, "I think that we had better go now to make sure that we have time to set everything up and be in place when Green arrives at the springs."

They arrived a little after four-thirty, which gave them over an hour for Kansi to find the most advantage spot up in the rocks. They got out of the Chevy and looked the place over. Satisfied that there was no one in the area, Kansi took the rifle from the back seat and slid the bolt back. He punched five bullets into the gun and chambered a round. He flipped the safety on and said, "Lets go up the hill and find a spot. They climbed until they were approximately fifty or sixty feet above the picnic area then turned and looked down. Kansi smiled because he could see all the way back to the main road. He could also see the entire vicinity below with an excellent view of the picnic tables. Looking around his immediate surroundings he spotted a tight group of small boulders that would preclude him from being seen from below. He walked over behind them and laid his rifle in a small crevice that formed a V in the formation. Once again he checked the view and found it to be excellent. This is the location from where he would shoot Green. Kansi put his hand on Mousawi's shoulder and said, "Go on back down and wait at the tables. I will watch closely though the scope and make sure that I see the transmitters before I shoot him."

"Right my brother," Mousawi replied as he started back down.

Before long Mousawi was sitting at one of the tables with his briefcase next to him. Now there was nothing to do but wait. Kansi kept a sharp vigil for the next hour and finally he saw a white four door BMW pull onto the dirt road. He hoped that it was Green. The car pulled up next to the picnic table and stopped. A tall thin man with sandy hair got out and appeared to engage in conversation with Mousawi. A short time later the man walked to the back of his car, opened the trunk and removed a fairly large box. He walked back around the car and set the box on the table near Mousawi. Kansi watched through the scope as the guy opened the box and produced some gadgets with antennas attached. Mousawi took one of the items and looked it over, then put it back in the box. At this point Kansi thumbed the safety off and trained the cross hairs on the tall man's forehead. When Mousawi leaned over to get the briefcase, Kansi squeezed the trigger and fire spat from the rifle's muzzle. Instantly the man's head exploded with blood, brains, and hair being blown backwards onto the BMW's grill and fender. He slumped back onto the car and slid to the ground. He twitched a couple of times and then lay still. Kansi stood and made his way back down to the picnic area. By the time he got there, Mousawi had already put the man back in his BMW and placed the transmitters on the back seat of the Chevy. Mousawi looked at Kansi with new respect and said, "I'm going to drive his car to the edge of the arroyo over there and then we can push it over."

"Good," Kansi said, and followed as Mousawi slowly eased the BMW forward. He stopped at the edge and got out. Both men put their shoulders to the car and shoved it over the side. It dropped about thirty feet and landed on it's top. Kansi hoped that it would not burst into flame and it didn't. They turned and headed back toward the Chevy. They were almost to the vehicle when a Dodge station wagon pulled up with a man, woman, and two children inside. The guy stopped the wagon and got out. He looked at Mousawi with a friendly grin and asked, "Are you guys up here hunting?"

Kansi continued to the Chevy and without hesitation opened the door and removed the rifle. He shot the man in the chest and then walked over to the wagon and shot the two screaming children through the back window. At this point the woman was almost in shock. He opened the door on her side and looked her over. She was Hispanic, and he guessed her to be around twenty-six. She was also pretty and petite. Wasting no time he reached down and with felt swoop, ripped her blouse off.

Mousawi, who had been watching, now spoke up. "Kansi, what are you doing? We don't have time forth is kind of thing."

"Shut up Mousawi. If you want some you can have her after I'm done." By this time Kansi had her skirt and panties off, and Ogar wanted his do.

The woman cried and whimpered as Kansi shoved her down on the seat and then screamed as he roughly entered her. With her pleading and crying, the rape continued until Kansi had climaxed four or maybe five times in quick succession, Meanwhile she had passed out. He would like to have had her someplace in private where time would have allowed Ogar to suck out her soul. However, this quick satisfaction would have to suffice. He got out of the car while zipping up his fly and asked, "Well Mousawi, if you want her be quick because we shortly must send them to meet Mr. Green."

Mousawi had been watching and was now aroused. He unbuttoned his pants as he got into the wagon. Quickly he fell on top of the woman and quickly began his part of the rape.

She became conscious and Kansi could hear her begging as Mousawi ruthlessly raped her. Finally Mousawi crawled out of the vehicle and then Kansi shot the woman point blank between the eyes. The two terrorists shoved the wagon into the ravine and watched as it bounced once off the Arroyo wall and hit the BMW. Leaving the carnage behind, Mousawi made a U-turn and drove away in a cloud of dust. As he maneuvered the vehicle along the dirt road he cleared his dry throat and quipped, "Kansi if we stay, we could open our own scrap metal yard."

"Quiet with the meaningless chatter and let me think," Kansi growled.

Mousawi said nothing more until they reach Las Cruces and took the onramp to Interstate 25. "Kansi," he said, "We have only a limited time before they are found."

"Mousawi, it does not matter. We do not live here so there is no connection to us. Besides, by the time they are found and the police start an investigation the Americans will have more to worry about than four or five dead bodies. Now to more urgent business, how many of our brothers still do not have transmitters and where are they located?"

Screwing up his face in concentration Mousawi said, "Lets see, there is Raheem in Odessa and –"

"Never mind. Mousawi. When we get back to Albuquerque I'm taking the next plane to San Francisco. I want you to box up the transmitters individually and Fed-Ex them overnight to the brothers who need them. They should receive them about the time I get to Frisco. Meanwhile, after you get them shipped, catch a flight to Dumas and check in with Souhadee. I want you to work with him. Mohammad Ramneshee in San Francisco has the phone numbers of all the brothers and we will start and coordinate the big bang from there."

Mousawi asked, "Why does it start from San Francisco, why not from Texas?"

Kansi looked at him for a moment then said, "The reason we do it this way is because the damage will be greater going from the destination to the origin."

Looking puzzled, Mousawi persisted, "But why is that. Does it have something to do with –"?

Exasperated, Kansi said, "Never mind my brother. It will enhance nothing for you to know and I just don't want to take the time to explain it."

Mousawi turned on the headlights as they sped along into the night.

The following morning at nine a.m. sharp Kansi was at the El Paso, Texas airport standing in line at gate five waiting to board a San Francisco bound South West Airlines flight. As his flight cleared the runway at nine-twenty, he leaned back in his seat and thought; *Allah's revenge will come soon.*

Chapter 22

Ryder awakened early to something buzzing around in his mind. He looked at Patricia's naked form draped across the bed and decided that she had a great body, almost as beautiful as Lisa. The buzzing in his mind grew louder and then exploded with pure unadulterated clarity. The pictures and words swirled around in his mind like a kaleidoscope and why had he not seen it before. The bloody papers he had found in Kansi's office back at Sidi Slimane and the fragmented words on them. Yes, trying to put the words in order he remembered they were: states, gas Western, and what was the other one, oh yeah company. He'd thought that the reference to 'company' was the CIA. How could he have been so wrong? He had seen the answer clearly on the maps that Patricia had lent him yesterday and overlooked it. In the correct order the words were: Western States Gas Company. It was a giant corporation that ran two, four foot diameter, high pressure natural gas lines from Dumas, Texas through Arizona, New Mexico and all the way to San Francisco. The company incorporates a series of pumping stations at intervals of every hundred miles to keep the natural gas flowing. *The terrorists are going to blow up the pumping stations* he thought. Ryder first let the concept sink in and then started to methodically think about how they could and would do it. After a moment he muttered, "Yes, that's where the 164.5 comes in. It's a transmitter frequency with a delay that they will use to sequentially set off conventional explosives at each pumping station one after another which would rule out just a couple of plants. The Arabs planned to take out the whole system. *Damn,* Ryder thought, *if the whole gas system goes it can't be rebuilt. That would mean no gas for households, no gas for factories, or gas fired power plants, etc,*

Hell, it would domino and put the west coast into chaos then spread across the country. The United States industrial complex is so interdependent that this could cause a national economic collapse and maybe even anarchy. As Ryder was getting dressed, Patricia awoke and mumbled, " Lance did you say something?" She rolled over and saw him putting on his pants and added, "So what do you do lance, love'um and leave'um?"

"Patricia I'm sorry but I've got a national security issue going on here." he said.

"Well I've heard a few, 'morning after, get out of the house excuses', but that is new. Are you going to be back or is this adios?"

He looked at her and said, "This is not adios, get up and get dressed. We are going to my hotel."

She smiled and replied, "Oh, so you're one of those guys that like to do it in a variety of places. Well I'm up for that and I hope that you are too." As she spoke she got out of bed and made her way to the shower.

Twenty minutes later they were headed downtown to the Hilton. Upon their arrival Ryder took her straight to his room.

"Yes, I'm going to love this," she said with a big grin.

Ryder keyed open the door and they stepped inside.

"Damn Lance," she said, "this place is a mess. All those maps and things that I lent you are scattered all over the table and bed. We're going to have to get all those things off of the bed before we can –"

"Patricia, not now. We have other things to do. I want to show you something and then for awhile we are going to concentrate on just that."

Her grin widened as she replied, "But Lance, you showed it to me last night and I think that it's wonderful. Drop your pants and –"

"Would you get serious for a minute," he said. "I need your help."

Her smile faded and finally she said, "OK big guy, get the map or whatever and show me what's got you so excited."

Ryder fumbled around with the documents for a minute or two and then exclaimed, "Here, look at this map." Shoving everything to one side, he laid the map out flat on the table and ran his finger along, tracing over a four state route.

Patricia looked at the map and said, "You're looking at the Western States feeder route. So what is so important about the gas company?"

"Well I was thinking that it could be vulnerable to say, oh, I don't know, maybe a lightning strike. That would be economically problematic for the state, right," he asked?

Somewhat quizzically she replied, "Well, yeah, I guess so. But I don't see the big deal. If one of the stations got lighting struck they would repair the damage and keep pumping, although they would probably loose quite a bit of gas to the resulting fire."

"This map shows the complete system but it shows very little detail. Do you have individual state maps for, Texas, New Mexico, Arizona, and California at you office showing the gas pipe route in more detail?" He asked.

"Yes," she said, "I suppose so but why do you –"

"Take my car keys," he said, reaching into his pocket, "and go get the bigger maps."

"Lance I don't even hardly know you and I'm already starting to think that you're some kind of a nut. OK, I'll do it but you are buying breakfast when we get done here." She took the keys, kissed him, and added. "I don't think you deserve a kiss but I'm feeling charitable." She slapped him lightly on the cheek and left the room.

Watching from the balcony, Ryder waited into she drove off in the rental, and then he stepped back into the room, picked up the phone and dialed OMNI.

The receptionist pick up on the third ring, "OMNI, may I direct your call?"

"Is Commander Power in," he asked?

"Yes he is. Whom shall I say is calling?"

"Agent Lance Ryder."

"Stand by one minute, Agent Ryder, and I'll put you through."

Ryder listened to the elevator music being piped over the phone as he waited and couldn't believe that a security agency like OMNI would set up their phone system in such a fashion. *It's almost comical,* he thought. The music stopped and a familiar voice said, "Commander Power, here."

"Alex," Ryder said, "have you found out anything on the wiretaps?"

"Oh, Lance, my boy, I thought that was your voice. Yes we have. I had to contact the local chief of police, a guy by the name of, Hal Hampshire and let him know what we needed. We also had to get a judge to sign a court order for the wiretaps. Back in the old days we wouldn't have to –"

"Sorry to interrupt sir, but I have a time crunch. Can you just tell me about the calls?" Ryder asked.

"Oh, of course. Lately there does seem to be more telephone traffic in the New York Arab community. We intercepted interstate calls between here and San Francisco and also some cities in Texas, Dumas I believe. There have also been quite a few calls to Blythe, Santa Barbara, Indio, and the list goes on. There seems to be a pattern of calls between, New York, Texas, New Mexico, Arizona, and California. We have analysts working as we speak trying to determine if it means anything."

"It does mean something, Alex. The terrorists are not going to explode a hydrogen bomb in New York or anywhere else like we first thought. That was just a red herring. Their plan is to destroy the Western States Gas Company by placing composition-4 Symtex high-explosive charges in each pumping plant between Dumas and San Francisco and using radio transmitters tuned to 164.5 frequency to detonate them sequentially. My guess would be at twenty or thirty-minute intervals to allow gas build up at each plant. They also probably plan to coordinate the action with a phone call the day or maybe even the hour before; so we need to stay on top of the wiretaps. Looking at the physics involved makes me think that they plan to start with the plant in San Francisco."

"Why do you say that, Lance. Why start in Frisco, why not Texas?"

"Because if they start at the point of origin in Texas, as soon as the Dumas plant blew, the breached pipes would drop the pressure thus depriving the rest of the plants fuel for an explosion sufficient to destroy them. In other words they plan to use our own natural gas to insure a big enough bang to take out the complete network of gas lines."

"My God, Lance, that makes perfect sense, but how did you figure that out?"

Ryder explained how he and Baronga had the shoot out at Sidi Slimane with the terrorists and he later found the papers that Kansi had left behind.

"That certainly explains our current situation," the old investigator commented. "However, now I think that we should contact the OMNI office in Los Angeles and have them round these guys up. Hell the wiretap guys got us a bunch of names. Some of the people mentioned in phone conversations besides Kansi were Abdul, Raheem –"

"Commander Power, it would do no good to arrest these people because we have nothing on them. The justice system would simply turn them loose and they would be free to bide their time and blow the gas lines at a later date."

"You're right Lance. I just wasn't thinking. What we need to do is start running surveillance on each of the pumping plants plus talk to the plant superintendents and find out if there are new hires and who they are."

"That's possible Commander Power," Ryder said, "but I believe that because of the sensitive nature of the gas company they would run background checks on new hires for citizenship and so forth."

"But, Lance if the terrorists are going to set charges that means they will have to come up with a way to gain access to the pumps, engines and pipes."

"Yes they will, and I believe that they will have to do it by getting peripheral employment that does not require a background check. A job that would give them periodic access to the plant on a short term basis."

"Like what, Lance?" the old commander asked.

"Like a Coke truck driver or candy vendor. You know someone who would fill up the soft drink and candy machines. They would case the plant on their first few deliveries and decide where they'd want to set the charges to do the most damage."

"Good," Power said. "We'll just send our guys out to inspect the plants for explosives."

"I hate to pop you bubble Commander Power, but I don't think they would find any explosives."

"And why is that, Lance?" Power asked.

"For just the reason that we're discussing. If the stuff is planted and left for an extended period there is a chance it will be found by either the plant workers or by law enforcement in the event their plot was discovered."

"So what do you suggest?" the old man asked.

"I suggest we go with your idea Commander Power." Ryder said to give the aging OMNI agent the feeling he was contributing.

"Uh ... yes, and ah, what was that again?" the old man asked.

"Why, run surveillance on the plants. Another thing Commander Power, when you call the L.A. OMNI office to request surveillance, ask to speak with the electronic whizzes there and tell them to build me an electronic frequency spectrum analyzer with frequency scrambler capability for a range of at least a half of a mile." Ryder recalled the business with the burning of Eddie Slade and added, "By the way, tell them that I need a flare pistol."

"Did you say flare pistol, Lance?" Power asked, not sure that he'd heard correctly.

"Yeah, the kind they have on ships and planes to send distress signals." Ryder replied.

"Will there be anything else Agent Ryder?" the commander asked.

"Well, you might tell the field chief that I'll be there to confer with him as soon as I can get a flight out to LAX."

"Sorry Lance, I dropped my pipe...Now what were you were saying?"

"Tell the OMNI bureau chief in L.A. to meet me at Los Angeles International. I'll try and be on the next flight. Also tell him to have the equipment ready when I get there because I'm only going to be in L.A. long enough to pick it up. I'll also have a quick coordination briefing with him and then I'll be catching a flight to San Francisco. By the way, what is the OMNI station chief's name in Los Angeles?"

"It's a man by the name of Jim Toby." Power replied.

"Thanks. It's been good talking with you again Commander Power. Good bye."

"Good bye to you, Lance, and get those bastards."

Ryder heard the receiver click on the other end and then he hung up. It was somewhat ironic he thought. Eddie Slade had met with a fiery end and now Ryder was faced with another adversary in which the two could come together in a similar volatile environment. The thought of packing a flare gun along with his P-89 seemed ludicrous, *still*, he thought, *one just never knows.* He looked back at the mess of maps and decided to try and glean a little more information from them. After scrutinizing them for another ten minutes it was obvious the map was of no further use. Another fifteen minutes went by and Patricia walked in with a smug happy face and a couple of more maps. Ryder quickly took the maps and began pouring over them. However after a couple of minutes he could see that they just provided more and bigger pictures but no useful information. He began gathering up all the maps and stacking them neatly on the table as he said, "The quicker we get the documents off of the bed the quicker we can use it."

Patricia didn't have to be told twice and pitched in to help. Just as she tossed the last map on the table, Ryder grabbed her from behind and swept her from the floor. She squealed with delight as he carried her across room and dropped her onto the bed. He fell next to her and began kissing her face, licking her neck, howling like a wolf and generally acting like an idiot. She laughed as she looked at his ridiculous expressions and said, "What in hell has gotten into you, you crazy man."

"To be more accurate," Ryder howled, "it's not what is getting into me but what is getting into you."

Still giggling she asked. "And what might that be you silly boy?"

Between licks he managed, "Me, I'm going to get into you."

She shrieked with laughter and said between labored breaths, "Damn it Lance, quit running you tongue around my belly button it's ticking the hell out of me and I can't stand it ... Ok that's Ok, you want to ... slide my skirt and panties down. Just have your way with me, you brute. You're bigger than I and I won't try and stop you. Lance, Lance ... you're not licking my belly button anymore. Lance ... you're licking my ... Oh, god you're licking my, oh my, yes, yes just keep licking right there!"

Patricia stood next to the bathroom sink, smiling into the mirror while she combed her hair. She dropped the comb back in her purse, dug out her lipstick and said, "Lance," and received no reply. She waited a moment then repeated in a louder voice, "Lance, I know you can hear me out there."

After another minute he appeared at the door with a knowing little grin and said, "And what else can I do for madam?"

She leaned over and pinched him on the arm and said, "Just what do you mean by that crack buddy. It's more like what I did for you." She pinched a little harder as she added, "I made your day didn't I mister Lance Ryder?"

With a mock wince of pain he replied, "Yes, yes you did Miss Patricia, now please don't hurt me anymore."

She let go of his arm and quicker than a fox slipped her arms around his neck and slid her tongue into his waiting mouth. Coming up for air he said, "Finish getting ready we have to go." Leaving her to her lipstick, he turned and walked back to the living area to wait for her.

Ten minutes later she joined him and asked, "Do I look presentable enough to be seen in public?"

"You look stunning," he replied.

Still fishing for compliments as a coy grin crept across her lips she said, "Well I'm surprised after the way you mauled me you sex maniac."

"Hey, look who's calling who a sex maniac." he rebutted with mock chagrin.

Demurely she replied, "I am not a sex maniac. I just simply have a normal, healthy sex drive."

He said, "That you have Patricia," as he slapped her lightly on her bottom and added, "Are you ready to go?"

Suddenly serious she asked, "Lance what were you doing while I was in the bathroom?"

"I was calling Kennedy International," he said.

"And," she asked?

"And I'm taking a plane to LAX," he replied a little sheepishly.

"And why didn't you tell me before?"

"Because I didn't know that I was going until ten minutes before you brought the second set of maps through the door. I didn't want to ruin our time together so I just put it off until now." Two things were going on in his brain, he was feeling pressured, and he was feeling like a dog. Both for what he had done to Lisa and now for what he was doing to Patricia, but wasn't keeping America safe his first priority? *If that's not rationalizing, I don't know what is,* he thought. "Pat there is some things that I have to do and –"

Quietly she said, "Stop, Lance. First, we hardly know each other and you didn't promise to marry me before we went bed together. We had a good time and we owe each other nothing so let's be adults about this. You have a life and I have a life. If you get back this way, look me up. Now let's get these maps back to the travel center before the boss finds out I took them."

They went about the business of gathering up the maps and packing his clothes. Before leaving he looked place over, locked the door and dropped the key off at the front desk as they left the Hotel.

The trip to the tourist center was completed with the usual small talk. After they had gotten everything back in it's place and the Center's outer door locked, she said, "Lance do you mind if see you off at the airport?"

Her request made him feel even worse. He had used her maps, took her to bed on a one night stand and not only was she not angry, she was even willing to see him off at the airport. Patricia was truly a remarkable woman. Almost at a loss for words he mumbled, "That would be –"

"Speak up Lance. I didn't understand what you said."

A little louder he repeated, "That would be great, but only if you will let me buy you lunch at the airport cafeteria."

"Good, I can use some lunch. Then it's settled."

"Airport food usually isn't this good," Patricia said between bites of her chef salad, "and the atmosphere is good. You can see the airplanes and all sorts of activity through all these big windows." Looking at her watch she asked, "What time does your flight leave?"

Ryder double check his boarding pass and answered, "Four-fifteen p.m. that's about a half hour from now."

They finished their lunch and headed for gate 21. Ryder noticed quite a few people milling around and figured it would be a full flight. They talked and laughed about a couple of funny things that had happened while they were making love, calling it 'the interlude at the love motel'. Finally the PA system announced the departure of his flight. They embraced, kissed deeply and said good-bye as he started the long walk up the ramp that ended with him taking window seat, 18a behind the wing. Ryder peered through the plexiglass window and spotted Patricia standing near the gate area window looking back at him. The tow tractor pushed the big 727 back away from the loading ramp and as the aircraft turned, he lost sight of her. He sat back in his seat and decided that Pat was indeed a good woman. The pilot fired the three General Electric J-57 engines and taxied out to the runway. After getting a tower clearance the captain applied full power, released the brakes and the plane thundered down the runway. At the eight thousand foot marker he pulled back on the wheel and the nose came up. After clearing approach, the pilot banked the plane to the west and continued to climb.

Chapter 23

The light came on and Ryder fastened his belt. He looked out and saw the sprawling city of Los Angeles below. The flight attendant stopped by his seat and said. "Sir we're in a holding pattern that will delay our flight about twenty minutes."

"Thank you he replied." The plane made several circles and finally lined up on final and made a smooth landing. Ryder kept a sharp vigil as he entered the general population area. He spotted a guy wearing a tweed suit, blue tie, and dark glasses standing with his back to the wall. Ryder wished he'd asked Powers for a description of Toby, but taking a chance he walked up to the man and asked, "Are you Jim Toby?"

"And you must be Ryder?"

"Did your people manage to get the equipment that I asked for?"

"Let's go to my office and talk, Agent Ryder."

The two men started walking toward baggage pick up, and were headed downtown a short time later. Toby parked near a large nondescript brown ten-story brick building. The men entered the building and took an elevator to the eighth floor. As they exited the elevator Toby Said, "The electronics lab is down the hall, three doors on the left. They entered the laboratory and found a number of people wearing white knee length lab coats involved in a variety of activity. Toby led Ryder across the room to introduce him to a technician. Toby looked at Ryder and said, "Ryder I want you to meet Debra Williams," and then glancing at the tech, he added, "and Debra this is Lance Ryder, the agent that has you working overtime, building the frequency spectrum analyzer and suppression unit."

F. Washington Brown

The woman said, "It's about time I got a look at the guy that's responsible for getting me out of bed at four this morning." With a slight smile she extended her hand and said, "Glad to meet you."

Ryder took her hand and replied, "Likewise Miss Williams. I'm sorry about getting you up so early."

"Don't worry about it Agent Ryder, it's happened before." Turning to the lab bench she continued, "This is the unit that we've produced for you. It's small and compact but incorporates the functions that you require." As she spoke she picked up a rectangular metal box approximately eight inches wide and fourteen inches long. It had a strength meter, two control knobs, a toggle switch and a red light indicator. Near the top an electrical cord extended out about two feet with a one-foot diameter parabolic dish connected to it. There was also a handgrip attached to the dish. She said, "I'm going to step you through the operation of this item. Turn it on and hold the analyzer in one hand and the dish in the other. The dish is directional so you'll have to point it in the general direction that you think the target frequency is radiating from. If the red light comes on that means it has detected the selected freq. Move it around until the signal meter gives you its highest reading. Then flip this toggle switch that converts the unit from signal detection to signal suppression and it will kill the broadcast freq that you have selected. Any questions, Agent Ryder?"

Ryder reached out and took the devise from her and guessed that it weighed about three pounds. Well Miss Williams I'm impressed. The unit is lightweight and compact. I was expecting to see something cumbersome and hard to operate."

Her face lit up as she said, "Why thank you Agent Ryder. Around here we aim to please." She folded the antenna like a Japanese fan, put everything into a carrying case and handed it to the blond spy. Then she said, "Agent Ryder it was a pleasure meeting you. Around here you're a legend as a field operative. Now if you guys will excuse me I have another project that I put on hold."

Hot Sand & Cold Blood

Ryder said, "It was likewise a pleasure meeting you Miss Williams. Thanks for the help. We'll get out of the way and let you get back to work."

Toby spoke up, "Agent Ryder why don't we step into my office next door and exchange the latest information on this situation." Leaving the lab the two men entered Toby's office. The room contained an office desk, three metal filling cabinets, a couple of chairs and a window behind Toby's desk that gave the viewer a look at the RCA building. Toby took a seat at his desk and said, "Have a chair, Ryder."

Ryder sat down and asked, "What do you guys have on this thing so far?"

"Power called and gave us everything that you and he had discussed," Toby said. "We took the info and enacted the standard procedures. We've rushed agents to all the areas near the pumping stations and are currently in surveillance posture. We are a little short on people so we borrowed some folks from the FBI. We have discreetly checked with soft drink and candy vendors in towns near the gas plant pumping stations and have come up with some interesting information. These companies all have men of Middle East origin working for them. Each city taken by its self is not suspect, but together it sends up a red flag. We also contacted law enforcement agencies in towns all along the gas line route to check for increased criminal activity or just anything unusual. Only a couple of things turned up that seemed out of the way. At the Blythe California pumping station an employ there become irate about his wages or something and threatened to beat the hell out of the plant boss. El Paso has a pumping station and near there was other incident involving a mass shooting. Actually it took place between El Paso and Las Cruces, New Mexico. It happened at a picnic park near a defense installation called, White Sands Missile Range. They found two cars in a deep arroyo. One contained an employ from the range. The other contained a man, his wife, and two kids. They had all been shot and it appeared that the woman had been raped and had some sort of word scratched on her head. We took note of this incident because the range employ had some government electronics equipment in the trunk of his car and a broken transmitter that had been tuned to 164.5 freq. Now this is probably just coincidental but –"

"Wait a minute. Are you sure about the 164.5 frequency and the dead woman with something scratched on her head?" Ryder asked, his voice exuding excited, puzzlement.

"Yeah," Toby said, "I had them check it twice."

Ryder exclaimed, "Kansi is responsible for this. He cut up some women in Lisbon the same way. But what would Kansi be doing in New Mexico? I thought he would go straight to San Francisco from New York."

"Maybe he was the bag man," Toby offered.

"What?" Ryder asked, his attention divided with trying to figure out this twist that didn't dovetail with his theory.

"Maybe he was the guy with the money that purchased the transmitters. As I give a little thought to the situation, it seems to me that the range employ could have been the source of the equipment and the one we found was probably just a broken spare."

Adjusting to the idea Ryder said, "Yeah that's conceivable. He could have detoured through New Mexico to take care of this business and then more than likely caught a flight to San Francisco. I imagine that Kansi arranged to meet the range technician there to make the exchange, shot the guy, then took the transmitters and the money. The dead man and his wife may have been a part of it. However, having the kids there makes me think that they were out for a little recreation and stumbled into trouble. How long have those people been dead?" Ryder asked.

"Two hunters found them this morning and the coroner puts their deaths at around twenty four hours." Toby replied.

"El Paso has the only airport in the area with planes flying interstate and international routes. Check all flights in and out of there in the last week. I'm looking for the name, Kansi, Amal Kansi, Mohammad Kansi, or any variation. I'm still convinced that Kansi is in Frisco as we speak. Toby, I think the phone activity and Coke vendor activity will increase in the next couple of days. Stay alert and call me with the airport info or anything else that will confirm that we are on the right path."

"We sure will Ryder," Toby replied, and then added, "Well if that's it, Ryder, I'll give you a ride back downtown to catch your connecting flight to Frisco.

Toby pulled the car to the curb in front of the passenger terminal and opened the trunk so Ryder could retrieve his belongings. They shook hands and Toby said, "I'd see you to the gate but I have a ten minute time limit on parking."

"Keep close contact with me and all the team chiefs on this one," Ryder instructed. "We have a lot of marbles riding on it."

"I understand, and have a safe flight," Toby said as he turned and started around his car.

Ryder went into the terminal and two hours later his flight was touching down in San Francisco where he was met by Bob Wesson, an agent that he'd met soon after coming to work for OMNI. Ryder extended his hand and said, "Bob, It's good to see you. How many years has it been?"

Grinning and shaking Ryder's hand, Wesson said, "It's been more than I care to count. Ryder what in hell are you into? The phone system has been lit up for the past twenty-four hours. The FBI has been called in, not to mention the CIA and you know the, 'Company' never gets involved with the domestic stuff.

"Bob, I think that we're down to the wire on this one. I guess that you've been briefed and you're up to speed on the situation?"

Wesson's face took on a serious expression as he said, "Yeah, we're pretty much on top of it. As a matter of fact we probably have more current info than you do. Your theory was right about Kansi. We checked airline passenger lists from here to El Paso and it looks like he arrived earlier this morning on an eleven fifteen flight. But before we take this any further let's get you down to the operations complex where we can keep up with everything in real time.

Arriving at the downtown OMNI office complex in Oakland, he and Wesson entered the building and went directly to the ready room. Wesson thumbed open the cipher lock and they went in. The vast chamber was dimly lit and there were banks of plot-boards and communication monitoring devices. They went to the briefing area and sat down around a large table. Ryder saw documents lying out on the table and among them were the blueprints of the entire Western States Gas Company system from Texas to California. There were three other guys already sitting at the table discussing the status.

"Ryder," Wesson said, "I want you to meet, John Crosby. He's the operations manager for Western States and he can tell you everything you want to know about the gas company."

A tall bearded man wearing a dark suit rose slightly, extended his hand across the table and said, "Pleased to make your acquaintance, Mister Ryder. I'm glad to see you. I understand that you were the government agent who discovered this problem. I hope you can help us get through this without loosing our business."

Ryder shook Crosby's hand, and then turning his attention to the blueprints, he said, "Likewise Mr. Crosby. All right I'll take the list in order. First, I believe the terrorists will try and initiate the attack here where the feeder ends for reasons the engineers have already explained. Secondly, I'm going to be the point man in the field, meaning I will lead this team and I'll be in or around the gas plant in the time frame that the monitored phone traffic indicates they are most likely to strike. I want this team to be extremely subtle and low key. I don't want the bad guys alerted and scared off. I want to meet the Frisco surveillance team right away and I want to be informed of any change in phone traffic immediately. When I leave here I'm going to get a bit to eat and get a couple of hours sleep and then go to the gas plant. I believe that it will take them close to twenty-four hours to get everything coordinated before they decide to stash and detonate the charges. You've all been briefed that it's likely they'll use a delayed timer and frequency transmitter to allow their people to get out before their particular plant blows. Is everybody OK with what I've just said?" Hearing no nays he added, "Alright let's go about our business."

Ryder felt somebody shaking him and then he heard a voice. He recognized it as Wesson's.

"Lance, get up man. The phone monitors are picking up increased phone traffic and most of the parties are speaking in Arabic. We think that it's going down shortly because our interpreter is catching snatches of conversation mentioning Kansi's name in connection with delivering Allah's plan. Our guys in the field are keeping a sharp eye out for vender trucks."

Now fully awake, Ryder quickly rolled out of bed and got dressed. Four minutes later the OMNI spy finished putting black grease paint on his forehead and slipped the ski mask over his face. This completed his ensemble, which matched his black sweater and fatigue pants, which was pretty much like Wesson's uniform de'jure. He pulled the P-89 Ruger from its holster and double-checked the clip. It was full of hollow-point hot loads. He slammed the clip back into the P-89 and slid it back in its custom holster. Next he opened the flare gun and checked the single chambered round. If Kansi were who or what Ryder thought he might be, regular bullets would not take him down.

They arrived at the plant and took up predetermined positions that gave them visual access to the entire grounds including the giant gas pipes coming into the plant from the Santa Barbara pumping station. The plant's grounds covered over ten acres with a tall mesh fence that went around the entire outer perimeter. High intensity floodlights mounted on tall metal poles stood every hundred feet, bathing the area in eerie bluish light. In the center four giant metal buildings approximately thirty feet tall, seventy feet wide, and two hundred feet long were arraigned like a row of army barracks. Inside each building, rested five giant natural gas powered ten cylinder engines that stood twenty feet tall and thirty feet long. There were metal ladders that connected to catwalks, which went around the top of each engine so maintenance people could reach the valve covers to perform service work. On the grounds and around the buildings, giant pipes, like overgrown anacondas, came out of the ground and bent and curled in various directions. Ryder looked at Wesson and said can you believe the size of those engines?"

"Yeah," Wesson said, "and there are twenty more plants just like this strung across four states. To top it off, they're all connected by two, four-foot diameter pipes filled with natural gas at pressures of over five thousand pounds per square inch. If that thing blows it'll be the biggest damn' Forth of July you'll ever see. Last year I went to –"

"Quiet," Ryder said. "Look at the entry road to the plant that comes off of the main street. Isn't that a candy vendor truck from Tom's peanuts and candies, pulling up to the gate?"

"Yeah, Ryder I see it. The two guys in the truck are clean shaven and wearing Tom's uniforms."

"The two guys," Ryder said, "does it not look like they are a bit dark skinned? I can't be sure from this distances if either guy resembles Kansi." Ryder lifted his walkie – talkie, pressed the mike button and said, "Listen up, people, two Arab looking men have arrived in a candy truck. There may be others outside the perimeter as back up, so look alive." Ryder dropped the walkie – talkie, pulled the P-89 from its holster and said, "I'm going to work my way to the right and around closer to the vending machine and snack area. You go around to the left side and be sure to keep out of sight."

"Sounds good to me, Ryder," Wesson said as he pulled his Glock-9 semi-auto and check the clip.

By the time Ryder had moved into a position near the machines, the two candy venders had already opened the candy machine doors and were loading them. Ryder was

Hot Sand & Cold Blood

straining his eyes to get a good look at the men, but they were standing between him and high intensity bright lights, making it impossible to get a clear look at their faces. As one of the men headed back to the truck to pick up more items, Ryder pulled the frequency analyzer/suppression devise out of his knapsack and turned it on. He swept the area and detected no signal. He figured that while one of the men kept filling the candy machines the other guy would get the explosives from the truck and sneak them in the engine room. He'd hide them somewhere out of the way, turn on the timer and then they would casually leave. On the other hand maybe Ryder had been wrong about his whole plan; maybe these guys were just candy vendors. He was just starting to seriously consider that possibility when, bingo the little red analyzer light came on indicating a 164.5 frequency had just came up. Ryder quickly flipped the toggle switch, turning on the freq suppresser, which immediately put the plants in four states in the safe zone. *What the hell is going on*, Ryder thought. Then it dawned on him that there had been three guys in the truck. The third guy had probably ridden in lying on the floor. *Damn, he thought, which means that Kansi is already in the building and has planted the explosives somewhere, but where? This is one big building.* He set the suppresser on level ground to make sure that it wouldn't tip over and be accidentally turned off. He came to his feet and ran toward the vending machines.

When the two vendors saw him coming toward them carrying a gun, they dropped the candy and reached into their coats. One man pulled a revolver and brought it up to take aim, when Ryder put a round through his chest and another through his stomach. He shot the second man in the throat. Not breaking stride, Ryder continued into the building. Holding his weapon in both hands he rapidly scanned left and right as he quickly made his way along. He looked up, checked all the catwalks and everywhere else in the hundred places a man could hide. He had made his way about two thirds of the length of the building when a shot rang out and ricocheted off the floor about four feet to his left. He ducked in behind one of the giant engines and panned the area in front of him but he could see nothing. He was about to ease around the other side of the monster engine when he heard a voice boom out.

"So Ryder, we meet again. You prevailed in our last encounter but now I know you, and I, Ogar will kill you. I am invincible and I will destroy America and I will rule the world or destroy it."

Immediately Ryder's blood ran cold. That was Kansi's voice but the rhetoric his voice was spewing forth was a replay of something he had heard two years prior. Ryder shouted back. "Which encounter are you referring to, the one in Sidi Slimane or the one two years ago at Long Binh, Viet Nam?"

"It doesn't matter Ryder because you are only a mere mortal and I will prevail. I know that you have found a way to stop my radio signal from going out because my transmitter is neutralized, but no matter for I have activated the manual timer switch. It is hidden so well no one will be able to find it in time to save this mammoth structure. I may not be able to destroy twenty gas plants but I will destroy this one. I will kill you and you will burn in this building."

"Ogar, you talk a good fight but if you were so damn' tough you would come out and face me." Ryder baited.

"You are right. Let's step out in the open like in the old west. But your bullets did not stop me before and nothing has changed."

Ryder leaned forward and looked around the big engine. At first the OMNI agent saw nothing, and then he thought he detected movement at the far end of the building. As it moved closer he could see that it resembled Kansi, but there was something about him that was different. Ryder couldn't be sure, maybe he looked taller. When Kansi had drawn to within about thirty feet of Ryder's position, The OMNI agent stepped out with the raised P-89 and started shooting. It was like shooting a paper target because he was close enough to see where the rounds were hitting Kansi. The bullets were knocking the terrorist around like a rag doll and a little blood splattered here and there but he was not going down. Instead he seemed to be looming larger as his face started to reshape and become reddish gray in color. Ryder kept firing until the Ruger's slide action slammed back and locked sending a wisp of smoke curling from the gun's chamber. The OMNI agent had hit Kansi with every round but the bullets had no real effect.

Kansi raised a .44 Desert Eagle automag and opened fire as his hideous sounding voice boomed out, "Now it is my turn, you annoying insect that has plagued me for over two of your earth years. Now your end has come."

Ryder yelled with pain as a .44 round tore through his leg. As he dropped to the floor, he reached into the utility pocket of his black fatigue pants and quickly pulled the flare pistol. With bullets ricocheting off the floor all around him he rolled over on his stomach and griping the flare gun with both hands he took careful aim as he thought, *gotta make it count because I won't get a second shot.* He squeezed the trigger and watched the trail of flame erupt from the big pistol's muzzle. The fiery round hit Kansi in the middle of his chest making the surreal looking terrorist drop his gun and bellow with pain. The unnatural sound of his wailing resounded around the plant with chilling echoes. Trailing flame and smoke, Kansi turned and loped off into the far reaches of the huge building to hide until he could recover, or die.

Ryder came to his feet drawing quick conclusions about two things: he could hardly walk much less run fast enough to catch Kansi. Even if he could the OMNI spy was in no condition to apprehend the terrorist/demon. Second and most importantly, there was a comp-4 hi-explosive bomb running on a short manual timer somewhere in the huge building. There would be no time to find and disarm it. He would probably be lucky if he could clear the area before it went off. He started for the door, limping as fast as his bleeding wound would let him. He managed to get through the door and was making his way across the grounds toward his parked vehicle when Wesson came running toward him.

Wesson grabbed Ryder around the waist and pulled the wounded agent's arm over his shoulder in order to expedite the quick shuffle toward the vehicle.

Wesson asked, "What happened, Ryder? I was on far side of you without a decent view of the vendor truck and then the next thing I know I'm hearing the sound of gunfire.

How bad are you hit?"

"Not now, Wesson. Get the area evacuated, there is a live comp-4 bomb somewhere in that building getting ready to blow."

"Don't worry about an evacuation, Ryder. Every body left the plant when the shooting started. The only people here are you and I. I relayed a call into the fire department as a precaution but if this place goes I don't know how much help they will be."

They reached the agency car and Wesson quickly helped Ryder into the passenger's side. Leaping over the hood, Wesson, in one fluid motion entered the vehicle and started the engine. He slammed the car into gear and sent gravel flying as he fishtailed out of the gas company compound. Barely making it to the main road, Ryder looked back just in time to see a fireball erupt from inside the main engine building where he had shot Kansi. As almost as if in slow motion, Ryder watched the roof being lifted straight up by the explosion while the walls went outward and up at an angle. The blinding light from the giant fireball was followed by a huge shock wave that went out in all directions knocking down trees and flipping gas company vehicles parked near the building. Ryder could see the results of the powerful explosion as it rapidly moved toward them, dissipating only slightly as it did and he yelled, "Put your foot in it Wesson."

At that precise instant, the car as if being lifted by a giant hand came off the ground and was hurled down the street. It spun in circles and finally, but none too gently came to rest against a freeway overpass abutment. The giant blast had destroyed or severely damaged everything in it's path for a mile in every direction, including bringing down a small plane that was passing overhead. The pilot and three passengers were killed instantly. Now three huge severed pipes protruded from the ground spewing fire one-hundred feet into the air like angry giant gas torches.

Feeling a bit groggy and disorientated, Ryder looked around and was totally amazed that not only was he not dead, except for the bullet hole in his leg, he wasn't even hurt. He looked at Wesson and saw that he wasn't moving. "Wesson," Ryder said, "Are you all right?" Still Ryder could see no movement from his fellow agent. Ryder reached over and put his hand on Wesson's shoulder. At Ryder's touch, Wesson recoiled. Ryder quickly withdrew his hand and repeated, "Wesson, I see that your eyes are open, are you alright?"

After another moment Wesson slowly turned his head and looked at Ryder with glassy eyes. His lips started to tremble and he finally managed to say, "Uh ... are, are we alive?"

"Yeah, Wesson. I think we made it." Ryder answered.

After a moment longer Wesson started moving his hands and showing more signs of life. He checked himself over and discovered that there was nothing wrong other than he had been paralyzed by fear. Wesson broke into a nervous little snicker and said, "I'm not hurt...yes, I am OK, alright. Damn what a rush!"

Grinning, Ryder said, "Well I'm not so sure about that Agent Wesson. Maybe you'd better hang on a second before you say that."

Suddenly Wesson became serious and asked, "What do you mean? Am I cut somewhere?"

"No." Ryder said, "but I think that I detect the distinct smell of urine in this car," as he burst into laughter.

Wesson grabbed his crotch and exclaimed, "Damn! Ryder if you ever tell anybody about this I'll steal your P-89 and toss it into the Ohio River.

Fire trucks were starting to arrive from Frisco and Oakland and began fighting to get the flames under control. It was a struggle but as the sun came up, the firefighters were starting to stabilize the fire. However, it would be a couple of days before they got the upper hand.

F. Washington Brown

Ryder and the other OMNI agents sat around the briefing table summing up the outcome of the operation. The chief of the OMNI San Francisco division stood between the table and a chalkboard, holding a pointer while recapping the outcome of the damage suffered by the gas plant. "Gentlemen," he said, "it looks like the material losses are not as great as it first appeared. This was mainly due to our being able to disable the bombs in the remaining facilities. As soon as things popped here that was enough legal proof to round up the terrorist suspects throughout the four state sweeps just as they had planted their devises. However, because of our electronic countermeasures the bombs never exploded. Now if there are no questions." Looking around, he saw no hands raised. He looked at John Crosby and said, "Now I am going to turn the briefing over to the Western States Gas Company representative and let him tell you a little about the damage to the local gas plant here in San Francisco." The chief waved a hand in John Crosby's direction and added, "John step up please and give us the details."

The gas rep rose from his chair, approached the chalkboard and took the pointer from the OMNI chief. He looked at the board and said, "Gentlemen, as you can see, I have a diagram drawn on the board here. Now, of the four main buildings that house the pump engines, all were severely affected ... destroyed actually and will have to be rebuilt. However, we were lucky to have sustained less collateral damage than we anticipated. Fortunately the fire department trucks from several locations were quickly on the scene and held the damage to a minimum. It will take some time but we will be back up and running. Meanwhile our San Jose plant will assume a heavier roll to offset our diminished capabilities here."

One of the agents spoke up and asked, "And what if the San Jose plant along with the others had been destroyed?"

John Crosby winced and replied, "I don't even want to think about that scenario." He continued with the briefing and when it was over Ryder got up, and favoring his right leg, went into the outer office to use the phone. He dialed

Hot Sand & Cold Blood

the OMNI office in Frankfurt and reached the embassy receptionist.

"American Embassy, Frankfurt, May I help you?"

"Yes. Agent Ryder here. Is Agent Dante available by chance?"

"Why yes sir, you are in luck. He has just arrived. I'll ring you through to him."

There was a slight pause and then Ryder heard a familiar voice.

"Agent Dante, and what can I do for you?"

"Dante. This is Ryder. How is everything going?"

"Good, Ryder." Dante replied. "I understand that you completed your investigation. Congratulations old boy."

"Yeah, that's what I was calling you about. Everything is pretty much rapped up here and I have a little unfinished business in the Middle East. I'd like to get some time to take care of it."

Well, I don't know, Ryder. We've had a problem crop up in South America and we'll need a couple of agents down there in Columbia. Something about some Contras and cocaine. You know that sort of nasty business."

"Dante, I really need some time." Ryder repeated.

"Tell me Ryder, what is this time for and is it official business?" Dante asked.

"I need to confer with a constituent that was instrumental in helping me solve this last case." Ryder explained.

"In other words, it's not official. Are you sure that this doesn't have something to do with some little piece of fluff you ran across in Germany or Beirut?"

Ryder growled, "Damn it Dante, can I have the time off or not?"

Dante laughed and replied, "Settle down Ryder. Hell yes you can have some time off. By the way, buddy, you have no secrets. Everybody knows about that little airplane driver that you got hooked up with. I understand that she's a real cutie. Take a month and then I want you to report to the CIA chief in Miami. He'll give you the lowdown on our problem in Columbia. I'd brush up on my Spanish if I were you. Good luck with Lisa I have a feeling that you'll need it. Later buddy."

"Yeah I know. She was a little upset because I had to leave Beirut without ... hello." Ryder slammed the phone down and mumbled, "Damn' it I hate that when people hang up on me."

Ryder relaxed with a cool rum and coke as the Lufthansa 707 plowed through the European skies. He was going to take Lisa into his arms and do nothing but relax and make love for a week. He felt the aircraft's nose dip down slightly as the plane started a shallow decent. He smiled, knowing that in just a matter of a couple of hours he would surprise her in Hamburg. He had called the Mid East Oil Company office and learned that she was currently on a short vacation. They had given him her temporary vacationing address as 341 Yeager Strauss in Hamburg.

When the plane landed Ryder made his way to baggage to retrieve his suitcase and caught a cab to the Hapbonhoff. The main train station was extremely busy and Ryder was happily jostled around in the crowd as he made his way to the ticket counter. After obtaining a ticket he headed for the track nine platform and hopped on just as the conductor was completing the boarding. The ride to Hamburg was pleasant and reflected Ryder's mood.

Arriving at 341 Yeager Strauss Ryder was almost beside himself with eager anticipation as he rang the bell. He waited a moment or two and rang again. He was just getting ready to ring the third time and the door came open and there stood Lisa, smiling and looking as beautiful as ever. He just stood for a moment drinking in her Venuses-like beauty.

"Lance," she said as her smile disappeared. "I thought you were ... I mean ... what are you doing here?"

Detecting something in her facial expression that said she was surprised but not exactly happy to see him sounded a small alarm in his mind. "Lisa," he said, "is there something wrong? I thought you would be happy to see me. I know that you were upset went I left without saying goodbye but I didn't have a choice."

A small tear appeared at the corner of her eye as she spoke with a quivering voice. "Lance," she said, "I told you not to leave me and you did."

"But, Honey, I didn't have a choice. I had a job to do. I tried to call you but you had already left." he explained.

"Lance, I thought about us for the longest time and wondered if we could make it work. I had doubts ... you must know how it can be when you're not sure about something." she sobbed.

"Lisa, I know what you mean. However my assignment is over. We can be together. We'll go back to –"

"Lance, stop," she said. "We can't go anywhere together. I don't know of any other way to say this, so I'll just come out and tell you. Lance, I've met another man and –"

"Stop," he yelled. "I don't want to hear it! Just don't say another word." Ryder was trembling with anger. *I've got to get hold of myself,* he thought. Taking a couple of deep breaths, he remembered a yoga breathing exercise he used to get control of his emotions when he'd found himself in dangerous situations. After taking a moment to gather his thoughts, Ryder said, "Lisa I'm sorry things turned out this way. I sincerely hope that you have a happy life. If ever there was a woman in the world who deserves it, you are that lady. I'm going to leave now, but I'd like to kiss you before I go. That is if it's all right with you?"

"I think it would be OK Lance. Step inside for a moment."

He stepped into the apartment's living room, took her in his arms and kissed her, slipping his tongue into her mouth.

For a fleeting moment she responded to his touch then abruptly drew back and breathlessly said, "If I let you continue, I won't be able to control my emotions and that will make me feel cheap. You have kissed me now please go before I lose control and start crying again."

Ryder had given it his best effort and came up with nothing. "Alright Lisa, good bye and good luck," he said as he turned to leave. He stepped back out onto the sidewalk and was headed down the street when he heard her call out. He turned and saw her standing in front of the open door, looking like an angel.

She raised her hand halfheartedly as if to wave, and sounding almost like a lost little girl, she said, "Lance, we did have a wonderful go of it didn't we."

A slight lump rose in his throat as he replied, "Yeah, Sweetheart, we had a great go of it ... Good bye, Lisa."

Good bye, Lance," she replied.

Ryder turned and with a slight limp ambled slowly down the street. *One in a million,* he thought. On the other hand, there was always Patricia ... and South America.

Lance Ryder in "Zombeast" is now available. Go online or pick up a copy at your local bookstore

CPSIA information can be obtained at www.ICGtesting.com
Printed in the USA
LVOW10s2304300116
472825LV00001B/18/P